BURGUNDY

AND

LIES

Carol A. Strickland

Other books by Carol A. Strickland

Applesauce and Moonbeams, wacky soft sci fi

Nothing Personal, even wackier soft sci fi

Touch of Danger, vol. 1 of the Three Worlds superhero fantasy saga

Lost in the Stars, vol. 2 of the Three Worlds superhero saga

Stalemate, vol. 3 of the Three Worlds superhero saga

Worlds Apart, vol. 4 of the Three Worlds superhero saga

Star-Spangled Panties, all about Wonder Woman!

With thanks…

…to the members of our local RWA group, Heart of Carolina. As always, so many helped me along. To those RWA people who put together all those great workshops, many thanks as well! And to Karen Dodd, Terry M. and Sarra Cannon, who convinced me back in the day when it wasn't, that self-publishing was a legitimate way to proceed.

…to Samantha Gordon at Invisible Ink Editing for the original edits.

Burgundy and Lies / Carol A. Strickland. – 2nd ed.
Digital ISBN 978-1-941318-00-3
Print ISBN 978-0-9912688-9-4
IngramSpark digital ISBN 978-1-941318-36-2
IngramSpark print ISBN 978-1-941318-37-9

1

Burgundy, France 1555

Family duty could weigh too heavily. Sometimes Abbie Bourgogne thought she would scream from it.

She twisted her cousin's blonde hair into a light, twining crown around her head and desperately wished she were training young grapevines onto an arbor instead. The grapes were what was important. Her family's reputation lay within wine. Why then must she waste her time like this?

"He kissed me," Babette said as she held the hand mirror to admire herself in the candlelight.

With a start, Abbie realized she hadn't been listening to her cousin's chatter. "Kissed you? Who?"

"Who do you think I've been talking about all this time? Michel, silly."

"Michel Silly… You don't mean Michel the Silly Fichaud?"

"That's not his name," Babette huffed.

Abbie herself never liked to be lectured, but she couldn't help doing so to this flighty girl. Nip the rot in the bud; that was always best no matter how much it hurt. "It should be. Or Michel the Inept, and leave off Fichaud. He may be handsome and talk sweetly to young girls, but he's no good for you or the family. He's ambitious beyond his skills."

"Take it back, Abbie. I love him!"

"Oh, you *love* him." Abbie chose a beaded pin to hold Babette's hair in place, trying not to roll her eyes as she did so. "That doesn't discount the fact that he's an idiot where wine is concerned. Why your brother ever hired him is beyond me. It's been two years now with Michel as steward of the winery and–"

"Wine, wine, wine. All the time with you it's grapes and wine. I am sooo tired of wine." Babette slumped in her chair, making it difficult for Abbie to work on the back of her head.

They thought that this was where she fit in, to be helpmate and companion to her cousin. This was her place within her uncle's family. It meant she had a home to stay in, a bed at night, and food when she was hungry. Others would have been well-pleased at such a situation.

But no one else now alive in the family loved the grape as did Abbie Bourgogne. No one else knew its temper, its moods both on the vine and off. No one else could coax it to full flavor and fame like Abbie.

Spring was so far away. Would she be home by then, caring for her vineyard?

Abbie pulled her cousin back up with a grunt. "Wine is what our family stands for, Babette. Family is the most important thing there is, and our burgundy is the best in all France– or it was when Papa was still alive. I'm afraid your brother hasn't the feel for it. I wish he'd take my advice. I do dread to see the Bourgogne family reputation fall."

Babette pursed her lips. "I'm sorry, but Uncle Robert is dead and has been for years now. It's time you came back out to see the world, Abbie. Speaking of brothers– Michel has one. Would you be interested?"

"Ah, I remember him. Pierre the Dolt, Michel the Idiot's brother. What a catch." Abbie gave her cousin a small smile in the silvered mirror and patted her shoulder. "All right, I'm sorry I called him an idiot. Enjoy your little crush, Babette, but remember: you're seventeen now. Time soon enough for Uncle Gus to be finding you a husband."

"You're eighteen and unmarried."

Babette had never been one for thinking before she made sharp comments. Luckily Abbie wasn't in a hurry to get married, and thus the arrow failed to hit its intended mark. Abbie had a more important goal than mere marriage.

"Able Abbie," some people called her. If Old Eric wasn't around, she was the one they turned to for instruction when it came to the grapes. While other children had been off running through summer fields, she had delighted in watching the vines and seeing God's handiwork grow before her very eyes.

"You'd better go and play or you'll set root, too," her father had often told her with his hearty laugh. But now her vineyard was far away, and Papa and Mama and her brothers were farther still, in Heaven. The grape was all she had left of her family.

Here they had grapes, but they weren't the same: pale chardonnay and pinot blanc instead of dark pinot noir, and they grew in such a tiny vineyard! It had been intended only for the family's use. Out of sympathy for the forlorn girl, Uncle Gus had given Abbie a spreading, sunny slope that was too rocky for growing his mustard, too steep to graze his cattle.

She'd planted cuttings from the family's vineyard and finally last year everyone had come out to wonder at what she'd grown. Holidays had been toasted to excess with her chablis. There was even enough left to sell at the spring fair this year and turn a tidy profit.

The vines thirsted for the same care she'd given those in her family's vineyard. She loved these, but what she longed for were the hands-filling clusters of the almost-black fruits of home.

Still she had a duty to the grapes here at her uncle's house. Family and its obligations must come right after God in life's priorities, even before the wine. Sometimes that realization made Abbie feel more than a mere year older than her cousin– or perhaps Babette seemed more than a year younger than she. Babette didn't understand the first thing about family, much less wine. Women comprehended these things; children didn't.

"I haven't a husband because I'm not first in Uncle Gus's heart," Abbie said. "He'll get to me soon enough. You should start seriously thinking of marriage. Once the contract is signed, there'll be no need for love. Women have no choice in the matter. We have no freedom to choose our lives, much less follow our dreams. Let's hope the Hereafter is different."

Abbie frowned as she brushed fallen hairs from the square neckline of Babette's good red wool dress. No choice to return home to her vineyard. All she was required to do was this trivial duty, that of being friend and– let her be honest– nursemaid to her cousin. She sighed and said, "At least we can be sure that Uncle Gus will find us the best husbands he can. Some fathers aren't like that, but Auguste Bourgogne is a good man who loves his family."

Unhearing, Babette closed her eyes and clasped the mirror to her bosom. "It was a marvelous kiss."

Abbie shook her head and bit her tongue on a more scathing comment. "I'll wager he's practiced on many a girl," was all she said.

"Oh, no. He's true to me alone. He kissed me and then said he loved me."

"He said–?" Abbie's hands froze in mid-air. What had Babette gotten into this time? How involved was she with this fool? "When was this? I thought Michel just arrived yesterday from the clos."

"It happened last night, down at the bottom of the kitchen garden. Michel kissed me at least twenty times. It was heaven!" With that Babette gave the back of her hand several loud kisses as a demonstration.

It sounded like suckling pigs going after their dinner. Abbie grimaced at the swooning girl. "You're asking for trouble. Perhaps Michel's a decent man, but you mustn't… bait him."

"Bait him?" Babette stuck out her lower lip.

"You know. Bat your eyes and smile at him like you do all the boys. They all worship you anyway, but someday one might take you seriously. They might want to go too far."

Babette swung the mirror around so she could try out her smile on herself. Blue eyes, pink complexion… and Abbie behind her, seemingly a faded version of Babette, her smile never coming into full bloom anymore.

As if she could read Abbie's mind, Babette said, "You need to smile at the boys. You need to have fun."

"Why bother? I just need to smile at Uncle Gus," Abbie said with a teasing glint in her eye. "You must teach me how to do it so expertly. Then he will find me a husband who lives near the clos, so I can work there again."

"Oh no! He wouldn't separate us!"

Abbie sorted through the small chest of jewelry for another nice pin. "Marriage will part us anyway," she reminded her cousin. The thought of the day years from now when the two of them would be married had hovered hazily in the back of her mind since she'd come to live with Babette. "There's nothing to be done about that. I promise I will write you each week and tell you everything just as we do now. We'll always be like sisters, no matter what happens or where life takes us. I only pray every day that marriage sends me back home. It would be– Babette!"

Abbie held up a thick golden crucifix necklace. "This was my mother's. What are you doing with it?"

Scarlet flushed over Babette's face, and she wouldn't meet Abbie's accusing gaze. "I just borrowed it. Oh, Abbie, don't be mad at me. I just wanted to wear it a day or two and then I would have put it back."

"It's part of my dowry. Uncle is holding it for me."

"It's still your dowry. I was going to give it back in a while." Babette pouted. "You can put it back now if it's so important. I merely wanted to look nice for Father Bernard. Papa said this was to be a very special dinner tonight."

"Oh." Abbie turned the cross over. Candlelight caught the edge of it. So clearly she remembered it upon her mother's breast. A far-off laugh and the fading vision of a warm smile came to her. "Well, just for tonight," Abbie said slowly. "Please return it before you go to bed. It's all that I have left of her."

"Oh, I had every intention to do so," Babette declared. Eagerly she took the valuable piece and made a great commotion as she tried to put it on by herself. Abbie had to help her with the clasp. Babette could be such a baby sometimes!

"And you aren't wearing it for Michel?" Abbie asked. "So he'll kiss you again? He'll be eating with the help tonight, not with us. You won't go down by the garden again, will you?"

The door burst open. "Abbieabbie!" her young cousin Thérèse cried as she ran in. She held her arms open for a hug, her little fists filled with ribbons of all colors.

Abbie knelt down to embrace the dear girl, knowing that it was a half-bribe, as children were wont to do.

"Don't you look nice," Abbie told her, and Thérèse preened. This was the first dress the girl had helped sew. Abbie and Aunt Danielle had waited one night until Thérèse was asleep, and then pulled out most of her seams and redone them properly. The girl had never guessed.

"Thank you," Thérèse responded to the compliment politely as she'd been taught. She stuck out her hands with those ribbons. "Do my hair." And as an afterthought: "Please."

"Abbie's attending to me right now," Babette told her sister.

Thérèse gave her a dubious look. "You're done," she decided. "Now it's my turn. Please, Abbie, please?"

"No!" Babette turned and pointed at Thérèse. "I go first. I am the oldest."

"No, me! Me first!"

"Me! Me!"

"ME FIRST!"

"MEEE!"

"MEEEEE!"

Both girls kicked their feet against the floor, screwing their faces into reddened knots.

"WHAT is going on up there?!" came Uncle Gus's bellow from downstairs.

"Nothing!" all three called.

Abbie planted both fists on her hips and stared down Babette. "Thérèse is seven years old. How old are you again?" Before her cousin could reply, she added, "Seven-year-olds have less patience than grown girls. Or perhaps grown girls should have more patience than seven-year-olds."

With that she squatted to reach Thérèse. "This won't take long, she assured Babette as her cousin pouted behind her. When all Thérèse's ribbons were secured to wave merrily at each movement, and the child had been delighted at her reflection, Abbie scooted her out of the room and returned to Babette.

Her cousin sat with her arms tightly folded across her chest. A frown tightened her face.

"Now, Bab," Abbie said, "I am ready to finish you."

"About time," Babette muttered.

"Or I could go downstairs and help Aunt Dani."

Another mutter, this one unintelligible.

"And what would Father Bernard say about this conversation?" Abbie asked. She put on a Bernard expression, puffing out her cheeks and looking around as if slightly unsure where she was. "A lay-die mother puts her, hrum, heh, chiiild-ren fust," she said as she wobbled in place.

Babette giggled despite herself. "Oh dear, he would. And just like that, too."

"He'd be right. Children can't help themselves, but we grow out of that."

Babette rolled her eyes. "Yes, mother," she said, and that made Abbie laugh.

"I do tend to lecture sometimes."

"Only sometimes, cousin."

They laughed their way through the final pins of Babette's coiffure.

"It was magic," Babette said as Abbie pouffed out the tops of her sleeves for her, batting at stray pet hairs that clung to them. "The moon was just setting and there was some star in the sky that was the brightest I've ever seen, and it was as if it were just for us. We made a wish upon it. Abbie dearest, I can tell you this." A trace of steel ice entered her voice. "I know you'll never tell Papa."

Abbie made a noise which she hoped Babette would take as agreement. This entire affair reeked of bad luck. A love match– if indeed such quick infatuation was love– was not in the family's best interests. Babette had never been one to use her brains. Instead she relied upon her God-given good looks to make her way through life, and a very good way it had been so far.

But the girl had no common sense at all. If sinful things happened to other young girls, it never entered Babette's mind to avoid the same fate. Tonight Abbie would talk to her aunt, Babette's stepmother Danielle, who would best know how to approach Uncle Gus about keeping that idiot Michel Fichaud from sniffing around his eldest daughter.

Abbie stepped back to inspect her work. Despite herself, she was getting better at this. Babette's hair shone like the gold she wore at her throat. Pretty Babette. Her eyes were as blue as a spring sky, her cheeks blushed like the primrose. Her figure was a willow in the wind, and her neck graceful as a swan's.

And her temper could be just as bad as a swan's, too. Spoiled, used to having her own way, keeping her father artfully under her thumb.

"Aren't you done yet?" Babette asked. "We'll be late for dinner and I need Papa's good graces. I'm going to tell him tonight."

"Tell him what?" Abbie asked as she tucked one stray curl back behind Babette's ear. Really, she had much more skill with grapevines than with hair. She had been taught the secrets of wine since she could first walk, but had only come to learn these more womanly arts in these past four years.

"That we're going to be married, silly. Michel and I. I think Christmas will be a good time, don't you? It's not all that far away. We'll have all winter to– you know." Babette ducked her head between her shoulders, her cheeks reddening.

Abbie straightened the pins within the jewelry chest. "Until recently Michel has merely been a farmer, and he's a younger son at that. He's only been in his position at the clos for two years. Just look at what he did to this year's pinot noir crop. We had fine weather, but the crop was eaten up by moths and what was left allowed to mold, barely good enough for *verjus*. All the other wineries are saying that this was their best year yet."

She shut the heavy wooden case with a decisive thump. "No, Babette, a marriage of you to him would just put him in the clos for the rest of his life, and we would never have a good vintage again. Clos Bourgogne Grand Cru would become just another burgundy wine. The family's reputation would plummet quicker than a fat goose under a hunter's arrow. Uncle Gus will never let you marry him, so don't get too attached."

I won't let you marry him, Abbie determined. If she had to run through the church disrupting the wedding mass so the vows were never declared, she'd do so and gladly. Cousin Christopher was on the verge of letting Michel go. If Michel married Babette, there'd be no way the clos could be rid of him.

The sudden sound of wagon wheels approaching sent them both to fling open the diamond-paned window onto the brisk late-October evening.

"It's Father Bernard at last." Abbie peered through the gathering darkness and bold purple silhouette of the cedars that lined the rutted drive near the house like thick, tapering columns. The shadowed wagon approached at a quick clip despite the puddles left from the morning's rain. Probably the horses as well sensed a visitor's supper to be had here.

Babette craned to see around Abbie, crushing one of Abbie's sleeve poufs as she did so. "How many men does he have with him? One, two… five. I'll tell Danielle."

"Who is that?" Abbie asked.

"Which? Oh."

A man sat next to the good Father Bernard up front in the priest's wagon, while the others slumped on covered hay in the back. But this man…

In the deep dusk his clothing stood out from the black of the priests and monks. Oh, his broad-shouldered, open gown would have marked him as a man of prestige anywhere, and Abbie could see the rich fur it was lined with even from where she stood. But underneath, his bright red hose and what she could see of his doublet were slashed again and again.

"He hasn't been in a fight," Abbie murmured to herself. Surely his gown would have been ripped as well? These tears looked too precise to be accidental.

"No," Babette agreed. "Look, he's wearing hose under his hose. I think it's supposed to be like that."

White hose peeked through the slashed red overhose, as did his white linen shirt through his doublet. A tall, wide-brimmed cap matched his ensemble, and it sported a red feather as long as an arrow climbing up its side. The strange fashion cast a deep, masking shadow over the man's face.

"Is he this evening's entertainment?" Abbie wondered.

Babette nudged her. "Silly. I think that's the way they dress in the cities. Some of the fellows told me about the Swiss look, how everyone's doing it."

"Some of the fellows? Who have you been talking to?" Abbie asked and turned to face her, but Babette pushed her shoulder to turn her.

"Look at that," she pointed.

It was not difficult to know what she referred to when the man shifted his position and spread his legs slightly. Abbie wanted to look away but curiosity and the bright contrast of red and white next to such a masculine spot froze her gaze.

"I hear the city men stuff them with horsehair to make them look bigger," Babette whispered to her.

"Uncle Gus will not like it. Remember that beggar clown at the harvest revels? He dressed like that, in rags, and stuffed them too."

"Oh, phoo; don't be so old-fashioned. It's a stylish suit. It shows that this is a man of some distinction. I wonder where he's from?"

"Beyond Beaune, that's certain," Abbie decided.

"Dijon, do you think? Maybe even Paris?"

"Clearly he's not a priest. Or are the Parisian priests wearing that kind of thing these days?" Abbie asked, and Babette giggled.

Together they decided that was probably not the case.

Abbie gave the man one more curious look before securing the window against the cold. Babette ran off in a flurry of skirts to inform her stepmother of the number of guests.

It did not take long for Father Bernard, his swarm of assistants, and the stranger to ascend upon the house in a great glut of good-natured shouting. Servants and family bustled around them, gathering cloaks and gowns and handing out warmed wine.

Abbie struggled with the weight of the stranger's gown. It seemed leaden with its fur lining and so much padding around the shoulders. This wasn't rabbit fur, either, but something even softer.

But it left him in just a finely embroidered jerkin over his doublet and shirt. Up close, Abbie could see the slashes were quite deliberate and his linen shirt had been pulled through them as if to show off the fact that he wore quality down to his skin.

The stranger turned to her, his hand reaching up to catch the brim of his hat, hiding his eyes from her still. Perhaps by surprise his mouth opened and then widened into a smile.

"Well, hello there," he said in intimate, low tones. "Please tell me you aren't Babette Bourgogne."

How was she supposed to take that? Still as a polite girl should, Abbie gave a quick, short curtsy. "I am Abbie Bourgogne, *monsieur*."

"Ah, very good," he said, and his words caressed her like his gown's own fur did across her cheek. She balled that coat in her arms to keep a safe distance away from the honeyed voice. Candlelight finally caught his crinkling black eyes, bright on hers, and the left side of his mouth twitched up.

He was youngish, well under thirty, with medium-dark hair that curled all over. His chin might be beardless but it was broad all the same, and speckled with an early evening's mist of whiskers. He looked like one of those devilishly handsome satyrs that Abbie had seen pictured in Uncle Gus's book of fables. The drawing there had shown pointed ears and furred legs with hooves, but the intent in the smile was the same.

This was clearly a man of the world, interested only in luring young women to sin. Obviously he believed all the jokes about farmers' daughters and expected himself to be the lucky recipient of the daughters' favors. He even advertised his role with this cosmopolitan costume and its padding.

Here was a man who needed to learn the fine art of subtlety. He could not possess the finesse that the boy who slopped the pigs had shown Abbie when she was thirteen. Oh, how that simple country boy had almost parted Abbie from her virtue! And now some ridiculous big city man thought to do the same to an older and wiser woman?

Abbie chuckled despite herself, and the stranger's little grin deflated.

"Hrum! Monsieur DuMonde!"

His head turned quickly at Father Bernard's call.

Someone stuffed another cloak into Abbie's arms so she had more time to study M. DuMonde from its protective camouflage. As soon as he'd been introduced to Uncle Gus and bowed, he handed over a letter of introduction. While Gus read it next to the hearth, DuMonde looked around. He soon found a sharp, sudden focus of attention: cousin Babette. His mouth did not smile but some quirk of it showed her that he was making a decision about beautiful Babette, a judgment perhaps.

Perhaps this man thought he could take Michel's place, hm? Best to keep an eye on him. That might not be too painful a task, and as Babette's nursemaid, it was her duty.

Now that she was a safe distance away from him he didn't seem such a satyr. That evening shadow darkened his chin, but it did not give him as sinister an air as it did some men. Instead it enhanced the delightful line of his jaw. Abbie was glad that he was not the type to wear a beard. It would surely be a minor sin to hide that angled, masculine face and neck.

For a moment those eyes– black and bright as a moonlit midnight– glanced at her, but they quickly returned to Babette. Why should they linger upon Abbie? Next to the beauty that was her cousin, she was plain. Babette's radiant blondness had darkened to a honey brown for Abbie's tresses. Babette's blue eyes took on a yellowish veil of mourning to become Abbie's green ones. The roses in Abbie's cheeks hadn't shown themselves since she'd come to live with her uncle.

Abbie hurried to put the cloaks away.

Heaven had been kind to her. It had provided a place of family, of protection, even of education where she could grow to be a woman. Her uncle had promised to find her a suitable husband someday. If Uncle Gus's devotion to family duty had not been there for her, her only choice would have been the nunnery. Though Abbie enjoyed quiet meditation upon occasion, she did not relish the idea for the rest of her life. Since she was not a man, she could not join the Cistercian monks who performed such wonders with the vine.

All in all, so much better to be the companion of her cousin. So much better to have a chance at least to help care for Uncle's small vineyard.

They took their seats at the dining room table. Another table had been married to it so all but the youngest children could find room. Abbie and

Uncle Gus settled old Nana into her chair, and then Uncle Gus helped Great-Uncle Ronald adjust his footstool until it was comfortable. Ronald was in charge of overseeing his son, poor Cousin Louis, and making sure he didn't cause a scene in front of their guests.

Aunt Danielle signaled the servants and lutist to begin. The timbered room seemed so much smaller than normal with all the extra people packed in. The servants– two of them borrowed from the Gilberts down the road– had to squeeze their way between the back of the chairs and the wall.

"Lovely, lovely," Father Bernard clucked about the food and the soft stringed melodies served to them. He had fine table manners for a priest and carefully wiped his hands on the tablecloth after each course. His assistants all used their sleeves. "Such noble hospitality you offer your guests, Auguste."

He leaned to catch the eye of the man in red and white sitting three places down from him. "Heh. Only good has ever been spoken of our host, M. DuMonde. Auguste Bourgogne is beloved of his people and his church. He's an outstanding member of the community and kingdom."

"Yes, I have heard the same," DuMonde replied. His voice flowed rich and even, and Abbie found herself longing to hear him discourse at length.

Uncle Gus and the men carried on a puzzling conversation. Instead of discussing the needs of the church or its parishioners, it seemed to Abbie that the priest and his men concentrated on praising Uncle Gus to the heavens. They detailed his many holdings, the richness of his lands, the superb varieties of mustards that came from this farm, the fine vintages he produced at the clos and now at home, as well as his holy virtues.

It seemed almost comical when Uncle, such a large, grand patriarch with his sculpted graying beard, dressed in his finest starched jerkin and flat cap, his best jewelry on display, would then tut-tut in a most honorable and humble way. The commander of this table, of this household and his many holdings, waved off the compliments despite the fact that indeed he was a good man.

The handsome stranger would smile and bow his head, making the long feather in his hat bob. He rephrased each compliment to indicate that he'd noted it, as if he were building a list.

And he kept glancing at Babette.

Realization began to grow in Abbie's belly. Babette was seventeen now. Beautiful, well raised, of a family displayed here as being a large and healthy one, signifying the chances of her bearing a similar one as being good as well.

Uncle Gus had commissioned some miniatures of Babette over the past year. Babette had preened in posing for them, thinking that her father merely wanted the honor of immortalizing her, when he must have been circulating them hither and yon to interest a young man. Like this one.

Oh, the poor, wretched creature! Abbie gave a snort and tried to cover it up with a small cough, but she'd attracted the man's attention.

He examined her up and down with curiosity and she tried to hide her laugh behind her hand. Arching one eyebrow, she flicked her gaze over to her cousin and then back to him, asking silently.

He inclined his head ever so slightly, and Abbie couldn't stop a quick cough of dismay. He looked a little wounded at that.

Poor man! Poor, poor man! To have to endure Babette intimately for the rest of his life!

Abbie loved her cousin, but she knew her faults all too well. She had too many unpleasant moods for Abbie's tastes. A day could be perfectly lovely, the sun bright and breeze light with flowers adorning the green hills and bees buzzing in the vineyard– and Babette would bring her own storm to sully the world.

Abbie could walk into a room where the servants smiled to each other and to her, some perhaps with a little tune to lighten their work– and when they stopped and looked at the ground and grumbled, Abbie would know that Babette was passing through, sharing a headache with everyone.

Babette was beauty itself. When she was happy, the land smiled with her. It made having to wait upon her whims day and night worth it.

And it made Uncle Gus her little puppet.

Suddenly Abbie felt as if someone had struck her with a cook pot. Babette was to be married.

Where did that leave her?

Yes, yes, she'd known that Babette would be married off someday, but that day had always seemed so far away. Where had the time gone?

Babette was Abbie's anchor to Uncle Gus's family. Abbie's duty was to keep an eye on her cousin. Without her cousin around, what would she be expected to do? She had gotten her little vineyard here because the family knew that Babette couldn't occupy all her time. What if they came up with something that would keep her away from her vines?

Abbie put down her dining knife and stared at her plate in consternation. She tried to think of some duty here that wasn't already being taken care of, some spot that she could fill, but the prosperous household was run efficiently. Everyone had their job to do. Everyone knew what was expected of them.

A sudden surge of hope bloomed within Abbie. She was a woman now, no longer a helpless girl. Might she ask to return home to the clos? Would Cousin Christopher let her work there, where she belonged?

After all, wasn't that where she was needed most? It would fulfill her family duty as well as her joy. Why, Babette getting married was the greatest of blessings. Abbie offered up a thankful prayer to St. Amandus. She could go home again!

That is, if Babette didn't mess up things.

"Papa," Babette said brightly when conversation had paused for some time as the plum pudding was served, "I would like to talk with you about— ouch! Why, Abbie, that hurt."

"Oh dear, was that you? I'm terribly sorry, Babette."

Aunt Danielle smiled a weak warning. She couldn't be more than six years older than Abbie. "Babette, please don't interrupt your father."

"But I wasn't. He wasn't saying anything and I have such an important subject to bring up." Babette turned quickly to her father. "It's about Michel. Michel Fichaud."

Uncle Gus's forehead furrowed as he humored his eldest daughter. "Fichaud?"

"You know. The master of the clos vineyard, Papa."

"Of course I know Fichaud. What is it, Babette? Do you want some more wine?"

"Oh, Papa– ouch!– we're getting married. This Christmas, I think. I–"

"You're what?" Uncle Gus blinked as he held his spoon ready to sample the pudding. He blinked again and his cheeks went red above his graying beard. "You what? Did I hear you say that–"

"Married, Papa. Isn't it wonderful? He's going to ask your permission just as soon as–"

"Married?"

For a moment Abbie thought that Uncle Gus would bound out of his chair, but instead he sank back into it and let out a huge laugh. "Married! Ah, my beautiful daughter, what a jester you can be!"

"It's not– ow!" Babette kicked Abbie back this time and gave her a dark look.

Uncle Gus still laughed, his large frame causing the table to shake as well. "I think our young Babette has discovered what we are up to tonight." He chuckled and winked at the priest, who tried to join in, glancing nervously at DuMonde.

The man sat there, seeming isolated from the rest of them. His eyes darted back and forth from father to priest. Then he searched Abbie's face and she looked away, straightening her countenance so she would not spoil things for her cousin. And for herself.

"All right, all right." Uncle Gus wiped his fingers on the tablecloth with some ceremony, a merry grin superbly masking the anger that still shone in his cheeks and nose. "Babette has guessed. Yes, we think we have made a match for you, daughter. A very fine match indeed, as good as I'd ever hoped. She is my diamond, my pearl, Jean-Marc." He nodded at DuMonde. "Her dowry matches her value to me."

"Details still wait to be resolved," Jean-Marc said, nodding to Babette. Surely he could read the horror in her face.

"But–" Babette sputtered.

Underneath the table Abbie reached for Babette's hand and grabbed it in a hard hold. Every time Babette opened her mouth, Abbie squeezed. Finally even Babette realized that for once she had to keep quiet.

Everyone was staring at Babette. Abbie had to do something until her cousin could compose herself. "May I be the first to offer my congratulations, Monsieur?" she asked quickly.

Again he inclined his handsome head to her, a thick curl falling onto his forehead. "You may offer them," he told her, "but it would be better to offer them to my employer, Philippe Dellamer, for it is his business that I am here to conduct."

"Philippe Dellamer," Abbie murmured, trying out the name. She nudged Babette. "Mistress Dellamer," she said as a peace offering. "Congratulations."

Babette's eyes flashed lightning. "Thank you," she said from between gritted teeth, as she did whenever she thought she was putting on a show of cool refinement.

Abbie knew that sullen look all too well. Babette would make trouble about this.

2

Jean-Marc DuMonde allowed himself to be ushered into the study. It was a comfortable size, as were all the rooms that he had seen so far of this impressive country house, made small only by the sheer number of people who crowded in.

He was used to business deals being made by two, perhaps as many as four people, quiet men standing in the stately offices of the Dellamer Company. Though most of these men were local priests, they talked loudly, laughed loudly, and had the unfortunate tendency to clap him hard across the back.

He liked it. Well, except for the pain part.

It was something different, a new way to deal. These were new people with a different way of seeing the world. They weren't the type to stroll to silent offices and sit there all day, poring over columns of numbers. These were men who got up in the morning and accomplished something real before they returned to bed at night, whether it be bringing in a crop or saving a soul or two.

Auguste Bourgogne poured watered wine for all except the middle-aged man in the corner who drooled onto his own shoulder. He received mostly water with a little wine mixed in to make it healthy. Jean-Marc's gaze rested upon him and then moved on. All families contained members who weren't quite right.

Of course there were all kinds of not quite right. This Babette… would she be right for Philippe? She was a little beauty, but already he could see that she was strong-willed. Spoiled, perhaps, though it was possible he'd caught her on a bad day. Even so, a wife needed to bend her will to her husband's desire. Philippe needed someone to help him, not a brat to pester him day in and day out.

What was all that about marrying the master of the vineyard? It didn't seem a very funny joke to Jean-Marc, if that was indeed what it had been.

Her cousin seemed to find a slight humor in the idea of Babette being married. Had that been pity he'd seen in her eyes when she thought that he was the intended husband?

Ah, Babette's cousin. Abbie, the intriguing one. Not too young, not too old. A figure that was neither too big nor too small. In all probability a virgin, a good country girl. Hair the color of honey. Eyes reflecting a stormy sea. Her pink mouth promised many things to the man who'd dare to kiss it. He looked forward to exploring her more personally, just as he explored all things new to him. How long would he be here? How much of a watchdog was Bourgogne over his charges?

Jean-Marc frowned at himself as Auguste reached into his desk for his writing supplies. This wasn't about sweet Abbie Bourgogne. It concerned the wedding of a shipping empire with a valuable product. The religious ceremony to ensure that the contract would last several lifetimes was merely a secondary clause, though an unwritten subclause would also grant him his own freedom.

At last.

Jean-Marc crossed his arms over his chest. "We will get both the October and February shipments," he began.

Babette paced the narrow hall in front of the heavy oaken doors of the study, her long skirt twitching behind her like the tail on an angry cat.

"They are bargaining my life away!" she hissed at Abbie. "*That man* and Father!"

"Father Bernard will oversee the contract," Abbie replied. "He's a man of God and will make sure everything is fair."

She sat in the warm nook that was bounded by the back of the kitchen fireplace. Next to her, frail, white-haired Nana snored softly, hunched under her coverlet while young Thérèse lay curled up at her feet in the tumbled folds of the same coverlet as if she were the family cat.

Though Abbie drew her book of psalms closer to the candles as if she were trying to read, she couldn't. For all her stillness, she felt every bit the anxiety as did her cousin. She didn't want these dear people who had been so good to her to think her a traitor for wanting to leave.

Her duties to Babette anchored her life here. With Babette gone, would Uncle Gus dismiss her because she wasn't part of his immediate family? Ah, God above, what if he didn't relent to her plea to return home? Why should he listen to her, a mere niece? Where could she go? What could she do?

She knew how to run a winery, but who would hire a woman, even a Bourgogne, to do that? Abbie couldn't imagine herself as merely a married woman. Neither Mama nor Aunt Danielle had ever taught her the duties of a wife. She had no idea how to plan meals or keep linens on hand, though she could follow the housekeeper's suggestions to keep Babette's room tidy and ready for her. Abbie didn't know how to organize a household staff.

Oh, she knew well enough how a wine should taste at each stage of its life, how to tell when the grapes were ready to be harvested. She knew when to drain off the fermented wine into new barrels, how to manage a vineyard's workers– but she hadn't relied upon that knowledge since she'd moved in with her uncle and his family. The clos vineyards where she'd grown up were far away now and no longer hers to work. They'd gone to her uncle upon the death of her father, his older brother.

No, with Babette gone a hole would gape within the household, and Abbie was terrified that she'd be the one to fall into it, never to emerge.

"I am going to bed," Babette whispered fiercely to Abbie, knowing that Nana would never hear her. "Don't bother to wake me when they're through. I can wait until morning to be told my sentence."

"I'm coming," Abbie said automatically and put down her book. It was her duty to ready Babette for bed, just as Babette did the same for her.

"I will see to myself tonight." Babette lifted her chin in defiance and turned on her heel.

An act of kindness or of sulking? Abbie tried to figure out her cousin. Of the few times in the past when she'd actually assumed the worst of Babette, it had turned out that she'd been completely fooled and discovered that Babette indeed held a goodly reservoir of kindness in her heart, kindness she'd been taught by her father and mother.

And Aunt Danielle as well. Abbie's aunt rounded a corner into the hall with weary step as she listened to the housekeeper beside her. Danielle wore her best dress of green and cream tonight. The colors set off the red in her coiled hair. She was a beautiful woman.

But Aunt Danielle always seemed listless. Abbie wondered if it was because she already had two children in her young marriage to Uncle Gus, or if it were something else. When Abbie had met Danielle for the first time on the day of her wedding, Danielle had seemed unhappy for a bride. Her lips had smiled at her new family, but nothing else had. Danielle was a quiet thing who only displayed enthusiasm around her own children.

Now with all the younger children in bed, Danielle sank into the chair next to Abbie's, dismissing the housekeeper for the night.

Danielle glanced around. "Where is Babette?"

"She's gone to sleep."

Abbie's young aunt shook her head. "If I were her, I would be anxious to hear my fate." She took up some darning work and bent to the candles to attend to it.

"Babette is probably plotting how she can get out of this," Abbie said. "She's quite taken with Michel Fichaud. She thinks to marry him."

"Well, she's wrong." Danielle clipped two threads quickly. "She has no choice in this."

Abbie wondered at the frown on Danielle's face. Surely she was not concentrating so hard on her work for her brow to wrinkle! "It seems a very good match," Abbie told her. "Babette loves her baubles, and apparently this Dellamer man is quite rich."

Danielle snorted. "Wealth doesn't matter. Men don't understand that. What is money next to a loving smile?"

"Like the way Uncle Gus smiles at you?" Abbie keenly watched her aunt, but Danielle said nothing, her face a mask of nonemotion.

"But Uncle Gus does smile at you," Abbie said. "He adores you."

Danielle put down her darning. "He is a good man," she said slowly. "He's a good provider. I can grow old here without worry."

Suddenly she seemed deflated. Her shoulders sank. "I can grow old here without love."

"But Uncle Gus loves you!" Abbie protested softly. "He always said that this was the marriage he took on for love."

"Yes. His love. Not mine." Danielle touched two fingers to her lower lip. "There was a boy back home… By now I suppose he runs his father's farm." She shook her head and picked her stitches back up. "We made our own promises to each other. We had our own future planned, full of smiles and children and happiness. And then Auguste made his offer to my father, and Jacques couldn't come close to being able to match it."

Danielle had never mentioned anything like this to her before. Abbie reached out to take her hand. "I didn't know," she said. "Were you very much in love?"

When Danielle turned to her, her eyes were full of tears unshed. "I will love him until the day I die," she said. "I will meet him again in Heaven. Let Auguste live with his first wife there. I will search for my Jacques and we will have a heavenly mansion to spend eternity in. This is the hope that keeps me going from day to day."

With a sniff, she returned businesslike to her work. "It could have been much worse, I suppose. Many men beat their wives or are drunks. Many men take lovers and thus make fools of their wives. Auguste is an honorable man."

"He does love you," Abbie said.

That made Danielle pause. Her pale face seemed a trifle sickly in the candleglow, a shadow rimming her eyes. "I know. I don't know whether to feel sorry for him or guilty for myself that I can't love him back. Every day and night I pray for him, but I don't know what to pray for."

Abbie jumped as the doors swung open with a burst of boisterous laughing from Uncle and Father Bernard. The stranger, Jean-Marc, held a satisfied smile on his face as well.

He made such a fine figure, despite the slashed clothes, as the many small flames within the women's niche caught him in chiaroscuro. Uncle Gus clapped him on the back– a gesture of no small force, as Abbie knew– and Jean-Marc took it lightly across his shoulders.

He glanced about the hall. A lock of dark hair fell upon his face. When he lifted his hand to brush it back, Abbie felt as if the world slowed so she could see every moment of his face turning, of his hair catching the light, of his gaze stopping at her. Her breath caught in the back of her throat.

That gaze traveled down and then back up her form. She could feel it like a solid touch upon her. His smile grew broader, warmer. She lifted her hand modestly to her enamel necklace even as she felt her blush start from there, or slightly below.

He inclined his noble head to her and then returned his attention to his host.

"Danielle!" Uncle Gus called. His wife dropped her work to hurry to his side. Gus circled his arm around her waist and patted her hip, pulling her closer to himself. Abbie stood to hear her uncle's announcement as young Thérèse roused herself.

"Babette!" Gus shouted. "God's teeth, where is that girl? I would think she'd be here all along."

"She was quite tired," Abbie explained quickly as she joined them. "The excitement, perhaps. She was too tired even to require my help tonight, Uncle. I think she sleeps soundly."

"Peculiar girl." Uncle Gus glanced at Jean-Marc and corrected himself. "Most special girl. Only she would do something like that, to be so content with any choice I might make. A dutiful girl, she is. Well, wife, we have made and sealed our contract! What a fine marriage we have crafted for our dearest diamond, eh? And gained a sturdy alliance in the bargain."

Again he clapped Jean-Marc on the back. Now Abbie could spot the slightest of staggers in the young man.

"Philippe will have an even more lucrative trade overseas now that he can sell your goods," Jean-Marc said.

"Absolutely. We will make excellent partners. His ships, my mustards, my wines. My wines! They are known throughout the country, and now they'll be prized throughout the world!" Uncle laughed again, and this time Father Bernard joined in as well.

"Come, come!" Uncle waved them into the dining room where the best goblets were kept. The various clerics and Grand-Uncle Ronald clustered in from the study. "A toast all around! I have been saving a few jars of great distinction. The wisest thing my dear departed brother ever told me is that aged wine is even better than this year's crop. Six years ago, we had such a vintage–!"

Father Bernard tut-tutted. "Aged wine? Hrum– Six years?" he asked. "Surely you can't be serious. It will make us sick!"

"Sick with pleasure." Gus granted him a back-clap as well. "Wines keep long in earthenware jars. My brother purchased a handful to experiment with."

The priest patted his belly anxiously. "Still…"

"No one has ever gotten sick on Bourgogne Grand Cru. In fact, I believe it's responsible for bringing several people back to the land of the living. Come, you all will taste and remember to tell your grandchildren about its magnificence."

The last of the guests had all been made comfortable. Father Bernard was given the younger boys' room while they shared with their older brothers. It had taken some time before they finally settled down for the night, but now they were fast asleep. Jean-Marc DuMonde's things were placed in the guest room, which now held the beautiful quilt from Uncle Gus's marriage bed.

He and Uncle Gus were still downstairs. The rest found cozy pallets waiting in the barn.

Abbie yawned as she opened the door to her and Babette's bedroom. She made no noise so as not to disturb her cousin and set the candle down where her body would block the light from Babette. It was an effort to untie her heavy sleeves and undress by herself, but she finally managed it. She hung everything in the armoire. How nice to see that for once Babette hadn't left her own dress lying around for Abbie to pick up. Unbinding her hair and brushing it, she then quickly braided and capped it.

With the candle out, darkness cloaked the room. Abbie pulled the quilt back and eased into bed. Babette liked to sprawl, and she searched for the arm that was always there to lift it so she could snuggle in.

But there was no arm.

Abbie reached out and patted down the bed.

No Babette. Save for Abbie, the bed was empty.

The door creaked as it slowly opened, silhouetted by a candle in the darkness. Huddled high on the pillows, Abbie held her breath until she saw for sure who it was.

"Where in Heaven's name have you been?" she hissed. "I've been worried sick! Are you all right?"

Babette placed the candle on the night table and then swept her cloak from her shoulders with a toss of her head. "I have been out. With Michel. We've been making plans."

"Plans!" Abbie didn't know which to be most frightened of: that Babette had spent night hours unescorted with a man, or that her declaration seemed to announce that she would counter Uncle Gus's decision.

"Yes." Babette plopped onto the edge of the bed. She twisted to look straight at Abbie. "So tell me: what did they decide?"

"You're to marry Shipping Master Philippe Dellamer at Christmastide. He lives in Marseille. Uncle is anxious to use his business to sell our wines more widely."

"Wider than they are now? Clos Bourgogne is known everywhere. Here, cousin, help me with this."

Abbie crawled over to untie Babette's gown. "The wine is known in France," Abbie said. "Uncle means to sell it in Italy, Spain… perhaps farther."

"Really? And this– Dellamer man. He can do that?"

Abbie was encouraged by the thoughtful look on her cousin's face. "Yes. His ships travel quite far, and very successfully. His man says he ships everything except a true cru wine. He wants an exclusive contract. His man says that Clos Bourgogne was his first choice because ours is the finest vineyard in Burgundy." Abbie paused to drive the point home as she hung up Babette's gown. "Uncle said in so many words that Master Dellamer is quite wealthy."

"Ah?"

With a few more jounces, Babette lounged in her night chemise against the bare sheets and then leisurely drew the blankets around her. As usual she took more than half.

"Perhaps I shall have to rethink my plans," Babette said as if to herself. "What does this Dellamer look like?"

Abbie shrugged. "I have no idea. What does it matter, if he's rich?" She knew her cousin's preferences.

"Is he at least young? Not a doddering old man who's spent a lifetime building his empire and is only now willing to settle down?"

Abbie didn't want to sound like she was badgering Babette. Babette could be so stubborn if she felt she was being forced into something. No, subterfuge was the better strategy. She must make Babette want this match. Babette *must* fulfill the marriage contract. The family honor– and Abbie's future– depended on it.

"I got the impression that he was quite close to his man, Jean-Marc," Abbie said easily.

"In a brotherly or a fatherly way, I wonder?" Babette settled back on the pillows. "How rich is rich, do you think?"

"Uncle said he added to your dowry to sweeten the vintage. You already had a sizable dowry, Bab, one any girl would be jealous of."

"But not you." With a warm smile Babette leaned over to pat Abbie softly on the cheek. "Dear cousin. I'm sorry that life has been harsh to you."

"It hasn't been that harsh, Babette. Family is the most important thing there is, and your family reached out to save me."

"Sometimes I wonder if I could have taken it all as well as you have." Babette sighed. "Rich. My father's idea of rich and my idea of rich sometimes only match so much. I will think of this in my dreams."

"I prayed for you tonight, Babette."

"And I will pray for you– in my dreams. I'm too tired to kneel right now. Let us both sleep and have wonderful dreams of wealth. Good night."

A puff of breath and the room lay in darkness again.

Abbie rubbed the last of her sleep from her eyes. As soon as the sound of the priests leaving just before dawn had reached them, Babette had arisen bright and glowing. She'd insisted on wearing her best morning dress and had sent Abbie ahead to breakfast while she picked among her jewelry.

It was a hopeful start to the day. Wealth meant a great deal to Cousin Babette. Perhaps her dreams had shown her the reality of a match to Michel Fichaud compared to the mysterious bounty that Master Dellamer held. Perhaps some angel had whispered to her the importance of doing what was best for the family. A scandalous match versus the match her father had worked so hard to secure– even Babette could see–

"And what is this?"

Abbie jumped when the raspy male voice came from behind her. She looked around to find Jean-Marc DuMonde with those penetrating black eyes– no, in the daylight they were quite rich and brown– and the slightest of mischievous smiles lifting the corners of his mouth. Still, he looked bleary as well. The shadow from last night was now quite heavy and dark on his jaw.

At least today he dressed sensibly in browns and golds, with not nearly so much fine white linen peeking through slits in his doublet. And instead of that overly-padded codpiece sticking out down there he wore a much more distinguished base that draped almost to his knees.

"That's porridge," Abbie told him. She made the offer with the serving spoon and he nodded, so she dished some onto his plate. Not enough for a full serving, though; he might not like such simple country fare. There were enough dishes lined up on the narrow side table that he could find something he liked. It wasn't often that they had honey-dipped fritters and sausages, much less *oeufs en meurette*– eggs with burgundy and onions– but it wasn't often that they had important guests for breakfast, either.

"Did you sleep well, Monsieur?"

"Please call me Jean-Marc. May I call you Abbie?"

Carefully holding his breakfast plates level, he gave a graceful bow, and she tipped a curtsy back.

"I admit that I slept too well and the morning came all too quickly." Jean-Marc grimaced at her, his eyes crinkling painfully. No wonder his tone held a slight gravel to it, unlike the silk of last night.

"Ah. You were still celebrating when I went to bed." Abbie picked among the choices at the buffet and poured a combination of liquids into a goblet, including unwatered wine. With a whisper to a maid, she received a small pottery bottle of dark granules, measured them out into her palm and then swirled them into the drink along with three drops of red liquid from another bottle. A vigorous stir, and the antidote stood finished.

"With the quality of wines we produce," she told Jean-Marc, "our family are experts in devising counter-beers as well, though ours use wine as a base. It makes them work faster. Drink up."

Jean-Marc studied the mixture with a frown, but set down his plates and upended the goblet. Two swallows without a breath and it was inside him. He clutched at the sideboard and gasped.

"Are you sure the cure for such isn't death?" he croaked. "Hot. Hot, hot!"

Abbie tore a piece of bread for him, and he grabbed it from her, rolling the morsels around on his tongue as she handed him a mug of cool buttermilk.

"The drink really should have had a raw egg in it," Abbie told him in amused concern, "but sometimes that makes matters worse."

"Uhh… Whew. Yes. That's a little better." He gulped and then made a horrified face as her words sank in. "Thank you for no egg. I don't think I could take that this morning."

"A minute from now you'll be feeling much better. Eating a hearty meal also helps. We have eggs enough that are cooked. Try the hard-boiled ones with mustard." She loaded some onto one of his plates and took it to the table for him as he handled his second one.

For a moment he held one hand on his stomach– and a fine, flat one it was– before sitting in the chair. "I believe you may be right," he said as he settled more comfortably. "Perhaps the dawn does indeed have rosy fingers this day."

"And perhaps you'd best start with the porridge just in case," Abbie said.

"You seem quite the wise young woman. And quiet."

"Only among strangers. Quiet, that is. Wise, often."

That brought a chuckle. He had a wonderful, deep chuckle that vibrated against her. His curly hair had slipped back down his forehead again, and Abbie resisted the sudden urge to restore it to its place.

She laughed at herself. It had been a long time since she'd gone all cow-eyed over a man. Well, this one wouldn't be here much longer. She'd enjoy looking at him and hearing his voice while the moment lasted.

"I promise I'll never drink like that again," Jean-Marc said, crossing his fingers with reverence. "It's a foolish man who doesn't learn from his own mistakes."

"But it was a special occasion," Abbie protested. "Surely when your own bride is contracted, you'll drink even more. Or has that blessed event already taken place?"

He busied himself dribbling honey on the pile of oatmeal as she had done. "Ha! That's a good one. No, no marriage for me. I am a free man, a man of the world. That's why I chose my name: DuMonde. I travel all of Christendom with no hindrances to bind me. No woman owns me, nor will one ever."

"How sad for the world of women."

They laughed like two old friends until he hiccupped suddenly with a burping afternote. He smacked his fingers over his mouth and had the presence of manners to look mortified.

Abbie laughed again. "I should have warned you about that effect," she said. "But one good belch or two and it's over. Everyone does it. You'll live."

Cautiously he removed his fingers as if testing the air. Abbie dug into her breakfast plate to set him more at ease. There was no one else at the table yet for it seemed everyone, except the dutiful priests and servants, was rising late this morn.

"Your cousin– she is your cousin, correct?" Jean-Marc waited for Abbie's nod before he continued. "She seemed to have another man in mind for marriage last night, and I did not think it was a jest."

"She did," Abbie said. "She's very young. A butterfly, flitting from thought to thought. I explained things to her last night–" Abbie tilted her head to give the word "explained" emphasis– "and this morning I believe her thoughts have settled in a direction more to your liking."

He made a noise as he poured himself some wine.

"I shall miss Babette." Abbie played with the food on her plate. "She and I have been such close playmates for these past four years. I think she may be sad to leave this country, but she will cheer up enough when she gets to Marseille. Babette was never meant to be a country girl."

"And you were, mademoiselle?"

She gave him a little smile as he tipped his wineglass in a small salute to her.

"I am a Burgundy girl," she told him. "I was born here. My family has been here for generation upon generation, working our vineyard. The Clos Bourgogne itself– the walled field that makes up the special earth that grows the finest pinot noir grapes in the land– that was always tended by my family. My father was the last one to truly do it justice."

She sat and swirled her own goblet, looking at misty memories before she shook her head. "Since he died, my uncle put Cousin Christopher in charge of the clos. Father was the older brother, you know, but there being no surviving male heirs in his line, the clos transferred to Uncle Gus. Chris does not have the soul of a vintner, nor has he chosen to learn the skill. And why he hired Michel Fichaud to–" She glanced up to see two newcomers. "Oh, good morning, Uncle Gus. And Cousin Babette. She always looks this lovely in the morning, Jean-Marc."

Babette positively glowed at the praise as she strolled in on her father's arm, her sapphire skirts sweeping against his shoes.

"It is a grand morning, isn't it?" Babette asked the two at the table. She beamed at her father.

"A most happy day," Uncle Gus agreed. "I have planned for this since before you were born, my sweet diamond."

Babette's sense must have returned over the night. Abbie breathed a sigh of relief. Michel Fichaud might be a pleasure to look at, but truly, wealth played the better game within Babette's heart.

Jean-Marc made some quite polite noises in both of their directions, which pleased Auguste even more. The head of the Bourgogne family hummed as he made his way down the serving table to pick the best tidbits of this breakfast feast.

He swirled a fritter in the honey at the bottom of its serving dish before setting it on his plate. "I've instructed Danielle to send for the dressmaker," he said, and Babette squealed.

"Real clothes!"

"Hm. It seems to me that you're always dressed very well," Uncle Gus said as he examined the sausages. "You've never wanted for anything. We'll get Abbie some dresses as well. We can't have the two of you looking like country bumpkins in Marseille."

Abbie's spoon stopped halfway to her mouth. "Marseille?" she managed to ask, though her voice seemed far away.

Babette seated herself next to Abbie. "Why yes," she said with a self-satisfied smile. "I convinced Papa to let you come with me. I need a maid and a companion– and here you are already! Oh, Abbie, we'll have such fun in Marseille! I know you'll love it."

"Not… Not Marseille." Abbie twisted in her chair to beseech Uncle Gus. "Please don't send me from here. This is all I have left–"

Auguste made clucking noises as he scooped up eggs and onions. "Let us hear no more of this," he said. "You will meet a fine choice of men in Marseille, Abbie. Plenty more than you'll ever see here, so far from civilization. And these men will be the movers and shakers of the world, caught in the bustle of the city. You need a clever man to wed, smarter than the ones around here. In Marseille you will find such men by the dozens. You write me and tell me which you have your eye on, and I'll begin the inquiries. You know that I have gathered a good dowry for you. I honor my obligations to my brother and my family. I have always been a good uncle to you, haven't I, my dear?"

"Yes… Yes, Uncle Gus."

Thank goodness she was sitting down, for the room went pale and distant. The table seemed to sway in front of her, and the conversation between Uncle Gus, Babette and whoever else had just entered seemed to take place in another world.

From her right a strong hand took hold of her elbow, shaking it a little. "Drink." Jean-Marc's whisper penetrated her haze. He pressed a cup into her hand.

"Drink!" he urged quietly.

She gulped the *vin ordinaire* and he refilled her cup, wrapping her fingers around its bowl for her. Another few gulps and the room cleared in her vision.

Her cousins and aunt made great noise as they approached breakfast. No one had noticed her lapse save for Jean-Marc.

Marseille.

How far was that? The other end of the world.

Aunt Danielle spied her at last. "Ah, Abbie!" she cried. "Isn't it so exciting for you! The city– What an adventure. We'll have you dressed so fine that no man will be able to resist offering for you."

Uncle Gus nodded. "We'll throw a big farewell party for you, daughter. Niece. Everyone will come to wish you off."

"When?" Abbie managed.

"Why, Sunday after next," he told her. "In ten days you'll leave for Marseille."

3

J ean-Marc sealed the letter with candlewax. There. The most important letter of his life had been finished, the letter that would trigger his ultimate freedom.

He wandered downstairs looking for anyone who could start the letter on its journey to Marseille. He came to a halt before entering the kitchen when he heard two familiar female voices.

"How could you, Babette?" that intriguing Abbie accused. "How could you drag me into this? You know I want to go home. How will I manage that from Marseille?"

"It's for both our good," Philippe's bride-to-be replied. "I thought about this very hard last night."

"Sure you did. You fell asleep right off."

"Well then, I thought about it this morning. As Papa said, you'll have more men to choose from in Marseille than here, Abbie."

"I don't want a husband of Marseille."

"It will work out the best this way, Abbie. You don't have any faith in me, do you? I may not be as clever as you in some things, but I have thought this through. I've figured everything out, and this is the direction that we'll both be the happiest. That's it. It's all been decided."

"I won't go!"

"And embarrass Papa? After all he's done for you?"

An oath that came very close to being unladylike hissed through the hallway from the room beyond.

Babette went on. "Why, I think this situation might be even better for you than me," she claimed. "Come, Abbie. You urged me so hard to go, the least you can do is own up to your own family duty."

Jean-Marc scrambled into the shadows of a doorway to avoid Abbie seeing him as she stormed past. Marching in quick-step she swept out the front door, slamming it behind herself.

Jean-Marc caught it before it could snap off its hinges and closed it gently after himself. He trotted after Abbie, approving of the way the sun caught her honeyed hair as she shook her head back and forth. She kept her dark woolen cloak closed to the chilled wind with tight fists.

"Beautiful day, isn't it?" Jean-Marc ventured as he caught up to her.

A muttered grunt died in mid-syllable. He watched her jaw clench before she said with the slightest of leftover growls, "The sun is out. It's been a week of clouds with a bit of rain."

The swallow she gave was visible. "I hope you didn't get the wrong impression of me this morning, monsieur."

"Jean-Marc. I told you to call me Jean-Marc."

"Jean-Marc."

He matched her long stride easily, hands clasped behind his back. He took deep draughts of the clean, if cold, country air as they crossed the rutted road toward the stone outbuildings. "All I know is that beautiful Abbie Bourgogne thinks of herself as a country girl. This is fine country you have around here, if you like the country."

"You don't?" she asked, turning at a gate to look at him at last.

"I never said that. I haven't seen enough of it to say," Jean-Marc replied. "As you pointed out, it's been a dreary trip these past few days. The land hasn't shown itself to the best." He met her gaze and held it. "But some people along the way have caught my interest. One in particular."

Her right eyebrow twitched at the same time the left side of her mouth did the same. "Some people are not interested in your interest, mon– Jean-Marc. I'm sure you're a, a…" her voice trailed as she clearly realized she knew nothing about Jean-Marc, "a trusted man for your employer to carry out such an important mission, but do keep your mind on your business at least as far as I am concerned. I am set for a different direction in my life."

They proceeded behind the aromatic barns, skirting the even more pungent pig wallow, and then uphill across a pasture at a quick pace. It had been a few weeks since Jean-Marc had had the chance to stretch his legs at length, and his breath came harder than he'd have liked. "I, too," he told Abbie, "have set my life on an interesting direction. I have plans."

"Mm?"

"I'm going to see the world," he declared.

They came to an abrupt halt.

"The world?" Abbie asked.

Jean-Marc nodded proudly.

"And what is wrong with where you are?" she demanded. "What makes you think that anywhere else is going to be better?"

"Better?" Jean-Marc resumed their trek though he had no idea where they were going. From up here the segmented fields with their variations of winter-brown splayed in all directions, bounded faraway by bare woods. The buildings behind them clustered at the end of a meandering, tree-lined road. "It doesn't have to be better. It just has to be different. Interesting. I like to explore. I like to discover the new."

The glance he gave her was exploratory.

How proudly she stood, her fist closing her cloak at her neck. Her flushed face bloomed above the dull wool. Jean-Marc fancied that perhaps the cold and exertion were not all that gave her cheeks that magnificent color. Locks of her loosely-bound hair flared about her in bolts of gold and amber.

Abbie rolled her eyes. "I can assure you that I am quite like any other girl from around here. Plain and ordinary–"

"Anything but," Jean-Marc assured her.

She seemed about to say something else but then said, "Thank you. And again: not interested. If you wish, I could point you toward some girls who might be willing to indulge in a short fling with a handsome city man."

"You think I'm handsome?" Jean-Marc grinned in triumph.

"I believe you know it," Abbie said. She didn't look at him now. "Your fine clothes alone would have some think you handsome, even if underneath you were misshapen and scarred by the pox. And as old as Methuselah."

"I can assure you, fair Abbie, that even without my clothing I am not displeasing," Jean-Marc told her with a sweeping bow. "Shall I demonstrate?"

She turned to him, hands on her hips. "I should take you up on that," she said. "But it might tempt me to steal your clothes and let you hike back to the house in your altogether— if you could keep from freezing to death between here and there."

"Someplace warmer, perhaps?" Jean-Marc offered.

"Not interested, thank you," Abbie repeated. She frowned at Jean-Marc's chuckle. "Why don't you go back to the house? I came out here to think."

"You came here to be angry. I heard the little fight you had with your cousin."

She frowned again, her gaze turned inward. "I'm sorry you had to witness that."

"You don't want to go to Marseille."

"I think I already told you that I was a Burgundy girl. I plan to stay here… somehow." She set her jaw and slammed her fist into her opposing palm. "Drat her anyway!"

He watched her curiously.

"She deliberately did this," Abbie fumed. "She knew I wanted to stay here, maybe see if I could get back home, and just because Uncle Gus ordered her to Marseille she can't bear to see anyone else happy."

Almost immediately Abbie's face smoothed to contriteness. She reached to lay her hand flat on Jean-Marc's shoulder. "Not that she's a terrible person," Abbie said. "Last summer Babette was the first to come to the aid of the Meuniers when their house burned. She helped organize all the neighbors, and gave their little girl her favorite doll, too. When Cook broke her arm, Babette got up before daybreak every day to help in the kitchen, until Aunt Danielle found a replacement. She's a good girl… when she wants to be."

Jean-Marc shrugged. "This way I won't have to hire a maid for her on the journey. She'll have a friend to keep her amused. And it's true, there are many more men in Marseille than around here. Some of them are quite rich as well, and a few of those might fancy a simple country girl from Burgundy."

"Not interested," Abbie repeated curtly. "I will find a way to return." She turned on her heel and walked away.

Jean-Marc gazed after her, scratching his head, before he returned to the house.

With all Abbie's attempts to deny that it was happening, the days passed as quickly as a dream. Servants and farm hands helped load Uncle Gus's largest wagon with the two girls' new wardrobes and favorite knickknacks, along with the first installment of Babette's dowry: massive jars of different kinds of mustards, for which the region was as well known as it was for its wines, three barrels of Abbie's chardonnay, various household items, and a written contract between the Clos Bourgogne and Dellamer's Shipping Company of Marseille. The latter was securely pocketed within Jean-Marc's impressive fur-lined coat.

The girls shivered in the icy November mists as they left the village church where the townsfolk had gathered. Between sniffles Father Bernard blessed them for their journey. Even Uncle Gus broke down and cried great tears, kissing his daughter as if he didn't want her to go. He hugged Abbie until she thought her ribs would break.

"Here, Abbie. It should remain here for safekeeping, but I give this to you," he said. He fastened her mother's cross around her neck. "This will remind you that there is a generous dowry waiting for whenever you are ready to use it."

He lifted her chin with a finger, noting the dark circles under her reddened eyes. They'd been there for over a week now though she'd never cried in public. "Let this be a comfort to you. I'm sure your father is watching you from Heaven. I think he'd want me to say that God works in mysterious ways, His wonders to reveal. This is your best chance at a good future. Do what you can with it."

Abbie couldn't open her mouth to speak, so she merely nodded numbly. Suddenly strong arms enveloped her.

"Abbie! Abbie's going away!" Cousin Louis sobbed against her shoulder. "Don't go, don't go!"

Abbie tried not to notice how messy he was getting her. She twisted in his hold, patted his back, and gave him her handkerchief to blow his nose and wipe his eyes.

"There, there, Louis," she said as she hugged him. "You'll be fine."

"My girls are going. No, no, no!"

His hug was too strong for her. She couldn't breathe. Uncle Gus pulled the man's hands from her.

"Gently, Louis," he cautioned, and Louis nodded through a sheet of tears and runny nose, crying all the more because he'd forgotten his own strength.

"You'll have all the younger children now, Louis," Abbie told her cousin. "They'll be your new girls and boys. You can play with them now that they're older."

But the children saw Louis's tears and theirs began, too. They ran to Abbie and Babette, pulling on their skirts and wailing.

"Children!" Gus bellowed. "Quiet down! Danielle! Do something about this squalling!"

Amid her hangers-on, Abbie motioned to Danielle, pointing at the waiting wagon. Soon Danielle pressed a doll into Louis's hands.

"See, Louis?" Abbie asked. "I'm giving her to you. You can call her Abbie."

Louis sniffed and wiped his now-grubby hand across his eyes. "Your dollie? Can I have her, Abbie? Can I?"

"She's yours now. You can talk to her and maybe I'll hear. Remember me with her."

Louis gave her a huge grin as he clasped the doll to himself. Then he skipped off, swinging the doll around him in a dance. He halted and turned. "Good bye, Abbie," he said, and then resumed his dance.

"I wanna doll." Little Marie pulled on Abbie's skirt.

"I don't have another one here," Abbie said. She knelt down to hug her young cousin. "You ask your daddy. We left some dolls behind. You and your sisters can have those."

Even with that reassurance, the children's wails reached ear-ringing levels. Uncle Gus wiped his eyes and gave the two girls a wan smile. "If we want to keep the peace of the churchyard, perhaps you'd best go now."

After a final round of desperate hugs to the people Abbie would never see again, the wagon set off quickly.

Frost on the final scraps of golden foliage glittered as the sun broke through the remnants of the morning's fog. The horses' hooves clattered with great bracks on the semi-frozen ground. Abbie sat on her makeshift bench in the back of the wagon, glad to be facing backward so she could catch the very last view of what had been her home for the past four years.

Round bales of late hay lay piled in the rolling fields along the road. There was the Broges's farm, and there the Veneurs's. They'd hugged her this morning at service as if she were family, and Abbie realized that they were. These were the people she'd grown up with. She swept tears from her cheeks as she remembered all the sweetness that lay in this vale, all the honest folk who had only been kind to the frightened orphan.

At last the tallest tower of the church disappeared behind a ridge. Gone were the familiar landmarks and hills. Abbie burst out with the tears she'd held so tightly today.

Finally she could weep no more.

"All cried out?" Jean-Marc asked her. He sat lounged on their bench, his legs propped up on a trunk and his arms crossed over his chest, which made the fur trim of his deep red gown bunch around his face. He actually seemed to enjoy the journey.

"Never," Abbie said, angry that he could be immune to such disaster. "I am not a woman of the world to travel all of Christendom like some people. Today they've jerked me by the roots from my native soil. I am dying."

"Perhaps your roots just need more room to grow," he said with a smile. "You'll like Marseille. All women do. It's very exciting, lots of new fashions and dancing and markets."

"And men," Babette chimed in from up front.

"You need those for the proper dancing," Jean-Marc said. He turned forward to regard Babette sitting next to the village boy who drove and would then return the wagon when they were done. "How are you doing, Mademoiselle? Resigned to your fate?"

Babette let out a single, loud chuckle. "I look forward to my fate, sir. Now tell us of Marseille. Tell us of the wonders of the city."

Jean-Marc thought a moment and then began to relate the secrets of Marseille as if he'd been hired to take them on an extensive tour. Huge churches and tiny, hidden chapels. Fresh produce marketplaces that took up areas the sizes of entire villages. Flowers that bloomed all year long. Exotic merchandise from the Ottoman Empire and beyond. Slaves of every color. Food for every palate.

"Barefoot?" Abbie asked at one point.

Jean-Marc nodded. "You can run down the beaches with no shoes and no worries of ever stubbing your toe. The sand is absolute white, and the sea a marvelous blue that– well, I am not an artist, but I'll introduce you to one who can tell you exactly how blue the Mediterranean is. There are times when the water is so warm–" he wiggled his eyebrows suggestively at Abbie– "it's a shame to wear clothes when one runs into it. So some don't."

"No!" Babette cried from up front.

"Oh yes. There are many secret coves where all measures of frolicks take place." Jean-Marc's face assumed an angelic expression, and he reverently crossed himself. "Strictly between God-fearing husbands and wives, of course, merely exercising their marital duties in the same innocent way that Adam and Eve did."

Abbie knew her face must be beet red. As a farmgirl she had an idea what those duties might entail. Jean-Marc laughed at her. His hand slapped her knee and stayed there while Abbie wondered what to do with it, until he rubbed it in a swift circle and took it back to himself. His eyes sparkled a wicked invitation. She turned away, pretending to study the landscape.

She could hear his deep, soft voice, only for her, behind her shoulder. "Ah now, I've frightened her. I didn't mean to do that."

She ignored him until he resumed his conversation with Babette. They chattered. Abbie wondered how her cousin could be so gay when she might never see her home and family again, when Babette said, "Stop here."

Abbie turned to check the road in front of them. A meadow that still sprouted brave green shoots amid the season's leavings fanned out from the road, so there wasn't a place for private personal relief.

"I want to pray," Babette said, and sure enough, a post with a tiny shrine to Our Lady stood next to the road ruts.

Abbie knelt uncertainly next to her cousin as Babette counted through part of her rosary in front of the shrine, murmuring quietly to herself. Somehow this didn't seem right. Oh, it was proper enough, but Babette had never been the road shrine type. Sometimes she even missed morning services if her father were gone.

Babette sat back up with a sigh and her eyes focused on her cousin. "Oh," she said, "you're wearing the cross. It's so pretty."

Abbie's fingers moved to it automatically. "Uncle Gus gave it to me as… advanced payment. A gift."

"Oh, may I wear it? Just for this morning. For good luck," Babette urged.

"I'd really rather–"

"Oh, please, Abbie. I don't ask much of you, do I?"

Reluctantly, Abbie let Babette put the necklace around her own neck and felt a little better when Babette showed it off to Jean-Marc with a sweet story about Abbie's parents.

They rolled on soon enough, and the pleasant conversation continued though the two pairs were sitting back-to-back. Babette broke out into a song of young love. As she hit occasional notes off-key, Jean-Marc made faces behind her. She couldn't make the slide down on the end of the refrain to catch the correct pitch. Jean-Marc learned to anticipate it and then mouth along with her, screwing his lips around the foul note until Abbie had to clamp her hands across her own mouth to keep from laughing out loud.

He was nice enough to applaud generously when Babette finished.

"Oh, here's another," Babette observed as they approached a tiny lean-to. They stopped and Babette prayed again. Abbie clenched her eyes shut and guiltily offered up a prayer for herself, that whatever this horrible trip offered would bring more good than bad. That it would be a way for her to go home at last.

When they came to the fourth shrine, Abbie was prayed out. "What is all this, Babette?" she asked.

"Pray that after all these stops we'll reach the river by dark, for now that would take a miracle," Jean-Marc muttered.

Babette raised her pretty nose in the air. "I just want to start this marriage off right," she declared. "I want all the angels in Heaven on our side and to bless us. I want us to arrive safely."

Abbie, Jean-Marc and the village boy crossed themselves and they went on.

The fifth shrine they stopped at already had someone using it. A horse and good-sized, empty wagon stood patiently as a cloaked man knelt before the wooden statue.

Eager to attend to personal needs, their driver leapt from the wagon and ran into the woods that grew right up to the road here between meadows. The cloaked man crossed himself and stood up. His hood fell back to reveal straight, light brown hair and a new beard.

Abbie blinked. "Michel Fichaud! Why, Babette, it's Michel. How did he–" She blinked again at her cousin as realization crashed upon her.

"Oh no," she said even as Jean-Marc was helping Babette down from the wagon. "No. Put her back! It's a trick."

4

"It is not a trick," Babette said to the puzzled Jean-Marc. As first one foot and then the other set on the ground, she turned to Abbie. "It's a plan. A very good plan for you and me, dear cousin. As I said, I have everything figured out."

"Do we know you?" Jean-Marc asked the stranger.

He stepped back when Babette threw herself at Fichaud. "This is Michel, my true love. We will be married tonight, won't we, dearest?"

"I have the priest standing by," Fichaud declared.

Babette ran one hand through his slightly scraggly hair and kept the other on his chest. He gave her a small smile and then they kissed.

Abbie had never seen anyone kiss like that, not in public. Not where they thought anyone could see them.

"Oh sweet Heaven," she whispered to herself and sank to her knees within the wagon. "No, Babette. You are making such a mistake here. You'll dishonor your entire family. You'll dishonor Monsieur Dellamer and your father and–"

"There will be no dishonor, because no one will ever know," Babette said. She strode to Abbie's side of the wagon and grabbed its edge as if she would shake it to its axles. "You will take my place. It's as simple as that. We look enough alike that it could be you in whatever portrait Father sent to Monsieur Dellamer."

"Me?" Abbie squeaked.

Babette reached to pat her hand. "See, I was thinking of you, too. This way I'll not only get the man I love, but you'll get a rich and powerful husband. Father will keep his contracts, and all will be happy."

Jean-Marc stood looking back and forth at everyone as the situation gradually sank in. He pointed at Fichaud. "You are her lover," he accused.

Fichaud sank into a country bow. He'd always had a satisfied air about him, but now he reeked of it. "That is me," he said with a swagger of his chin. Whenever he'd visited Uncle Gus's home the household had come alive with the squeals and giggles of women who loved to fancy the handsome young man. And of course Babette had been the prettiest, the richest girl in the house.

Jean-Marc now turned his pointing finger to Babette. "You are backing out of the deal," he said.

"I did not make the contract," she replied icily. "I leave a perfectly acceptable substitute in my place."

"The contract was for one Babette Bourgogne." Jean-Marc's voice grated dangerously low.

Abbie covered her mouth in surprise and then released it. "My Christian name is Babette," she told Jean-Marc. "We were both named after our grandmother Bourgogne. She went by 'Abbie,' so I did as well. When Babette was born a year later, everyone said she couldn't use the nickname or they'd get us confused."

Babette directed Fichaud to the back of the wagon as Jean-Marc chafed, slapping his tall hat with its red feather against the side of the wagon.

"Take that and that," Babette instructed. Fichaud obediently hefted a small chest from the top of the pile.

"Here now, what are you doing?" Jean-Marc cried. "Are you stealing from us as well?"

"You can't, Babette!" Abbie pulled as Babette pulled, playing tug-of-war with another small chest that Abbie knew contained Babette's jewelry. "This is stealing from your future husband. It's not right. It is his. It is your father's gift to you!"

"So shouldn't I have it?"

"It's dishonest! I can't believe you'd do this. Think, Babette. An honorable marriage in Marseille. A wealthy marriage in Marseille. With all of society to admire you."

"And an ugly old man to share my bed." A final pull and the chest was Babette's prize. Abbie fell backwards, catching herself against some barrels.

Babette clamped both arms around the precious chest. "No thank you very much. Michel is leaving Clos Bourgogne to go to a very prominent position with his cousin in Dijon. We're going to need some things to help us get started in life."

"A thief, Babette–!" Abbie gasped. "You can't steal from your own–"

"Monsieur Dellamer will notice the lack of a dowry," Jean-Marc said. He leaned against the wagon, only his eyes moving as more boxes and trunks left in Fichaud's well-muscled arms. Fichaud had to step around him to get to his own wagon.

"We're only taking a little. The shipping contract is the main thing, isn't it? I doubt if anyone will notice," Babette said as Fichaud grunted under the strain of one of her wardrobe barrels.

"Dellamer will notice. I'll tell him."

Babette turned to shine her brilliant smile upon Jean-Marc. "Oh no you won't. What does he pay you to bring his bride to him? I'll pay you twice that, right here, to deliver her and keep your mouth shut."

Jean-Marc's eyes slid from Babette to Abbie and back. He kept silent and Babette smirked.

Abbie couldn't stand it anymore. "I cannot believe any of this! I will tell if no one else will. I will–"

"Bring dishonor upon our family?" Babette said coolly. "I think not. You go along with this, Abbie. It's for your best good. Where else could you find a husband of such a standing as Monsieur Dellamer? You, an orphan girl whose only dowry comes from her uncle's whim?"

Abbie tried to say several things and failed. She whirled to Jean-Marc. "And you– I cannot believe you would dishonor your employer in this way. I thought you were a trusted man, but I see now that you are not!"

A small smile came to his lips. "No," he said, "your cousin has convinced me that she is quite right. She is in love, and who am I to stand in the way of true love, especially if she is going to pay me well for stepping out of its path?"

Babette chuckled quietly at that.

"And if I understand things aright," Jean-Marc continued, "she is spoiled goods. She gave herself to this good man." He bowed to Fichaud, who didn't pay him any attention. "Monsieur Dellamer is expecting an innocent virgin to be his honorable wife. The most honorable young woman I've seen these past few days is our own Abbie– I mean, Babette Bourgogne." This time it was to Abbie that he bowed.

"I can *not* believe this." Abbie sat down with a *thwunk* to seethe in her own anger.

"And having met you, dear Mademoiselle Bourgogne," a bow to Babette, "I see that you are not at all of the proper temperament for Monsieur Dellamer. He requires a mature girl, a kind woman who is interested in others and in raising a family. A woman who won't spend all his money before her first month with him is up. I see none of those qualities in you. Abbie here, though, seems a woman who would do a man like Dellamer proud. She is my choice for him, and if we can slide her legally through this contract," he bowed again to Babette, "all's well that ends well."

"I see myself as not receiving many compliments in that speech," Babette said as she gave her chin a jerk. "But the sentiment comes out the same. Abbie will continue to Marseille. There she will marry Monsieur Dellamer, and if anyone can be happy with such a man as he must be, it is Abbie. She can find the good in anyone."

With a rush, Babette leaned over the side of the wagon to catch Abbie's hands in hers. "Oh believe me, dearest cousin," she said, "I did consider your happiness as well as mine. I know this is the best possible end for you, as it is for me. Please try not to think harshly of me for doing this. I know it is a shock, but as Papa always says, 'Abbie is the sensible one,' and you will get over it soon enough. You'll come to see as I have that this will be good– no, *wonderful–* for you. I wish for you all the happiness that I know I'll find myself. Dearest Abbie, forgive me. I do this for the both of us."

"And what about the stolen dowry?" Abbie asked, her face etched in stone. "How will I explain–?"

"Tell them thieves stole it. Tell them you don't know anything about exact quantities. Dellamer won't notice."

"He will." Jean-Marc's voice echoed between the trees lining the road.

Babette glanced at him and then shook Abbie's hands gently between hers. "And if he does, just write to Papa and make up some story."

"I don't lie to people I love."

"Well, do so just this once." Babette added hastily, "For the good of the family."

"So now you make me a thief? From the uncle who took me in when all was lost? How long will I have to stay in Purgatory for that, Babette?"

"No time at all. He said he'd provide you with a good dowry. Just think of this as me taking about what he'd give you, so when you ask– oh, and you can ask as if you'd found someone and it will be true, see?– it will be only him giving you what you are due. Not thievery."

"You are sacrificing your family, Babette. How could you even think of that? Family and honor are everything. Everything!"

"I will make a new family," Babette told her. "When Papa sees how well we are doing, he will welcome me back."

She touched Abbie's cheek and Abbie reluctantly looked down at her. "Our best good," Babette said firmly. "You will forgive me someday. Perhaps you'll even come to visit. I will name my first daughter after you. You bring yours to me sometime so she can meet her cousin Babette who loves her dear Abbie so much."

Babette dissolved into tears and tried to hug Abbie. She could not reach her, so she pressed her cheek against Abbie's hands instead.

Abbie sat there.

Still weeping, Babette chose a box from next to where she'd been sitting up front. Fichaud handed it to Jean-Marc.

When he opened it he frowned and turned some things in it over, examining them. It was mostly glassware packed in straw. "More," he finally said.

"Thief," Babette muttered. She and Fichaud went to the smaller wagon and fished through it, returning with some jewelry.

"Better? Are we through?"

"Deal," Jean-Marc said, and pocketed the extras. "This is where you leave forever. Get out of here."

"Oh, Abbie!" Babette started on another crying jag as Abbie refused to look at her. Fichaud pulled Babette away and stuffed her into the front of the wagon next to himself.

Their driver returned from the deep woods in time to see the smaller wagon roll away.

"Mademoiselle Bourgogne will be taking a more roundabout way to Marseille," Jean-Marc said, his arms crossed over his chest. "Come, it's time we got moving as well. We'll have to travel in the dark as it is. Into the wagon with you!"

Jean-Marc rearranged what boxes and barrels were left into a more stable mass as Abbie prayed to St. Amandus and the Virgin as hard as she'd done in her life.

"What shall we do, what shall we do?" she finally groaned against the hand she held over her mouth. Mustn't let the driver hear the truth. She'd seen the boy hiding at the edge of the wood toward the end of their encounter, but he'd likely been out of earshot, only able to hear raised voices.

"We'll proceed exactly as planned." With a final huff, Jean-Marc maneuvered the large trunk farther forward than it had been, and the wagon steadied as it lumbered down the little-used road. The lowering sun flashed at them from between thick stands of trees.

Jean-Marc plopped onto their makeshift bench and stretched out a kink in his back before donning his bulky gown again. "You have a clever cousin–at least for what she planned for you. It truly is a better contract. Oh, we'll have to finesse the dowry contents, but I agree that your uncle does indeed owe you a dowry of your own that should make up for it."

"Traitor."

"Tell me that in three years, when your babes are happily yowling around your feet in your new home."

"Oh! Oh!"

Abbie clutched at her neck, her face turning white.

"What is it?" Jean-Marc demanded.

"My mother's necklace! Oh, she has taken it! She deliberately stole my mother's necklace!" Abbie broke down into tears as if her life were ending. She tried to breathe and wound up emitting soul-filled howls of pain.

"There, there." Awkwardly Jean-Marc patted her shoulder. "There, there."

"She… She's a thief!" Abbie finally whimpered.

"Yes. Good riddance to her," Jean-Marc said.

"And I will be a thief and a liar if I go through with this," Abbie said miserably. She hid her face in her hands.

Jean-Marc gave her a chaste half-hug. "No, you're just what Philippe Dellamer needs. If we can divert his attention from the dowry until it's paid in full, he will be quite satisfied with the contract."

With a great sniff, Abbie raised her head to glare at him. "You're heartless."

He shrugged. "I'm realistic. I have my own plans, and you fit them very well. I look forward to seeing Philippe with a herd of squalling brats." He laughed and then laughed again. "Yes, it will be good for him. Your cousin has helped you and him in one stroke. Excellent work." He glanced north toward Dijon. "I should have thanked her."

But he didn't feel so thankful that night as they finally reached the river valley. It was too late even to load the boat.

Now Abbie Bourgogne was contracted to Philippe Dellamer. Jean-Marc scowled as he paid for the night's lodging at a stone inn.

"Miss Babette's not here, sir," the boy who drove for them pointed out.

"No, she wasn't going to meet us here," Jean-Marc told him. "She'll catch up with us later."

The boy nodded, clearly troubled by whatever explanation of events he'd made up for himself. Then his face lit up when Jean-Marc gave him three sous for dinner and told him that he'd ordered a room for him so he wouldn't have to sleep in the stable.

"Thank you, sir!" The boy clasped his hat to his heart. "You're very generous!"

Generous, Jean-Marc thought sourly as he watched the boy scamper off to a hot meal. Generous enough to give up a girl like Abbie to Philippe.

He'd set his sights on her. For the past ten days he'd watched her, admiring the way she moved and being astonished at how she commanded the help around her vineyard. She'd worked as hard as a man, yet when she came in in the evenings she was all woman. Disheveled, perhaps, but a woman looked her best disheveled, like she was ready to be disheveled more before the night was over.

His mouth had gone dry as he followed the graceful back-and-forth rippling of her skirts across the fields. He'd squinted to get a better view of the way the sun lit up her hair from behind, making it a golden halo around her sweet face.

She was so damned busy all the time he never had a chance to get her alone, save for that one aborted attempt in the fields. Whenever it seemed he might steal a few moments with her, someone would come up to him and say such a shame, sir, that Abbie's leaving us. They didn't seem to be that broken up about Babette's imminent departure. Such a shame poor Abbie's to leave her home. The girl knew her grapes, she did, and everyone loved her wine.

Abbie Bourgogne was a vintage Jean-Marc ached to discover, and now she was promised to Philippe. There'd be no question of trying to seduce her along the way to Marseille, or of catching her alone once they arrived at their destination.

Abbie Bourgogne was off-limits to him.

"Come in now," he told her. When she didn't respond, he put his arm around her waist and led her into the warmth and light of the riverside inn. She moved like a mourner at a funeral, as if her world were unreal and she was trying to track her way through it. "Follow me," he urged and was rewarded with a small nod.

The innkeeper immediately noted Abbie's state and summoned his wife. They built up a nest of blankets and hot bricks around Abbie and brought her warmed wine and soup to take the chill off.

"Has someone died?" the innkeeper's thin wife asked, wringing her hands with her apron in quick, nervous strokes.

"Yes," Jean-Marc replied. So others saw the same look, too. "Her cousin. They were quite close."

"Poor dear, poor dear," the woman said even as Abbie blinked, dimly hearing the lie. The woman clasped Abbie's hands in her own. "It'll get better. Just give it time. The angels will see to your dear cousin. You don't have to worry about her." She nodded to a side door. "We have a little altar in the back of the kitchen, if you'd like to light a candle and say some prayers."

Abbie tried to speak, but Jean-Marc had to respond for her. "Thank you," he said. "That's very kind. If she feels better in the morning, she will certainly do just that."

"The angels will watch over her," the woman repeated.

From another group of diners, her husband snapped his fingers twice. "Wife," he called, and the woman whirled to scamper to his needs.

"The angels will make sure Babette feels the heat from the flames of Hell for a few years for this," Jean-Marc muttered when he was sure he wouldn't be heard. Even so, Abbie shuddered next to him.

The chill lay heavy on the slow Saone River as their barge lumbered downstream. Gray drizzle sucked the color from what remained of the fall foliage and covered the low country to either side with an early, foreboding darkness.

"You'll catch sick from the river if you stay out here," Jean-Marc told Abbie. "Come inside. It's warm there."

Abbie's face was drawn and pale on this third day on the river, but the circles no longer showed under her eyes. Two straggles of hair lay wetly against her forehead as she searched the western shoreline.

"Come with me," Jean-Marc urged. "You'll do no one any good if you're dead from fever. You being dead won't fit my plans."

At that she turned to acknowledge his presence with a stony stare. "And what are these great plans of yours? What other treachery do you mean to foist upon your employer?"

"Treachery?" Jean-Marc leaned back against the deck railing. "I mean him only the best. He's been as good to me as I am to him. After all, I am fetching him a beautiful bride, one who will make him an excellent wife."

Abbie settled her cloak more closely around her neck. "And then?"

"And then." A far-away look came to Jean-Marc's eyes. "And then when you provide him with heirs to help him in his business, *then* I can leave and see the world. I can travel as far as I want, and I won't have to answer to Philippe anymore."

He stood up and raised his arms, taking in the entire world. "Free at last!" he said. "No more responsibilities. I can explore like I've always wanted to. I can barter and trade my way from Marseille to the North Sea. Perhaps I'll journey to Iceland. Maybe I'll see India instead."

"Why would a sane man want to do that?"

He leaned down into her face and laughed. "Perhaps I'm not sane at all. Philippe certainly tells me that when these urges come upon me. He has always said I'd grow out of them, but I never have. I never will!"

He took a brave pose on the deck, heedless of the staring man at the helm. "I am a man of the world. Jean-Marc DuMonde, that's me. I intend to live up to the name."

"And what does your family think of this?" Abbie asked.

"Jean-Marc DuMonde has no family to tie him down. Jean-Marc DuMonde is a trader-explorer, just as those Portuguese and Dutchmen are. Perhaps I'll join an expedition to the New World, I don't know. Anything can happen to a DuMonde." He shook his finger at her. "You and Philippe will have to get very busy very soon making those babies, so I can leave while I'm still young."

"Look where you are. Why would anyone want to leave this place? Why isn't here good enough for you?"

Jean-Marc frowned at the oppressive grayness that cloaked the low river valley. The bottommost flecks of indigo clouds scraped the distant hills so he couldn't even see their tops. "Who wouldn't want to leave this?"

"You're not seeing it right," Abbie insisted. "You should be here in the summer, when everything is lush and green and flowers fill the meadows. Or in winter, when even this old river runs wide and fast and is eager to be about its business. Or in early fall– that's my favorite season– when the vines are bursting and everyone comes out to help with harvest and we dance every night until we drop."

He settled beside her, squinting at the shoreline. "I've never been up this far before, it's true," he said. "Tell me what spring is like here. You know this country well?"

"This is where I belong," she said. "There. There it is." She pointed at the far slopes of the misty valley toward the orderly lines of what Jean-Marc knew were grape vines, weeks past harvest. A high stone wall enclosed how many acres of vineyard? He could only see its beginnings on this side of the hills, but it was large– very large for a vineyard of the Burgundy region.

"Clos Bourgogne," Abbie whispered. "It's been in my family for generations, since before Burgundy was a land unto itself, even before France was France. Centuries ago people put up the walls marking the clos because the earth grows such miraculous grapes within it. Others had to split up their vineyards, but my family has always kept our plot intact. It is only in a few spots here and there that the greatest burgundies can be fostered, but one of those spots is the Clos Bourgogne, the finest vineyard in France. Or it was once. It can be again."

"So this is where the Grand Cru Bourgogne is made," Jean-Marc said reverently.

"When my father died the lands went to my Uncle. He chose to stay on his farm and has given the responsibility of the clos to my cousin Chris."

"Your uncle makes a fine chablis," Jean-Marc said. "One of the finest I have ever tasted."

"My uncle does not make chablis," Abbie retorted. "That was my work. And the chablis is good enough, but our burgundy is the best there is. Or it was, until my father died. Chris doesn't understand wine or grapes or anything to do with the land. His brother did, but poor Henri died even before the plague came through. My father spent many years training Henri and my own brothers and didn't mind when I watched and listened. But after Henri passed and Christopher was sent here, I saw that Papa's lessons didn't sink in with him."

"With wine like yours, that's criminal," Jean-Marc murmured, but Abbie shook her head.

"Some people know the grape and others don't. Some people hear it, some people have wine in their blood. It's not a crime not to have it, but it is a crime not to hire a competent steward. Christopher would not reason well with our master vintner." Abbie sighed, her fingers curling around the edges of the damp bench. "I think Chris wanted to establish himself as the man of the estate and make a point, you know, assert himself in command here. He hurt Old Eric's pride. Now Old Eric is quit and Christopher hired that idiot Fichaud, who talks a good game but knows less than Chris does."

"And now Fichaud is gone."

Abbie drummed her fingers against the wood. "Perhaps that can work in my favor," she said slowly.

"Don't be getting any ideas in your pretty head. I don't see how this vineyard can have any bearing on your future life as Madame Dellamer," Jean-Marc said.

Abbie's mouth crooked and her eyes squinted at the foggy hills. "Perhaps I still have a turn to play."

5

Hugs and kisses had been exchanged, though the children still squealed from excitement and refused to pay attention to their mother Madeline's attempts to shoo them away from their guests.

"This is Henri and Bab and Lon," Abbie introduced the children to Jean-Marc, who knelt down to greet them.

"Let me guess: another Babette?" he asked.

The little brown-haired girl stuck three fingers in her mouth. "Bab," she said around the obstruction, only to giggle at the funny face Jean-Marc made for her.

Abbie's fair-haired cousin Christopher with the generous beard reminded her of her dear uncle. He was still slender with youth but showed early potential around his middle of the robust figure his father made.

"But where is our Babette?" Chris asked, peering out the door past the new arrivals. Only two small bags of clothing that they'd brought up from the river to the sprawling house sat there. This stone manse with its red-tiled roof seemed so old it almost grew out of the hills. "Isn't she supposed to be with you? I don't understand."

"Fichaud is gone," Abbie burst out. "Your so-called wine master has quit, to your good luck. You can do much better: me. I offer my services."

"What are you talking about?"

"Children! Children!" Madeline batted at them and they slipped out of reach, hiding behind folds of her wine-dark skirt. She pushed strands of errant chestnut hair behind her ear with a huff, her pretty lower lip jutting out with her determination. "Settle down or you're going to bed. Right now. That would mean no supper for you tonight. Come, Monsieur, Abbie. We've been waiting dinner for you."

They settled in a dining room deliciously warmed by the wall that formed the kitchen's fireplace. The room glowed with candles in every corner. The savory smell of fresh bread and *pôchouse*, fish stew with onions, completed the sense of homecoming. Despite Madeline's threats, the children ate with them.

"This is a tale that should be told away from the children," Jean-Marc said.

"They are too young to understand. Now tell us straightaway," Chris said as he passed some *friture* to his wife.

Between caterwaulings and mild exhibitions from the children, Abbie and Jean-Marc managed to relate their story.

"I can believe many things of Babette, but I can't believe she would go this far," Chris muttered as he sat leaning on his fist in wonder.

"I was there," Jean-Marc said. "Believe it. She had things worked out thoroughly. I'll give her this: this is a deal that, with a little tinkering, will go through just as well as when it was originally contracted. I will talk with Dellamer if he finds out. He listens to me. I will convince him that he's much better off this way."

Abbie slammed the flat of her hand down on the table, almost waking the youngest. "I am not going to marry Monsieur Dellamer! That was not the intent of the contract, and I will not defraud either Dellamer or my uncle."

She leaned toward Chris. "You know that my father taught me as well— no, better!– than he did Henri. I learned both from Papa and Old Eric. Eric said that if I were a man I'd have been his first choice for steward here, but if I were a man I'd have inherited anyway."

Chris sighed. "Yes, he always did joke about that. But it was just a joke, Abbie. You are not a man."

"But I know the grape. I can run this place– secretly, if we must. I can make it truly a Grand Cru again. Hire me. Give me one year to prove myself, Chris. I'll do anything for the chance. Anything."

Chris looked up as his wife entered with another pitcher of spiced and watered wine. She set down the pitcher and then picked up one sleeping child, took the next oldest by the hand, nodded to the oldest, and led them away to bed.

Chris sat in silence for a while. Jean-Marc tried to break it with a joke, but Abbie glared at him and he shut up. Instead he poured himself another round of the wonderful wine the house vineyard produced.

"I am almost tempted," Chris said as Madeline returned to join them. "And when I think of that, I think about returning home to Father and helping him."

"You'd leave all this?" Jean-Marc asked.

"Father is getting older, and my brothers are still quite young. Besides, I've never been all that interested in wine. Drinking it, yes. Making it–" He shrugged his shoulders.

Jean-Marc took a sip of the dark drink. "A shame to let the burgundy suffer by your absence."

"It wouldn't suffer under my hand," Abbie said quickly. "I would treat the vineyard as if it were my own, Chris. I would hold it in stewardship for you, but give me the chance to let the clos produce what it was meant to. You know this is home to me."

Madeline ventured an opinion. "Perhaps we could get some more cows. The meadows down to the river are hardly grazed at all, Chris. If we could get some boats while Abbie oversees the vineyard, we could make a good living selling the beef downriver."

"Downriver?" Chris's eyelids half-closed in interest. He scratched his beard slowly.

Madeline seemed afraid to meet Jean-Marc's gaze, so she spoke to Abbie. "Chris loves the river," she said. "Sometimes I think he wants to be a fisherman instead of a vintner, just to do something that would get him out on the water."

Chris gave his wife a pat on the hand. "Not much of a life to be made in fishing, Maddy," he said. "There are too many others in the business. Fishing isn't something Bourgognes do. But the burgundy wine– A clos is a rare thing to own."

"I'm not sure I understand the problem," Jean-Marc said as he pulled on the chin he'd shaved so closely this morn. "You take grapes and put them in a wood cask. They make wine." Jean-Marc shrugged, knowing that Abbie would be appalled. But it was Chris who contradicted him much more gently than Abbie wanted to.

"There's a little more work to it than that. And there are subtleties. When you produce a Grand Cru, you must pay attention to those. Experimentation has always been a foundation of this vineyard."

"It was founded on Cistercian methods," Abbie told Jean-Marc, as if that would explain everything. Everyone knew the monks excelled in wine production.

Chris said, "I admit that hiring Fichaud may have been a mistake. I've been denying it for some time, but I think I'd come to the decision to let him go. We've had two bad years here, and our reputation is already suffering locally. Another year, and–" He shook his head. "It's just that there's no one else who could come close to doing the job."

"You should apologize to Old Eric," Abbie said. She turned to Jean-Marc. "He was a dedicated monk when he was very young. He studied all their records and then decided that for him the wine was more important than God. The other monks must have sensed this as well, for they expelled him."

Abbie crossed herself, as did the others at the table. She took Chris in her regard. "He's dedicated his life to the pinot noir. Underneath the sacrilege and foul temper, he's a good man. Once you've salved his ego, he'll be eager enough to get back to work. And I can assist him so that when he's too old– and that can't be too long now– I can take over."

Chris gritted his teeth and Maddy reached out to touch his arm. "That old man said some nasty things about me and my abilities. I refuse to apologize to him. It's he who must come on his knees to me. I want his apology in public before I'll let him back– an apology delivered in front of a priest, at least."

"What could have been that bad?" Jean-Marc asked.

"They didn't kick him out for his sacrilege," Chris countered. "They kicked him out because his sourness would have infected the entire order!"

Abbie waved the opinion away. "Old Eric is always cranky. You have to ignore him when he gets like that. He always insults people. He doesn't know any other way. All he knows is the grape."

Chris took a drink and glanced at his wife, then at Abbie. "So he should be the last person a good woman should work alongside," he said.

"At least I know when to put the wine and my family first."

"Abbie!" Madeline scolded.

"I'm sorry," Abbie said quickly. "It's just that I've been backed into a corner by hunters. I must fight or I am lost. Chris, think of the clos. It's the most important thing here. It holds the family honor."

"How can land hold a family's honor?" Jean-Marc asked. "It's just dirt. Your honor lies in the contract your uncle signed."

"A contract for my cousin and not for me. Right now that so-called honor is only a sheet of paper."

Christopher pulled his hair straight back and sighed at the wall, then at Jean-Marc. "I don't know what to do," he said. "It's true; the grape is the foundation of our family. The family is the grape. The burgundy is our name. Without it, who are we? And yet– and yet–"

"And yet I am a woman." Bitterness burnt Abbie's words. "I cannot decide my own fate."

"The family decides all our fates, cousin."

"All except Babette."

"Babette is now renegade. What we do must be what's best for the family. How we act today will affect those who come after us." Chris again sat silently for some time. "I will pray on this tonight. Let me sleep late, for I do not think the answers will be quick in coming."

With a sharp scrape, he pushed back his oaken chair on the stone floor, then rose and left for the family chapel.

Madeline gazed after him. "I'll show you to your rooms," she finally said. "If you need anything, please treat this as your own home and serve yourselves. I will join my husband at his prayers."

Christopher and his wife were not the only ones who had a long night. Jean-Marc tossed in his bed, becoming trapped within the blankets until he wrestled them off. He paced the lightless room.

Philippe might not have any bride come morning.

It would be easy enough to summon a priest and witness that the contract had been broken. Would that harm Master Bourgogne's reputation? It seemed a shame to sully the man who was such a benefactor to his village and family, but he was responsible for his daughter's actions. It was he who had raised her to be so willful.

How much of a scandal would there be? In Marseille such news would be ripe gossip for a few weeks, perhaps a few months, before some new scandal wiped it from people's minds. Out here in the country where time seemed to slow to stillness, where nothing changed except the seasons, how long would a scandal last?

Still, any scandal was the Bourgognes' problem and not the Dellamers'. If Philippe's bridal contract fell through, Jean-Marc would have to return to the starting line to find him another girl who would come with a lucrative product they could use. Another girl who would be robust and young enough to produce heirs to take over the company.

A girl who would trade her life for Jean-Marc's freedom.

How much time would it take to find her? How much time before the first boy babe, before he was old enough to help with any kind of real work around the company? How long before Jean-Marc could leave his part of the business in the boy's hands, knowing that the company and Philippe would be safe in his absence?

How cramped was this room! Jean-Marc strode out into the long, narrow hallway that ran the length of the back of the house and paused before Abbie's door.

A light shone underneath it. He was not alone in his sleeplessness.

Abbie.

If she was rescued from this contract, she would be free, also— as free as any woman could be. Of course she'd choose to use her freedom to live here. She'd have to find her own husband among what was available in the countryside hereabout.

But for right now she'd be unencumbered.

Not Philippe Dellamer's.

Jean-Marc leaned against the cool stone wall and pondered the implications.

A hard frost lay on the vineyards the next morning.

"Lon! Henri! Bab!" Abbie called as quietly as she could to the children who frolicked through the long lines of twisted vines that came right up to the sides of the stone house. "Slow down! You don't play where you can harm the canes. And you must be quiet for a while more. Your parents are sleeping."

Young Lon ran to his cousin, showing her a scratched hand. Abbie knelt down, dusted it off and then kissed it.

"There now, see what comes when the grapes want to sleep and you wake them," she chided gently. "Go to the barn if you want to play. I'm walking here."

"But I want to be with you, cousin Abbie." The boy leaned against Abbie, slyly smiling up at her.

"Because I give you sweets."

"Do you have any sweets, cousin? Hm?"

"I have this," and Abbie kissed the boy.

With a laugh Lon threw his arms around Abbie and kissed her soundly on the cheek. "That's not the kind of sweet I want!"

Abbie reached into her cloak and pulled out a dried sugared fig, and another and another. "These are to share," she told the boy sternly even as they were snatched from her hand.

Lon ran from her with the treasure, laughing wildly and waving the figs in the air. His siblings made a beeline for him and the gate from the vineyard, and Abbie stood again to watch them.

"Do you have any sweets for me?" Jean-Marc said behind her.

Abbie stiffened for a moment. Then she said, "I thought I was for your employer." She turned to see that the remarkably clear sparkle again lived in his eyes. His mouth held the same sly smile that her little cousin had managed.

"It occurred to me sometime last night that if you stay here you are fair game," Jean-Marc told her as they left the relatively small vineyard to circle the old stone house. "And if that's the case, we can go play in the barn as well. There are very good games to be had in the warm hay."

"I doubt if I would like those games, monsieur."

He sidled closer. "Ah, now we're back to 'monsieur.' Well, mademoiselle, I think you shouldn't make up your mind so quickly about games you know nothing about." Jean-Marc paused and took the opportunity to run his thumb up the side of her cheek. She watched it warily out of the corner of her eye.

"A man may play such games, monsieur, but not a woman."

"But it takes a woman to play the game."

They gazed at each other, and his hand slid around to cup the base of her head even as he drew nearer still. He leaned down and lightly touched his lips to hers. Withdrawing for a moment to judge her reaction, he returned to press a solid but gentle kiss against her mouth.

Abbie had quickly kissed a few boys in her life, but never a man, never something like this that lasted for a second... Two... Five. How soft his lips were, while a few bristles from his hastily-shaven jaw scraped against her skin. How strange to have someone breathing on her face, to have him twining his fingers through her hair.

She opened her eyes to find him watching her. So close.

He pressed her against himself so she could feel his body through his thick coat. She was tense, ready to bolt, and yet he pulled her closer still, one hand reaching under her cloak to grasp her by her back and pull.

Maybe once more. After all, it was not like she was truly promised to Monsieur Dellamer. That was Babette. This was Abbie's chance to show that she would not abide by that false contract!

Abbie tilted her face up to him, her lips slightly parted to fully experience this new sensation, and she gasped into his mouth when he took her hungrily. His spread fingers dug into her back though the other hand kept a firm but gentle hold on her neck.

This was what it meant to be kissed by a man. This was a man's passion. And a woman's response, Abbie realized, as she became warmly aware of the pressure of their bodies together, even under all their clothing. When she reached to spread herself closer upon him, her fingers could only wrap around the padding of his shoulders. They sought to know his true contours. Abbie's skin tingled all over, sending a sudden rush of heat and tightness deeper within herself.

Jean-Marc kissed her as Michel had kissed Babette.

No, no, this was not right. Not proper at all, that his tongue sought entry.

She pushed hard at him, and he immediately stepped back. His breath came out in easy pants of frost, but so did hers. That soft mouth twisted into a triumphant grin.

"See?" he said. "It works much better when there are both a man and a woman. I can show you more in the barn. It is too cold out here."

Abbie shifted her cloak about herself to hide her blush.

"Come along," he urged.

"No," she said. "I won't be tempted by a man who will be traipsing off in a few weeks to see the world." She thought to hold him in a hard gaze but had to look away. "When I do settle down, it will with someone from Burgundy, someone who lives here."

She strode to the thick walls of the ancient house and pressed her hands against the cold stone. "This is where I was born," she said. "My brothers, my father, my grandfather, and his father before him– all born and lived here."

Abbie turned to face Jean-Marc. "Papa always said that the wine forms a Bourgogne's blood and these stones our very bones. He was right. Come with me." With that, she turned and walked quickly down the farm lane, past the outbuildings and high stone walls that marked the clos. She turned into a narrow path that ran between two walls and opened an iron gate.

A level patch of yard lay there, shaded by the hills that would leave the rest of the clos open to the sun. The grass was neatly clipped here, and uneven rows of gravestones protruded from the earth. A small stone chapel sat to one side, embedded in the boundary walls.

"This is hallowed land," Abbie whispered. "Here we are born, and here we wait for God to welcome us into Heaven." She pointed at a group of newer stones. "My parents. My brothers. If I can convince Chris, I will be buried here someday as well."

Jean-Marc helped her close the gate behind them when they left.

As they entered the clos itself through another gate, this one of wood, Abbie said, "Even though my body may leave, my soul, my heart will always remain here."

Jean-Marc gazed about the Clos Bourgogne. It was enclosed by shoulder-high, blue-black rock walls and stretched along two rolling hills before turning off to be obscured by the wall itself. How many generations must it have taken to build just the walls?

And yet people must have been here before the walls to discover the wondrous grapes that could grow here. Rows of thick, twisting vines carefully tended on trellises formed long, ancient lines along the contours of the hills.

As they walked the land rose, opening a view to endless lines of grapevines below them.

Abbie nodded approval at the wonder that shone in Jean-Marc's face. "As much as the graveyard is hallowed ground, so in a way is this. God has blessed this place for us. We have been given this land in holy husbandry, to care for it and to make it prosper. This is my family's honor," she said. "This is our pride, our skill, our very lives."

She gazed out over the clos. "This is why I must stay here. If I leave, I will disgrace us all before the eyes of God. The ghosts of my forebears will chase me down and surely find me. I can't let the family down!"

"Will they chase you even though the family has told you to leave?" Jean-Marc asked.

She shook her head. "Not me. Babette. They are probably hounding her even now for forsaking her duty. I hope they are," she added bitterly. "Coward."

"Love is a powerful thing."

"Love? You call that lust, that greed on Fichaud's part, love?" Abbie's laugh chilled the air. "Who marries for love, anyway? When you are born above a certain station, you must marry to suit the family's needs. Peasants and servants can marry for love, for that's all they have to offer. We can't. We've both known that since we were toddlers."

From behind Jean-Marc's hand settled on her shoulder. "So now you marry to suit your family's needs."

"The contract was for Babette. I have skills that must not be lost."

He turned her to face him. "So you'd back out on the contract so quickly?" He outlined her jaw with his forefinger and considered her lips. "I could live with that."

He pulled her to him. "Come with me, sweet Abbie. Tell me about your wine and let me taste it on your lips. Make me forget how I'll have to deliver the bad news to Philippe."

As he shifted, his furred gown opened. Something flashed white within and then fell to the ground. Abbie disengaged herself from Jean-Marc to pick it up.

Folded paper: an opened letter. A name in address:

"Jean-Marc Dellamer."

As if it were afire, she dropped it and Jean-Marc knelt to retrieve it.

"Dellamer," she hissed at him. "Not DuMonde. What are you, a cousin? Someone after his fortune to play with his honor as you have?"

Slowly Jean-Marc straightened and tucked the letter back within the lining of his gown. His jaw worked stiffly. "Philippe is my brother," he said at last. "My older brother, the head of the family."

"And you would blackmail him with the wrong bride?"

"I thought I was choosing the better bride for him."

"Whom you would take into the barn and… and…"

He drew himself to full height and put his fists on his hips, staring her down. "I thought you were staying here. I thought you were going to pull out of the contract and bring disgrace on my brother and your uncle and never mind who got hurt. I thought we could have a little fun before I left."

"Fun!"

"Yes, fun. Have you ever had any fun in your life, Abbie? Have you ever allowed yourself to enjoy freedom?"

"I am a woman. I am an orphan. What freedom can I have?"

With a quickness that caught her unawares, he swept her into his arms and pressed his mouth against hers. He pulled her to him as tightly as they could join.

Her mouth was already open in shock and his tongue took advantage of it, exploring her. His own breath swallowed her exclamation.

He held her off-balance so she had to put her arms around his shoulders to steady herself. Her heart beat in her throat at the sudden closeness. When his mouth shifted to kiss down the line of her jaw, it felt only natural to stretch herself back, to hang on tight to his neck so she could feel his own pulse racing underneath her fingertips.

His hair curled so tightly under her hands as she twined it around her fingers. It was Jean-Marc's slightly rough, dark hair that was always falling into his face. Now she brushed a lock back off his forehead only to find him gazing at her again.

Oh.

Oh!

"You are his brother," she whispered.

Was that pain in his eyes? "Yes."

Her mind was spinning. The world was not the same world she had stood in minutes ago. Jean-Marc held her in her own home.

"You must decide," he said. "Honor the contract or stay here. Go to my brother or come into the barn now with me." He leaned forward to nuzzle at her ear.

Abbie thought she might faint, her heart raced so. Despite the frost she felt as if her veins were on fire.

"I promise you: you'll like my game," he whispered in her ear, right before he pulled on it with his lips.

"Abbie!"

It was moments before she realized that it was her cousin calling from the gate.

"Abbie!"

6

There was no way anyone could have seen them through the thick grape vines, but Abbie's face still flushed deep rose from embarrassment and anger when she met her cousin and his wife at the clos gate. Chris and Madeline were bundled in simple, heavy cloaks that seemed so countrified next to Jean-Marc's brocaded finery.

Before Chris could open his mouth, Abbie said, "He's his brother. Jean-Marc DuMonde is really Jean-Marc Dellamer."

Christopher took a step back. "Are you planning on revealing Babette's treachery, Monsieur Dellamer? Is that why you represented yourself falsely to us?"

"I…" Jean-Marc glanced at the accusing stares. "I meant no deception. DuMonde is a name I use… so as not to fall under my brother's shadow when dealing with people who have never met either of us."

"Does family mean so little to you, sir? Are you feuding with your brother?"

"I love my brother," Jean-Marc said quickly, holding out his hands as if opening his heart. "He's a fine man and worthy of our family name. But I am going to leave the company business as soon as he has sons old enough to carry on the work. Making business transactions doesn't interest me. Freedom does. Shipping has always been the family interest, but I don't care for it. I don't plan on spending the rest of my life at a desk keeping track of boats and shipping contracts and portsmaster bribes."

Christopher scratched his reddish beard. "I know how that goes, not to have a talent for the family business." He sighed. "Dellamer, eh?" Then he considered Abbie. "Our Abbie here has wine in her blood. She has an eye for the vine and how it needs to be treated. But she also needs a husband, and this brother of yours seems a fine candidate, despite the dishonesty involved."

"Anyone could make a wife for Dellamer," Abbie retorted, "but only I can help out here. Chris, it's worse than I thought. You had black rot here this past year, didn't you? Isn't that what took most of the crop?"

Chris nodded, surveying the even rows of trellised naked grapevines that ran up and down the contours of the hills like an artist's charcoaled lines.

Abbie gestured to them. "The rot hasn't been cut off. Last year's canes haven't even been pruned."

"Are they supposed to be?" Chris asked.

Abbie pulled up two vines from the trellis nearest them and showed him the differences. "Next year's grapes will come from this year's growth. There's still dried grapes out there that haven't been picked off, too. As long as you have the rot, use the grapes in next spring's compost and they'll help ward it off."

"Really?"

"Yes. But you must cut out the sickness before winter sets in."

Chris scratched the other side of his beard and glanced at his wife, who returned his serious look. This was their livelihood.

"Come, Abbie," Chris said, and the four began to walk the clos.

Abbie pointed out the rot so they could recognize it. She took Chris's knife and showed him just how far to cut into the precious vines to remove it.

At the end of one row she sniffed and then leaned down to poke with a discarded cane through compost piled around a root.

"Fresh manure," she grunted.

"Not that fresh," Jean-Marc said as he peered from behind her at the brown stuff, but she wrinkled her nose.

"It's too strong for the vine," Abbie told them. "Keep this here and next year the vine will run wild with growth– but the grapes will wither. You have to feed the vines but not overfeed them. A fine balance is needed so the plant produces both leaves and grapes. This manure should be composted in the main piles until spring and then applied without so much generosity."

"Ah," Chris said. "Yes. The main compost piles."

The way he said it made Abbie rise up and turn around, her eyes sweeping the grand landscape. "You've moved them," she said. "Where are they?"

"Michel said we could compost at the source, like this," Chris told her. "That way we wouldn't have to drag everything to the compost heaps and then move them out on the fields. We'd save days of sweat."

"And just think: you'd save days of harvest as well since there'd be so few grapes. Chris, Michel Fichaud is an idiot. He has no idea what he's do-ing, but he talks as if he does."

This time Chris scratched his neck and looked skyward. "He certainly didn't do the clos any good," he admitted.

"This year was a disaster!" Maddy muttered under her breath. She pulled on Chris's sleeve. "Don't you think– I mean…"

Chris covered her hand with his. "The wine is our family's pride, and perhaps it's our honor as well."

"I haven't seen the winery yet," Abbie said as she slapped the dirt from her hands. "What has he done there? Perhaps he built fireplaces in the caves to keep himself warm while the wine ferments?"

The laugh Chris gave her was weak. "No, no, even I know not to do that. Give me a little credit, cousin."

She gave him a small smile instead. "You were already thinking of dis-missing him. That was a very good decision. Now make another one. I won't be much trouble. I'll sleep in the barn and even play with the children so you and Maddy can be alone when you want to."

Madeline smiled at that and rubbed Chris's arm encouragingly. He just looked down at the ground and kicked a fallen, shriveled grape leaf.

"This is what I had to decide," he said, "between the good of the family business or the good of the family. Where does one begin and the other leave off?"

He pulled himself up straight and took a deep breath, though his eyes were closed. "In the end, wine is only wine. It is here only for our mortal lifetime, while a marriage lasts even unto Heaven for all eternity." He opened his eyes to fix his gaze on his cousin. "Abbie, you must go to Marseille and take Babette's place in this wedding contract."

"No."

Chris shushed the words that were to come next by touching Abbie's lips gently with his fingers. "This is for your own good. This is for your happiness. Even if you do not love this man, you will love your children."

"Don't tell me this, Chris."

He nodded as if he'd expected that. "If the good Lord takes your husband away for whatever reason, you are always welcome here, and if you come we will put your knowledge to good use. But that will be God's decision and not mine. You will marry the Dellamer man."

He nodded to Jean-Marc, who bowed back to him, not letting his disappointment show.

Abbie was Philippe's once again.

Abbie stood on the river landing staring back at the far-off stone walls that shone almost turquoise in the bright noon. Jean-Marc could not see her face for she had worn a hood with her heavy cloak today. She had it pulled tight around her features, even though the day was warm for November.

He surreptitiously peered at her as he passed by once, just to make sure it was truly her within that cloak and not someone she had convinced to take her place. These Bourgogne women were too clever by half.

Another small but heavy wagonload of barrels pulled up to be loaded onto the barge by the winery's workers and boat crew. This was the primary portion of the dowry as well as the first shipment for the contract.

He had sampled the wares with Chris in the chilly caves just below the clos before making arrangements for shipping. Conversations these past few days about the condition of the crop had concerned Jean-Marc.

Instead he breathed a contented sigh after his first swallow of the unwatered drink. Warmth spread through his insides like liquid gold, honeyed with the most luscious fruits of harvest. He let the fragrant bouquet sink into his senses, savoring it until the end. It was so ripe, sweetly pure and chaste like a beautiful virgin girl. "Now that is a wine for a rare occasion," he said. "Not something to drink lightly over lunch."

Chris's face had held a thoughtful look. "It's still good enough," he finally declared. "But Papa and the others are right; it's not up to our standards."

As Chris made sure the barrel tap was completely closed, he said, "Do you suppose that brother of yours would consent to send Abbie back here in the spring? Just to make sure that we're starting the vines off as we should. Or in the summer, when the rot and the moths come. It would be to his benefit, you know. If we prosper, he prospers as well."

"If I were my brother, I wouldn't let a woman like Abbie out of my sight," Jean-Marc replied.

"I don't think I like the way you say that," Chris said as he straightened up. "Not with you two traveling alone. If you stay another day, I could arrange a chaperone. Perhaps." His brows furrowed and his eyes moved back and forth as if he tried to think of likely candidates for the job.

Jean-Marc put his tin tasting cup back on its shelf. "I don't dishonor my contracts, either," he said. "One Bourgogne virgin will arrive quite safely in time for her wedding."

"Still–" Chris said.

"She will be safe with me. She's to be my sister, after all."

Chris nodded and waved his hand to show his men that they could take the next load of barrels.

Now down on the docks Chris watched the stowing with interest, but not for the wine's sake. "This is your family's barge?" he asked Jean-Marc.

"It is. We have two barges that we use now and then when we have business upriver."

Chris patted the deck railing. "I don't know about the lower river, but it's a fine boat for the Saone. Low and well-balanced. Sturdy. Still, it needs some cleanup work if you want to impress passengers." He pointed to a rusted cleat along a door sill mottled by mildew and the general sad state of the corners and crannies of the vessel. "These days many people of means want to go up to Dijon or down to Lyon or even Avignon and beyond. Businesses everywhere seem to be expanding." He glanced at Jean-Marc and gave him a nod. "Or perhaps more people are thinking about becoming men of the world."

Jean-Marc cracked the barest of smiles at that. "There are too many stories of faraway places nowadays for a man to be happy sitting at a desk," he said.

"Aye, you're right enough about that," Chris said. On impulse he crossed the loading ramp, asked about cargo weight, and then explored the barge's passenger facilities.

He whistled with approval.

"We keep our barges in storage until we need them," Jean-Marc admitted.

"You shouldn't, not if both are like this. There are never enough barges, and those that have acceptable quarters for passengers of substance are very few. Underneath all this dirt, this is a fine boat. A man could make a stout living off one of these. And you say you have two?"

They came back out to the brilliant day and stepped quickly out of the way of the crew. "You seem quite knowledgeable," Jean-Marc said.

Christopher nodded. "I've had to make enough river trips by now. I know how to stay away from disreputable crews and rat-infested boats." He ran his hands lovingly over a barge pole. "I suppose I've always envied those who work these vessels up and down the river. It has always seemed to me that they must enjoy so much more…"

"Freedom."

Christopher shared a grin with Jean-Marc. "Yes. More freedom than you or I. You understand that too. Yet you are part of an international shipping company. There must be freedom in sailing the high seas."

Jean-Marc stood next to him, gazing off into the sharp distance as the noonday sun revealed slow-dancing glints of bright light within the ripples of the lazy river.

"I sit in an office," he told Chris. "Merchants come to me with lists of what they want to ship or buy, and I write figures in a book. I schedule. I walk down the street to bargain with insurance agents. Sometimes I get far enough to go down on the docks and talk to the captains of our ships. Sometimes I am called to speak to the harbormaster."

"That doesn't seem a good life for an active man."

"It isn't. During the winter the walls depress me until I can't stand sitting there one more minute. I think up any excuse to be out. If I had my freedom, I would run out of there and never return."

Christopher nodded. "Yes," he said softly. "The family's chains are heavy."

"And Abbie is the key to my shackles." She couldn't hear them from where she stood. "Once she gives my brother a couple of sons and they grow knee-high to being taught the business, I can be away."

"What will you do then?"

Jean-Marc chewed his lip. "I don't know. Perhaps I could become a traveling salesman through these parts. It is a pretty country here, even in this season. Abbie tells me it is even prettier in others."

Christopher laughed. "That's it, then. I will build a boat and you can travel up and down the Saone on it, selling your wares."

"Deal."

"Deal."

The men both laughed softly at their dreams.

One of Christopher's men came to tell him that the loading had been completed. Chris nodded and the man returned to the dock.

Jean-Marc brushed down his cloak offhandedly only to find that a piece of grapevine as long as his index finger stuck to its furred hem. He was about to toss it into the river when he thought again, and tucked it inside his doublet.

"Tell that brother of yours to take care of our Abbie," Chris told Jean-Marc. "She is very dear to us. She's been through too much these past few years. I remember when she was younger, she was never anything but laughing and smiling. She would start the day off singing– she had a sweet voice– and whenever she worked among the vines, she seemed to lessen everyone's burden with her kindness. I haven't heard her sing for four years now."

He shrugged with just his right shoulder. "Of course, I haven't been around her much these past four years, either, but I can see the changes. My sister Babette, she was always the jewelry, the bright bauble that shone if you polished it just right, but Abbie was a flower. You wanted to admire and treasure it because it was God's work."

He gave Jean-Marc a rueful half-grin. "My wife has been reading me poetry these past few weeks. I think some of it may have rubbed off. She's trying to educate me, I think." He chuckled.

"She is also a fine cook and has given me happy, healthy, and very spoiled babies. In the beginning I wasn't too sure about the marriage, but I went through with it because it was the proper thing to do. Now I've come to the conclusion that a wife is a very good thing to have, but you must be sure to pick the right one, like my Maddy. Someone with a good, sensible head on her shoulders," and here he gave a crooked smile, "as well as having other fine features of note."

Jean-Marc nodded. "That's exactly why I choose to go along with this deception," he said. "I believe that Abbie is the better marriage prospect. If anyone can bring a smile to Philippe's face, I think that it will be Abbie. He needs to smile."

He watched Abbie as she clutched her hood around her cheeks and gazed at the vineyards on the slope above them. She stood in shadow, silhouetted against the dying colors of the land, her cloak riffling in the stiff breeze.

"That is, if someone can start her own smile first," Jean-Marc said almost to himself.

7

They came upon Lyon by hearing the river roaring far ahead of them before they saw the actual city.

"Here we meet up with the Rhone," Jean-Marc told Abbie as the barge's captain maneuvered in to the city's quay. "The Rhone's a wild river. It runs downhill from the Alps and seems eager to get to the ocean."

He stretched hugely and took in the view of one of the crossroads of Europe with its ancient stone-walled houses and shops and great confluence of people. Tall, columned buildings came up to the very edge of the river, crowding onto a thin island that was bounded on one side by the Saone and on the other by the Rhone. From a quay-front inn, a savory perfume of roasting meats hung in the air to cover the slightly sour smell of river's edge. Rolling hills still dotted with green stretched out beyond the city.

"I don't know about you," Jean-Marc said, trying to hide his eagerness, "but I'm going to look around. I mean, as long as we're here, right? I had no time to dawdle on the upriver trip. I've heard great things about Lyon. Do you know they have remains from the Roman Empire here? Churches and theaters and such."

"Would they be interesting to see?" Abbie asked. Her eyes were wider than usual as the magnificence or perhaps sheer size of the great city dazzled her.

He was cheered to see her coming out of the dark womb she'd hidden in these past few days. "Interesting? Perhaps we'll spot some ancient Roman's ghost walking around."

That definitely caught her attention, and she crossed herself.

"Lyon calls itself the gastronomic capital of the world," Jean-Marc continued. "And I've heard of plazas that sell every flower known to man. They've been brought here by world travelers. Surely we can find someone to tell us their tale of faraway places."

"I'm not interested in–"

"And silk. They have looms here making the most marvelous designs. Have you ever felt silk, Abbie?"

The slightest of creases marred her forehead. "I've heard of it. It's an infidel material. Is it very sinful?"

"Sinful? How could silk be sinful? But some of it's worth a king's ransom. It's moonbeams that you can touch. It's– How should I describe it to you? Ah. The way everyone else's wine is compared to your burgundy– that is the how the finest linen is compared to silk."

Now he had her attention. "And speaking of wine," he said as he helped her off the barge, "they say there are actually three rivers that wind their way through the city: the Saone, the Rhone, and the wine! Even you would say that's something we should investigate, wouldn't you?"

Abbie had never seen so many people, so many wonders in her life! Narrow streets ran between houses that rose three stories high and more. These modern homes had balconies and cunningly carved columns where saints helped support the roof. There were tall, pointed arches over front doorways and bold patterns displayed in the very colors of a building's stones.

And everywhere were peddlers. Hot pies, spices, cloth, silver, relics… Anything a person could ever dream of was sold on the streets of Lyon.

The hill up from the river eventually led to the most awe-inspiring cathedral Abbie had ever imagined. It was broad enough to require seven double doors above the long steps leading to it. Supporting towers like flower spikes blossomed everywhere above, seeming fragile even though she knew they must be made of the strongest stone.

The poor clustered around its base, seeking alms from the newly-purified and those who wished to atone for their sins. Their dirty rags seemed to soil the great holy house. Abbie wondered if this was what the Gates of Heaven looked like: the pure wall marking the boundary to Paradise with the clamoring sinners of humanity seeking a way in.

And yet a part of her wondered why the poor were here. Surely with such an over-abundance of wealth on display, this church and its city could have done away with poverty.

She ran her hands over the carvings around one of the lesser doors, marveling at the workmanship and piety on display. "Look!" she cried to Jean-Marc. This saint held a wine cup in one hand and a bunch of grapes in the other. "It's St. Amandus." Such a serious face the saint had! Was he looking at her?

"I need to go to confession," she told Jean-Marc. "Over the past few days I've accrued a great many sins, and it seems I may be headed for more."

"They aren't sins if you're upholding your family's honor," Jean-Marc said as he held the door open for her.

"I'll let the priest decide that. Surely the priests here are great and holy."

"I hear they sup with the Pope himself on occasion."

Jean-Marc's remark was lost upon her as the marvels of the inside of the church assailed Abbie's senses in a riot of color and opulence and space. Great panes of rainbow-hued glass told the stories of the Bible, illuminated by the sun itself. She stood within a golden glow upon the floor and turned and turned so she could take it all in.

There was John the Baptist. There the angel Gabriel speaking to the Virgin Mary, held in heavenly light. Over here were the Apostles at the Pentecost, so real she could touch them if she wished…

And the church seemed to stretch so far above her, perhaps the angels themselves slept in the rafters.

"Oh," she kept saying. Even Jean-Marc was held silent by this holy place.

Eventually she made her way to the confessionals. When she disappeared behind the door, Jean-Marc had a quiet conversation with a priest to the side of the hall.

Abbie emerged in a sober mood. She had found the father sympathetic to her but he also counseled her for the good of her family to continue her deception. She only needed to make sure that in all other ways she led a virtuous life and raised her children as good Catholics. He also suggested frequent contributions to the church as a way she could expunge her lie. If her future husband were rich enough, perhaps she could sponsor an abbey.

She reported some of this to Jean-Marc as soon as she'd finished reciting her Hail Mary's before a small side altar. And he made sure that the same priest he'd talked to saw him drop a generous handful of sous into the poorbox.

Walking through the city on such a fine, warm day returned Abbie to a good mood. A city square held a troupe of traveling entertainers: jugglers with bells on their caps and sleeves, singers and even a magician. Abbie crossed herself and watched, wide-eyed, hanging onto Jean-Marc's arm.

"Do you think it's really magic?" she whispered to him.

Jean-Marc had been trying to keep track of the cups and balls. "It was on the left, I know it," he said after the magician had produced the ball from the center cup. "It must be magic. That's the only explanation."

The mage waved a curtain in front of a young woman, and then– she was gone! Only a puff of purple smoke remained where she had stood.

Abbie gasped in terror until the same woman reappeared. Rattling a tambourine, she danced among the crowd and gathered the coins they threw.

"How did he do it?" Abbie asked Jean-Marc. "Is it evil?"

"Do you think the holy priests would stand for evil to be called upon so close to their church?" His quiet laugh reassured her greatly, as did his arm around her shoulder.

So many young men dressed the way that Jean-Marc had when Abbie had first beheld him, but even more so. Cloaks slung rakishly around chic, bright suits. All their outfits had been slashed almost to rags with luxurious inner layers showing through.

And the women seemed so fine in their dresses heavy with embroidery, even gold. These too were often slashed, though less so than the men's. The ladies' skirts also seemed somehow different. Abbie tried not to stare, but they didn't fall in folds. Rather, they made a neat cone shape around their legs. How did they do that?

Such a rainbow in the November streets! It was not only the people, not just the activity that ran such riot. Someone fostered a thick planting of trees and bushes in one cul-de-sac that still held onto colorful leaves this far into fall. Behind a nearby fence grew a healthy garden of greens, late squash, and root crops that drew Abbie's interest.

They passed a group of soldiers with their uniforms smartly slashed, and crisp underlinens carefully plucked to fill the voids. Their short bases were organ-folded, creating a marvelously starched air about an otherwise rumpled look. Their sword scabbards flashed in the sunlight, drawing the attention of dozens of young boys who swarmed around them asking interminable questions.

"You wouldn't go off and join a war, would you, Jean-Marc?" Abbie asked. She clutched his sleeve so she wouldn't be drawn away in the fast-moving crowds.

"If you'd asked me ten years ago, I would have said yes," Jean-Marc told her, eying his would-be brethren. "But I'd rather not tempt fate and my own mortality. Let God take me when He will, and I won't give any man the chance to hasten my departure. I'll see the world on my own whims and not to the orders of some general."

Jean-Marc stopped talking when a well-dressed but raucous couple nearly mowed them down in the street. *She* was shrill and demanding; *he* cursed at her and landed a good slap on her cheek, which only caused her to shriek even more loudly at him.

"A love match," Abbie noted dryly. "I wonder how much her father sold her for?"

"There goes a woman who doesn't know how to make the best of her situation," Jean-Marc countered.

"So it is all her fault."

"Maybe it is. Maybe this was a meek and well-tempered man who has been driven to near-insanity by his shrewish wife," Jean-Marc said.

"And perhaps she was a sweet maid who found herself in a situation where the only way she could survive was to clash with her husband," Abbie said with a frown.

Jean-Marc patted her hand on his arm. "Philippe is the mildest of men," he told her. "When he gets angry, he locks himself in his office for days. But he doesn't get angry much at all. Three years ago last Easter is the last time I can recall that he did that." He gave her a smile and a reassuring squeeze. "He doesn't drink to excess or indulge in any vice that I can name. Such things would keep him from his work. He is a very serious and God-fearing man."

"Oh." Her eyes moved as she considered the information.

They strolled further before she ventured to ask, "Jean-Marc, what's an indulgence?"

He looked about to see what she had spied. "I suppose it's an extravagance. Do you see something you want?"

She shook her head. "That's what I was thinking, but it doesn't make sense," she said. "The holy father told me that I should purchase an indulgence a month for the lifetime of my marriage."

Jean-Marc stopped, bringing her to a halt with him. "Indulgence," he growled. "That's a different kind. An indulgence for the priest."

"But he said it was for me," Abbie protested. "How much are they? Do they have them in Marseille? If I do go through with this and if your brother finds out the truth, will I still have to buy them?"

"An indulgence is a fraud," Jean-Marc said in a flat voice.

"But the holy father–!"

"Some priests are holier than others. Some priests like to line their own hidden pockets with the hard-earned money of the poor."

Abbie hastily crossed herself, and Jean-Marc drew her from the more crowded portion of the fast-moving street traffic.

"It's a scam," Jean-Marc told her. "The Germans started it, I think. Leave it to the tight-pursed Germans. They're telling people that they can buy their way into Heaven."

Abbie's eyes widened and she crossed herself once more. "No man may buy his way–"

"That's absolutely true. God is not interested in money, else why would there be so many poor here on Earth?" Jean-Marc nodded to note two filthy beggars down the way from them. "Nowhere in the scriptures does it say anything about making deals with God through money or anything besides faith and good deeds. Nowhere does it mention anything called 'indulgences.'"

Jean-Marc shook his index finger at Abbie. "That priest was a charlatan. He should be reported to his bishop, unless his bishop's as big a crook as he is."

"Jean-Marc!" Abbie jumped at the shrillness of her own voice, looked wildly about to see if she'd captured anyone's attention, and then went on in hushed tones. "That's blasphemy. You'd best watch what you say."

His dark curls shook with his vehemence while the feather in his cap bobbed up and down. "It's not blasphemy if it's the truth. I've seen a few priests up to their armpits in the blackest of sin, and their superiors didn't do anything about it. If you ask me, that's why this Protestant business is causing such a stir. Not just because it's heresy, but because some priests seem to bring it on themselves. People don't want to have to put up with a devil masquerading inside the Lord's own house. Even God-fearing Catholics know that the church needs to clean itself up."

Abbie examined his face. "Are you a Protestant?"

He frowned at her. "Of course not. Would I be bringing a good Catholic girl home to my brother if we were Protestants? Would my family enjoy the honor it receives in Marseille if we were Protestants? Don't speak nonsense, Abbie– and don't listen to that priest again!"

"But what about the indulgence? He said that was the best way I could atone for my sin."

"I'll introduce you to some true priests when we get home," Jean-Marc assured her. "They'll set up penance for you and me and whoever else needs it. And perhaps they can figure how to deal with this false priest of Lyon."

His answer comforted her and she hung close upon his arm. It made sense of some things she had heard here and there. Imagine: a darkness within the priests running the church! Priests were supposed to be above the rest of mankind. They should be better than ordinary people. It was almost unthinkable otherwise. With a wave of sadness, Abbie wondered why it wasn't completely unthinkable. Priests should live up to their vows.

As a wife or a promised virgin should live up to hers.

Was this contract a true vow? Did it really pertain to her now instead of Babette? Marriage was a holy sacrament. Shouldn't it be entered into with as little sin as possible? Shouldn't it be maintained in the same way?

She was still quietly considering her position as they supped in an uncrowded shop whose only business, it seemed, was in serving food to well-mannered customers. Such a very cosmopolitan concept! Seven long tables more than half-filled the room while two servers moved up and down the aisles with their heavy trays of food and drink. As the evening deepened a small brass and drum band settled in to entertain, and the number of diners swelled.

"Tomorrow we'll go see the ruins," Jean-Marc said from over his grilled eels. The waitress arrived with a new pitcher of wine, this time a pretty claret for them to sample. "And we need to see about showing you some silk. It's made from spiders' webs, I hear. Spiders' webs or fairy stuff. It's magical."

More vintages came and went. Jean-Marc told Abbie about some of the people he'd met on this trip. He seemed fascinated by their ordinary lives and how they viewed the world. In learning how he felt about them, Abbie thought that perhaps he revealed his own opinions about how the world was run.

He enjoyed being outdoors and talking with people. He liked things that were different from what he was used to. He loved being surprised by life.

He took shocking chances that caused her to cry out with concern until he related the comical outcome of some of them.

"Tell me, Jean-Marc," she said after one discourse, "is your brother as nice as you?"

He raised his newly-filled goblet to her with a small smile, and then rec-ollected another interesting acquaintance, a fellow who owned a mule who could talk.

Just as Abbie was about to venture her opinion about that, dancing broke out opposite them in the room. A robust man and woman dressed in the Ger-man fashion put down their wine, moved to stand in the center of the open area of the room, and then performed a quick-stepping, light dance around each other. When they were done, they bowed to the room and held each other's hand above their heads, the woman holding her skirts daintily to show off her velvet dancing slippers.

Then four tables over, another couple– or rather, the man– had to show off. He was stouter than the first, and when he pulled his wife from her chair she had no choice but to follow him. Hesitatingly and then with more will, she let him spin her around himself only to catch her so they could tip their toes and then hop together, laughing.

The room's customers encouraged the dancers by clapping to the beat. The restaurant encouraged them by serving more wine. Jean-Marc bobbed his glass in time to the music as he sat sideways on the bench.

"You can do it!" he called to a man who danced by bouncing into deep knee bends that ended with a kick. He was a trifle old to be so boisterous and huffed his way through his turn. When he sat down he made a great show of catching his breath and calling for more wine.

Jean-Marc and Abbie both sang along when the band started a familiar tune, though some of the words they sang were different from each other's version. At one point Jean-Marc seemed to forget the words entirely, so he sang "la-la-la" at the top of his lungs and clapped until his hands turned red.

Taking advantage of their almost clear section of table, he jumped up on it and performed a jig. Abbie scrambled to save their drinks from his stamp-ing, but Jean-Marc didn't notice. He had enough room to take three steps and click his heels in the air, then take three back and click them again. He gave a grin to the room's cheers and waved his outstretched hands to encourage more. It took three men toward the door climbing up on their own long table to draw attention away from him.

Abbie helped him down when it seemed doubtful he could make the journey without incident. He sagged against her for a moment and then reached out behind her, grabbing a mug of Swiss ale from a passing server.

"Isn't this a great place?" he shouted at Abbie so she could hear him.

After more music, dancing, and wine, he paid their bill and stuffed some extra coins down the bodice of their waitress, who didn't seem to mind. Abbie dragged Jean-Marc out into the snappy night air.

"Oh yes," he wheezed. "Better. It was getting warm in there."

His face was flushed over his crooked smile. "Lyon," he said. "A city towering above others. I must come back again."

"Perhaps a time when you'll remember it?" Abbie asked him.

"I am not drunk," he declared. "I am merely taking advantage of the abundance that I find around me. Who's to tell when I'll ever taste the like again?"

Yet he was still unable to walk an absolutely straight line an hour later, after Abbie had plied him back and forth in the squares and plazas of central Lyon. Cold settled on the night. A hint of near-frost hung in the air. She shivered not just because of the temperature but because of all the strange people on the streets.

Abbie had been in villages after dark. The streets were empty. Good people stayed in their homes unless some task or emergency sent them outside. Here some of the people didn't look that virtuous. Some of them wore rags and furtive looks. Didn't they have homes to go to? Didn't the church at least provide safe housing for them?

A group of three well-dressed matrons with their husbands hurried through the night, talking loudly though their words seemed muffled and confused between the close buildings. Abbie caught the word: "Protestants," and froze.

Could there be Protestants in the area? She glanced to her left and right as she clutched Jean-Marc. Did such people lurk in the shadows, waiting to carry off godly Catholics?

"Jean-Marc!" she whispered frantically. "We have to get out of here!"

"No Protestant would show their face in this Christian city," he reassured her. "Although with the people we've seen today…" His face screwed up in hard-won thought. "There do seem to be a lot of Germans and Swiss here." He chewed the inside of his cheek. "And who can tell a French *Protestor* from a normal French man?"

Abbie huddled hard against him, thankful when he wrapped his arms around her. Father Bernard had taught them that Protestants had horns and cloven hooves, just like their master. "I'm afraid," she confessed.

"I am here. I'll protect you." He pointed at the candles in the windows of a rambling building down the road and walked them toward it, almost in a straight line. "Look, a proper monastery. No Protestant will venture here if they value their safety."

"Let's go back. To the boat."

He stopped them and looked about, taking stock of their location. "It's getting late," he said. "We're too far from the docks. The riverside streets are notoriously raucous well into the wee hours. They may be dangerous to travel– and not because of Protestants. I've kept you out too long, Abbie. I'm sorry."

"What will we do?"

"I could–" He turned and spotted a brick-and-stone mansion whose entry steps were flanked by stately lanterns. "There. A deep bed would be a welcome change."

It was a sumptuous hotel. Jean-Marc hired two fierce-looking boys and one of the maids to bring bags from the boat. "Tell the captain 'Dellamer,'" he instructed as he gave them coins. "Half now, the rest when the goods are delivered."

The boys ran off with high spirits while the maid followed at a brisk pace.

"I must have overpaid," Jean-Marc mused. He took a deep, cleansing breath and examined their hotel, approving of the public accommodations.

Clean and open, it held a modern decor of wood-trimmed chambers within its ancient exterior. A well-mannered staff had greeted them. There were no drunken louts lolling at dice to interrupt the patrons' sleep.

Their host ran a dust rag along a counter as he went to the back on an errand, and one of his maids took care of some spots he'd missed. An alert, short-haired tabby cat stuck its nose into a corner to check a shadow. Jean-Marc doubted if a rat had been seen within a block of the place.

"We can breakfast here," he told Abbie when he saw the small dining area next to the large, welcoming fireplace.

It was only three small glasses of Candian malmsey later that the boys returned triumphantly with two cloth bags, the little maid scurrying behind them.

When Abbie saw her hotel room, she whispered to Jean-Marc, "Surely this is much too extravagant." It held a bed big enough for three and a china lavatory upon which was painted sprays of roses. There were thick rugs and enough sweet-smelling candles to light a gentleman's library. The tall window overlooking the river Rhone was draped with curtains worthy of a prince. Heavens– they matched the draperies around the bed perfectly. She walked around the small room exclaiming at the exquisite touches. Jean-Marc followed her.

"If you wish, I could save some money by just taking the one room," Jean-Marc said with the slightest of slurs. "It could be quite cozy."

Abbie turned to him. "Jean-Marc, you've drunk far too much tonight."

He bent his head so his lips were mere inches from hers. "It's not the wine I'm drunk on. You are a beautiful woman, Abbie-Babette." Wrapping his hand around her waist, he pulled her hips closer to his. "I think you're the most intriguing woman I've ever met. I want to know more about you." He ran his thumb from her jaw to her collarbone. "Let's learn about each other tonight."

8

Abbie caught his roaming hand in hers. "I think I've learned that Monsieur DuMonde can't hold his wine. There's a contract between me and your brother, remember?"

"No no, sweet Abbie. Between your cousin and my brother," he whispered into her ear.

His wine-warm breath sent sparks all through her body, and where his strong hand held her waist, her flesh heated.

"Per... Perhaps you'd like to explore your own room?" she managed to say.

"Your room is so much more interesting." His soft lips fastened on her neck, right below her ear.

Abbie felt her knees weakening as she closed her eyes.

"Madam?"

With a start, Abbie's eyes flew open as she pushed Jean-Marc away. A young woman stood at her door and curtsied even while eying the situation curiously.

"Madam, I was sent to see if you needed any help... preparing for bed?" the woman said as she gave Jean-Marc a thorough, admiring scan. "Or is that taken care of?"

Abbie turned burgundy red. "No!" she said quickly. "The gentleman was just leaving, weren't you, Jean-Marc?"

He said nothing but bowed to both of them and then quickly left. Abbie put her hand to her neck, to the spot where his lips had touched her. As the woman came in to turn down the bed and then fuss with the fastenings on Abbie's gown, Abbie could only stare at the door, where the image of Jean-Marc seemed to linger.

She would have felt uncomfortable the next day in seeing him in the dining room but for an old married couple with whom he sat, who had traveled down from Geneva.

Jean-Marc straightened when he saw her and waved her to them. He introduced the two, Master Levesque and his wife, Eva. Jean-Marc leaned toward Abbie as the couple were occupied with their order, and said softly, "Lucky for me the master d'hotel has every bit as much knowledge of hangover remedies as your family. I feel fit enough to explore today. How about you?"

"Are you sure?" Abbie asked. Slightly purple patches circled under his eyes.

"I won't be making that mistake again," Jean-Marc told her. "I've been drunk twice in as many weeks. That's once too many. Perhaps the solution is moderation?"

She had to chuckle at that.

"And perhaps instead of sampling every new vintage as soon as I lay my eyes upon it, I should buy a keg and keep it for more leisurely sampling later. Perhaps in the presence of a lovely lady?" He nodded to her.

The couple turned back to them. "Master Levesque is a copper smith," Jean-Marc announced. "And his wife is the finest baker of Italian pastries in all Geneva." He gestured toward Abbie. "This is France's leading expert on the legendary wines of Burgundy."

Together they all had a marvelous, chattering breakfast at which Jean-Marc insisted that the couple tell them everything about their city, their people, and the lands they had traveled through.

Images grew in Abbie's mind of towering hills– mountains– and heavy winter snows. Of crisp summer air and sailboats on crystal-clear blue lakes.

All her life she had heard the stories of her family for generations back told a hundred times. Here were new stories. They were familiar but they held different, surprising twists to them.

These were people just like her, but they were different, too. They pronounced their words with an accent and sprinkled strange ones into their stories. The way Eva twined her hair from side to side instead of around her head seemed eccentric though pretty enough.

They spoke of different kings and of their youth in another era as well as their foreign country. Abbie began to see that they weren't as alien as she thought foreigners would be. The basic stories they related sounded of home. Work, family, life and death, and love.

Perhaps traveling the world wasn't that shocking a thing to do, if all people were alike in this. Why, here she was talking casually to people who had never visited France before. She smiled to herself. How cosmopolitan was she now?

By the time they were finished, Abbie knew all about the couple's family back three generations, as well as the families of Geneva's leading residents. She also learned a little about making *cassata*.

Master Levesque left carrying with him a note from Jean-Marc telling the captain of their ship that he had bought one barrel of Clos Bourgogne Grand Cru.

Abbie and Jean-Marc headed out to the streets of Lyon. "Yes, this is going to be a very profitable match." Jean-Marc smirked to himself as he patted the heavy purse he'd acquired for his brother.

"That was an astronomical price," Abbie protested. "You cheated the man!"

"Did I lie to him? I merely pointed out each and every fine quality of your wine. I do believe he was drooling there toward the end. I told the truth, didn't I?"

"Well, yes," Abbie said slowly. "But I've never heard of charging so much–"

"That's because you are a vintner. I am a salesman," he replied as he stuffed the purse safely into the interior pocket of his coat. "Someone should have taught you how to sell your wine when they were showing you how to make it."

That made her frown.

"Come, let's get you to smile. Lyon has a splendid Roman amphitheater. Let's go see it."

"I think I'll return to the boat."

Jean-Marc pulled at her, beckoning a small carriage. "You'll enjoy this. You've been cooped up in the same spot far too long. Time to see that there's more to life than grapevines and wine presses, Abbie."

Abbie had never been in a carriage, much less a fancy one like this with an upholstered leather seat. "Maybe," she started, but the carriage had already taken off, the single horse clop-clopping through the cobbled, ancient streets.

People looked up as they jounced past. The height of the vehicle allowed some splendid views. Strange how just a few feet could make the world seem different. More exciting.

Abbie pointed at a small street market, its wheelbarrows piled with strange-colored fruits. "I wonder what that is?"

"We'll investigate when we return," Jean-Marc told her, surprised that their excursion had changed her mood much quicker than he'd have guessed. Perhaps the soul of an explorer hid inside Abbie.

Just past a hill hardly outside of the city lay the remains of the civilization that had ruled this land not so long ago. The two of them strolled through it, Jean-Marc imagining what kinds of savage rituals the pagan populace had cheered for. Abbie ran her hands over the great columns in awe.

"These people probably lived in stone houses as well," Abbie said.

Jean-Marc shrugged. "Perhaps. Certainly their upper class did. There are still some of their homes in Marseille."

"Babette doesn't like stone houses. She prefers modern wooden ones. So does Maddy." Abbie fondled the creases carved deep in the column. "But stone is solid. Stone is permanent. I grew up in a stone house. You saw it, Jean-Marc. It's as wonderful as they come."

"I grew up in one as well," Jean-Marc told her. He bought some bread, cheese, and beer from a vendor whose cart sat on the edge of the great tourney field, and they settled on one of the long seats.

"You'll see it, too," he told her.

"How can you want to leave such a place, then?"

He shrugged. "There are other stone houses. Other styles of houses to see. Reasons why the people built them the way they did. Why, we'd still be building our homes with columns and friezes if the barbarians hadn't toppled the old Empire."

"Do you really think so?"

They munched quietly for a while. Jean-Marc watched her as she clearly daydreamed, her eyes sweeping the broad amphitheater in a hazy, unfocused way. The left side of her mouth relaxed, then began to curl up as if she imagined something pleasurable.

"I like to think of the people who were my age back in those times," Jean-Marc told her. "I wonder how they lived. What did they do for a living? What did they think about it all?"

"Did they sign away their girls' lives for marriage contracts, too?" Abbie asked.

"Probably. It seems the way the world operates most efficiently. Merge two families and their businesses through marriage. Why, isn't that what kings and queens are all about? Merging countries?"

Abbie had just bitten down on a hard chunk of cheese, but now she stopped chewing. "I hadn't thought of it that way," she said around the food. "No one escapes."

"Everyone does it unless they're too poor and can only marry for love. Be thankful your family is prosperous."

"Yours is very prosperous," Abbie said. "Wealthy."

"I suppose."

"How did they get that way, Jean-Marc?"

Jean opened up the second small jug of beer and refilled her mug. "My father's father's father's…" he counted on his fingers. "No, that's it. Father's father's father, he was a sailor from Italy. By chance– well, there's more to it than that, really– he came to own the ship he sailed on and began the business of import and export. He fathered sons who were good at selling and keeping track of the accounts."

"And a great-grandson who was good at trying to sail away from the family," Abbie observed.

He gave her a regretful grimace. "I respect my family," he said. "I support the business. I'm an excellent salesman. But I need my room. I can't be stifled or I'll die."

She nodded, gazing at the arches on the farthest side. "But your brother likes to be stifled?"

Jean-Marc tried to chuckle. "Philippe has never known any other life. Papa and my uncle brought him into the business very early. It was obvious that he had great talent. But…" Again with the sad frown. "I don't think he had much of a childhood. The pox came through and took my parents. My uncle was very ill for years, but had enough time to finish training my brother. And Philippe had me to worry about as well, to raise me as if he were my father and not just a few years older then me."

"Just a few years," Abbie murmured.

Jean-Marc didn't hear her. "I owe him everything. He didn't have to keep me. There were places that would have taken me in until I was an adult, kept me out of his way. He didn't mind if I hung around his office when I shouldn't. He made sure I had the proper tutors and I was dressed well, and he insisted that I play between my lessons."

"Did you play with him?"

That produced a low, mirthless laugh. "No. He was too old to play with a little boy. Besides, I don't think Philippe knows how to play."

"Too old?" Abbie asked. "Just how–"

"These ruins are delightful, *si*?"

Both looked up to see a woman not much older than they step daintily down the steps that doubled as seats. She was visibly pregnant yet she still grasped her loose skirts against her stomach in the popular way that would make an unpregnant woman seem with child. The result made her look larger than she probably was, a properly fertile woman.

Jean-Marc stumbled to his feet to offer her a supporting hand.

"You are so kind." She smiled, her eyes flitting across him to take his measure.

Abbie realized that she was grinding her teeth. How dare anyone look at Jean-Marc that way! Especially someone who should have a husband of her own somewhere.

"*Cara!*" a man's voice called from behind. The woman looked past them toward its source. Abbie distinctly saw her eyes narrow before her mouth smoothed into a smile.

"Oh, there you are, darling!" the woman said as Jean-Marc glanced around. "This kind man was just helping me, weren't you?"

The gentleman who ran up with refreshments in his arms was gangly as opposed to Jean-Marc's solid figure. He struggled to balance everything in one arm so he could use the other to help her. He was balding, his hair an unassuming brown compared to Jean-Marc's thick, dark curling locks.

"I think I shall settle here, if it's all right," the woman told them. "Really, I am quite exhausted."

As her husband bustled about to make sure she was comfortable and to arrange the food within easy reach, the woman looked over his shoulder and matched gazes with Jean-Marc. She gave him a lazy, coquettish smile. She passed her petite hand over her braided crown as if she were caressing a lover, and then touched her index finger to her lips, pursing her lips around it.

Abbie hated her. She didn't know exactly what she was suggesting, but she knew what it was about.

The woman introduced herself: Isadora, and her husband, Gian-Carlo, both from Rome and visiting Isadora's mother, who would oversee the birth.

Rome! In exultation Jean-Marc sat across from the couple and began his interrogation of them as to the wonders of the holy city as well as all of Italy.

The woman tried to flirt with him when she thought her husband wasn't looking, but seemed confused when she found that Jean-Marc's interest lay only in learning about aqueducts, the Via Venito, and how often a Roman would worship inside the walls of the Vatican itself.

She'd tilt her head and flutter her eyelids, and Jean-Marc would ask if this amphitheater resembled the Coliseum in the slightest. She slid her hand dangerously near his own but he was too engrossed in Gian-Carlo's description of the Tyrrhenian coast.

When Isadora deigned to glance Abbie's way, Abbie rewarded her with a smug grin that would have done Babette proud. Isadora stuck her tongue out at her.

"These steps are too cold," Isadora interrupted. Immediately her husband helped her up and then out of the amphitheater to a place of more comfort. They didn't offer any goodbyes or good wishes in their wake.

Jean-Marc scratched his head. "I wonder what all that was about?" he asked. Abbie didn't answer him.

On the way back to the city Jean-Marc used his silver salesman's tongue to finagle them a tour of a silk merchant's warehouse. There, amid the spools and looms that dwarfed Abbie, the foreman regaled them with tales of far-off Persia and deserts so distant from France as to boggle the mind. Brown-skinned people and cats the size of men; giant fish that walked on land, and wizards who could vanish into smoke or grant you your fondest wish. Spiders who could spin material fit for kings and emperors.

Abbie ran her hand over a length of smooth burgundy and gold cloth. Spun moonlight indeed. Was it magic?

The sun was a finger-width high in the azure sky the next morning when they left their hotel. Jean-Marc casually said, "I think perhaps I shall do a little confessing as well," and they returned to the great cathedral. Abbie took time out from her prayers to go back to the outer doors so she could admire the relief of St. Amandus once again. He made her both proud and humble to have wine in her blood. Hers was a holy calling.

It was quite a while before she spied Jean-Marc exiting through a far door. She found him engrossed in a man's story of Ethiopia, which apparently lay somewhere around Egypt or India, which Abbie knew was very, very far from here. Far enough to have given this man skin the color of walnut wood.

The world settled to a more familiar closeness as Abbie stood next to her escort. He'd cross his arms in front of him, leaning on one foot, then shift to take another pose, then shift a few minutes later. Even his body couldn't bear to be in one position for very long.

Abbie thought that perhaps Jean-Marc's dreams of traveling those magical lands were not so far-fetched. There was life to be experienced beyond the vineyards of Burgundy. When the man from Ethiopia spoke of the sun being directly overhead in Ethiopian skies, Jean-Marc glanced up at the position of their own sun and let out a mild oath.

"We must be on our way!" he said, and excused them hurriedly.

Jean-Marc helped her into their barge. "The Rhone's a rough river, completely different from the Saone," Jean-Marc warned before he inspected the safety of their cargo.

Under the protective shadow of her palm at her forehead, Abbie watched him. Adventurer though he wanted to be, he still held a businessman's knack to checking off the details as he instructed tighter ropes around several casks.

The captain had been changed for the lower river, but two of the crew stayed the same, while an extra one signed on. Abbie quickly unpacked in her quarters and ventured back outside to see what this Rhone would be like.

Almost immediately they ran into wakes of whitewater, the Rhone sloshing and overrunning the slumbering Saone. The Rhone rushed to the sea, not minding whom it pushed out of its way to get there.

The boat bobbed at an alarming angle, then suddenly switched to heave into another deep bow before rising up, ducking under, and settling into its new course. The crew scrambled with poles and the captain hung onto the wide tiller bravely. Their shouts were a definite difference from the laconic conversations of the Saone crew.

Abbie lurched with the boat. It was like sledding down a steep, hurly-burly slope in winter without the security of soft snow to fall into if you made a bad turn. Breathlessly she hung on for dear life to a great horizontal post fastened on the wall of the passenger compartments, but another roll of whitewater tossed her away.

Before she could fall, strong arms caught her. Jean-Marc pulled her to a long, secured box high enough to sit upon. He swung her onto his lap. While using one arm to lock around her waist, he took sturdy hold of the deck railing behind them. They whirled around in the uncertain currents.

"These men have made this trip hundreds of times," he assured her over the roar of the river. The ship lurched and he pressed himself around her in a protective embrace.

Quite suddenly they came out of it and the ship bobbed into smoother waters. The roil of the Rhone visibly commenced just a few yards behind them, then farther, then farther, and Abbie sighed with relief.

Jean-Marc's arms still held her in an iron cage. "I think you can let go now," she told him.

He eyed the waters critically, peering ahead and to the western side of the ship. The crew had calmed. One man swung a long pole back inside the hull for storage. He grinned at a crewmate and then over at them.

"All clear!" he shouted with a wave.

Jean-Marc relaxed and then his gaze darted back to Abbie. The corners of his mouth twitched into a small smile. "It's a cold wind," he said. "Perhaps you need warming?"

It was true, but it was truer that his arms were strong as well as warm. He wrapped her cloak around the two of them and settled, watching the river. His hands didn't seek out any indecency.

It was nice. It was rather a thrill to be in a man's arms, a man who wasn't her father. It wasn't at all like the boys back home.

Abbie leaned against the solid structure of his chest, held within the warmth of him. The padding of his gown's shoulder was comfortable as a sturdy pillow. White birds spiraled overhead, screaming at them, and Jean-Marc imitated them to amuse her. When one of the birds landed on deck a few feet from them, Jean-Marc and it traded insults until Abbie laughed out loud.

A sudden lurch and she threw her arms around his chest under the cloak, but the waters steadied after that. They held that warm embrace for some time, watching the world and not each other, especially once Abbie realized that Jean-Marc's chin was scratching up against her cheek.

He hadn't noticed, it seemed. She sank her senses into her hands and arms, which lay against him. The wide, smooth satin collar of his coat lay over layers of doublet and shirt, but even so she could feel his heartbeat. Yes, she was sure it was his heartbeat, because she could feel her own so strongly to compare.

She eased her right hand over and sure enough, the contours of his skin and muscles revealed themselves slightly to her. From before she knew that underneath the wide padding of the coat were shoulders that needed no padding to be impressive. The legs that showed under the smooth knit hose were long and well-shaped, and allowed Jean-Marc to stand with an assurance that other men must envy.

He'd helped out loading the wagon when they left Uncle Gus, and he'd had no trouble working side-by-side with the other men. A strong man, a pleasing body when draped in his more modest but refined clothing.

Thrice she'd seen a group of men swimming after a hard day's work, and often during the hottest part of summer they would do their work without shirts, sweat and dirt streaming down their bodies but not covering them up.

Jean-Marc would look like that: all long, sculpted muscles punctuated by rows of smaller ones. She leaned close to his neck, inhaling the musk of him and watching how he breathed. Without thinking she ran her fingertips across his nubbly chin. Whiskers. Not smoothly-shaven, not a beard yet.

He sat perfectly still. His breathing stopped. It took a moment for Abbie to realize where her hand was, to snap out of her reverie.

What to say? What to say? She tried to put a laugh in her voice. "You'll have to decide if you're going to shave or not, monsieur. I mean, if we are going to continue to sit this way. This in-between is rough on my skin."

"Are you warm enough?" There was a catch in his voice. "Shall I let you go?"

She quickly said, "The wind is cold. If you don't mind, I don't mind."

"I don't mind," he whispered and his eyes found hers.

9

He had marvelous brown eyes with a ring of gold in them. Darker brown flecks evened the color from a distance, but this close the gold stood out clear and bright. It was probably what endowed him with that devilish glance of his. His eyebrows were well-shaped, not too heavy, not joined together like some men's. They could be extraordinarily mobile as they expressed his emotions, she'd seen.

His nose was… distinctive, she decided. It held subtle curves like the statues of the saints in the cathedral. His mouth was truly the mouth of a saint. It was capable of grinning and snarling, of sneering, and of laughing in great guffaws. Right now it ever so slightly curved into a wary, small smile.

He had lovely ears, too, but they were hidden under the soft curls of his hair. So deep and rich and brown, yet the edges caught the light as if they were spun gold from a fairy tale.

Acting on impulse, she smoothed one of those curls back, and her hand lingered against the side of his forehead. Jean-Marc didn't object, and when she had held his hair back too long she slid the heel of her hand down the side of his face. Downy hair. Smooth, warm skin. Prickly beard. Smooth skin again on the side of his neck, and then the crusty embroidery of the neckline of his shirt scratched her.

His own hands squeezed her waist where he held her.

"Am I still the bounder you thought me?" he asked her quietly.

She shook her head. She knew her cheeks were flushed because she could feel the heat in them. Heat coursed everywhere through her: veins, skin… especially where his hands touched her.

He eased forward to kiss her under the cover of her hood, and she let him. Such sweetness, such warmth. She felt so close to him, though they were just as close as they'd been before. Abbie ran her hands over his solid chest as he kissed her again and again.

And then his lips were gone. She opened her eyes to find his mere inches away. A disappointed sound escaped her and he smiled. Such a lovely smile, especially so close, so targeted directly at her. She basked in the glory of it.

"We are in public," he told her and with a start she realized where they were, how they were seated.

"Oh!" She pulled her cloak into a semblance of order and then slid off his lap, causing another quick repositioning of her cloak. The extra material on her hood flapped across her burning cheeks.

"Maybe we should go in to continue."

Was that man over there laughing at her as he secured a rope? Why was the captain smirking at them as he stood on top of the passenger compartment?

"Oh!" Abbie gathered her cloak around her and ran to her room.

"Abbie?" came Jean-Marc's voice from outside her door. "Abbie, let me in."

"No. No, thank you, Monsieur Dellamer."

"Ah, so it's that way, eh? No one can see us in here, *chérie*."

"I– I am very tired from the day's travel, Jean-Marc. I think I'll take a nap."

For a few minutes she didn't hear anything. Then she heard the door to the common area close, hopefully behind Jean-Marc, and she drew a deep breath of relief.

Abbie needed a chaperone. She'd always thought that chaperones kept men at bay from innocent girls, but now perhaps chaperones also kept the lusts of those so-called innocent girls leashed to propriety.

Babette should be her chaperone, and she, Babette's.

But by now Babette was wedded and bedded. Having Abbie's supposed fiancé's own brother accompany her should have been safe enough– but it wasn't.

Her fiancé's brother.

The priest had told her that her morals must be perfect for the rest of her life for her to pull this off without consequence. It hadn't been two days since then– and now this!

She pushed the idea of having bussed her fiancé's brother– all right, of having kissed him at length and thrilled at it, too– to the back of her mind. She was getting off-track here. She had to keep the important things in mind.

There was no way she was going to marry Philippe Dellamer. Despite what Chris and the kind father had said, it would be immoral to lie one's way into marriage. Marriage was one of the most holy of sacraments. She was not going to go to Hell or even Purgatory by such an easy thing to get out of.

Surely she could just sit down with Monsieur Dellamer when she met him and explain. It was all so reasonable, once you thought about it. And it really, truly didn't reflect badly on Uncle Gus, did it? Babette was the villain in this piece. She would make Monsieur Dellamer see that, so that no trace of scandal would touch Uncle.

And that way perhaps her own feelings toward Jean-Marc wouldn't be so much of a sin.

Her uncle's words came back to her now, about her finding a man who pleased her. Jean-Marc's was a name that she put into her definite consideration list. Uncle might not approve, since Jean-Marc was a younger brother and he had plans to leave the security of his brother's company, but maybe she didn't have to tell Uncle that. He didn't have to know all about Jean–

She stopped her thoughts right there. He wouldn't know about Jean-Marc because she didn't know much about him at all. Who was he? Where was he going in life? She knew his kisses sent fire up and down her body, and that his eyes could captivate her– but what was that? Would that get her back to Clos Bourgogne?

She knew he wanted his freedom. He would probably hop one of his brother's ships one day and sail off to… to… Abbie tried to think of the farthest place she'd ever heard of. China. Oh yes, that was precisely the kind of place he'd sail to. He'd become a silk trader, a merchant of mysterious spices. He'd grow a long, dark beard and wrap his head in a turban.

And he'd have seventeen wives, just as they did in China. Wives and concubines, children and bastards, he'd go off and leave them as well.

No, she was going about this all wrong. In her mind she crossed the name "Jean-Marc" off her potential husband list. Instead, she had to learn the names of eligible men who lived around the Clos Bourgogne. They must be men who had no family vineyards of their own, for the Clos Bourgogne must remain within the Bourgogne family.

Though she could think of a few possibles among the young men she had known while growing up (but they were all dullards!), she could also write a letter to Christopher or Madeline and ask for names. Chris would do this for her. He wanted the vineyard to succeed, and he knew she could make it do so. Yes. Yes, this was a good plan.

Tell Philippe Dellamer the truth, make sure he placed no blame on Uncle, and find a man that Uncle would approve of who lived near the clos.

When the boat stopped beneath an inn that evening, she stepped forth from her cabin with new determination and half a letter already written.

"You look pleased," Jean-Marc told her as he helped her to the dock.

"I am. Quite pleased. I have a letter I need to send. How difficult will it be to get it back upriver?"

"Not difficult at all. There's lots of traffic going back."

Yes, Abbie had seen the long gangs of oxen, mules, and men along the shore struggling with towlines against the Rhone's current, pulling barges upriver. "Good. How soon will it reach my cousin?"

"I thought you weren't speaking to her?"

"Christopher. I've written Chris."

Jean-Marc scratched the back of his neck. "Can everyone in your family read?" he asked.

"Many do," she sniffed. "We must read the wine records. Old Eric taught those of us at the clos, even me. And I managed to teach Babette enough to get by."

He shook his head. "That's dangerous. See what trouble she got into? Too much schooling gives a woman ideas."

Abbie let herself be mysterious about the letter as they supped at a small inn. There weren't that many patrons. As Abbie and Jean-Marc sat at a private table, Abbie caught a glimpse of the members of their crew wolfing down their food in the ever-so-slightly larger public room.

Just to be sure she stayed true to her new resolve, she special-ordered a familiar dish of hard-boiled eggs with mustard and greens, which turned out not quite like the way they made it back home but close enough. Jean-Marc took the Lyonnaise-style roast pork that everyone else ate.

"As long as I've unpacked my writing tools and we had such an unusual adventure in Lyon," she said as the serving girl refilled their wine cups, "I might as well write everyone."

"Even Babette?" Jean-Marc asked with a crooked smile.

Abbie opened her mouth, closed it, and then said, "Perhaps I'm not ready to write her yet. Not until this is all over and settled."

"That's a sensible girl." Jean-Marc leaned back on his bench and patted his stomach. Though he had eaten generously, it still rumbled. "Chris was telling me that most barges don't offer our level of comfort for their passengers. Tonight I think I'll appreciate my soft bed. Shall we take a walk before we retire?"

With newfound confidence in her ability to ignore improper thoughts of Jean-Marc, she agreed. They strolled along the paths around the cluster of family and farm buildings and little kitchen gardens. Lights peeked out the cracks of windows shuttered for the night.

The stars twinkled in the crisp night air, but none seemed as bright as the one Babette had told Abbie about. They were just normal stars, and Jean-Marc was just an ordinary man. When he tried to put his arm around her waist, she eased away from him in a smooth motion and he didn't try again.

Even so, he again was considerate in helping her onto the boat as the choppy water made it bob up, down, in, and out from the dock. Jean-Marc was a kind man. The world was full of kind men. Abbie would find one at the clos whom she could call her own.

There was a common area just outside the six passenger rooms, and the crew had their own quarters just behind this, which explained the two tendrils of smoke from two different small stoves within the deckhouse. Tonight the warmth was quite welcome, and she took off her cloak and hood almost immediately. She ran a hand across her hair to smooth it.

"Perhaps I'll write those letters before turning in," she said.

As Jean-Marc took off his scarlet winter gown, he rummaged through its pockets. "I know it's here somewhere," he muttered. "Ah. Here. Mustn't lose this."

He pulled out a small bundle wrapped in soft cloth. "I got this for you while we were in Lyon."

"What? For me? What is it?" Abbie took the package from him and unwound the wrapping. The cloth was a length of jewel-colored silk, large enough to make a beautiful shawl. But inside–

It was a necklace. Gold wire wound about a narrow stoppered glass bottle, tying it to the vertical member of an intricate golden cross. There was something inside the bottle…

"What is it?" she asked as she peered.

"I told the priest that it was a piece of wood from Golgotha that a pilgrim had brought back from the Holy Land," Jean-Marc said with a straight face. "I will say ten extra prayers tonight for my lie, but I thought you needed a crucifix to replace the one that Babette stole. Inside it is a sliver of those vines of yours."

Clos Bourgogne. Inside that bottle and protected by the Cross was her piece of home. Her grapes. Now she could see the distinctive patterning that showed it was a vine.

Her eyes filled with tears as she clutched the precious necklace to her breast. "Oh," she said. "Oh!"

Abbie threw her arms around Jean-Marc and kissed him full on the lips. "I can't thank you enough. I can never–" and she kissed him again, very hard. "You are such a–"

This time he kissed her.

His lips pressed fervently against hers and his tongue opened the way into her own mouth. He pulled her tightly against him, one hand above her waist and the other lower.

He had shaved. His skin welcomed hers.

Abbie hung on as hard as she could to try to quell the quivers that ran up and down her body. Wonderful, wonderful man! His fingers dug deeper into her. Now she could clearly feel the length of him right up against herself, and she ran her hands over what she could reach to get more of him.

Such delicious decadence, his tongue in her mouth. She felt her secrets flowing to him as he explored her teeth, then her tongue. Why loose her own secrets without tasting his? In a burst of resolution she tangled her tongue with his and slid her hands under his brocade doublet.

When his lips left hers to trail down her neck, Abbie arched to accommodate him and a soft, sighing moan escaped her.

"Quickly, *chérie*," he whispered in her ear. "Into my cabin. Now."

Abbie clung to him, hugging him with all her might. His lips rained tiny kisses over her face with each halting step he took, closer and closer to the door to his cabin.

Abbie tried to slow him down so she could reach him better. She took his face between her hands and tried for another long kiss, but he turned his head to pay attention to the door latch.

"Here," he said, and then, "There. At last."

The door swung open and through a haze of happiness and adrenaline Abbie saw his room.

Not hers.

She was going into a man's room, alone with the man.

Abbie froze. When Jean-Marc pulled at her, she resisted. She had to prop her hand on the door frame not to be drawn in by his little tugs.

"Come on," he urged. "It's just my room."

"I… I can't."

"We won't do anything. I promise. It's just for privacy."

It was true enough, for what if one of the crew happened into the passengers' side to ask Jean-Marc a question? Perhaps a door between them and everyone else would be a good idea.

Besides, she was going to tell Philippe Dellamer the truth. She wouldn't be held by the contract. She was a free woman.

"We can just lie on the bed," Jean-Marc said. "It won't go any further than that. He caught her in one of his delicious, drawn-out kisses and Abbie closed her eyes in ecstasy.

This was what Heaven was like.

She took a step into his room and he kissed her the same way again. She let go the doorframe and was rewarded with another kiss.

When she put her arms around him, he kicked the door shut.

"That's better, *chérie*," he whispered. "Oh yes."

Now that they were alone he held her so tightly she almost couldn't breathe. "Let me loosen that for you," he kindly suggested for the laces on her dress, and she did the same for him, just a few that felt so good when they released.

The heat in the cabin stifled her. She was on fire with desire for Jean-Marc and his mouth, his hands. She'd never felt this way before. Now she drowned in her passions, groaning her emotions.

"Let me help," he whispered, and more laces loosened. She threw her leg over his lap because that way she could feel more of him and revel in the way his breathing, too, seemed out of control. The way his skin gave off heat as well as hers.

Suddenly she realized that her hand had gotten inside his shirt because she encountered the bare skin of his chest, ticklish with a thin graze of hair. Beneath her hand, his heart hammered. Beneath her hand, she felt nipples and layered muscle.

"Oh, Jean-Marc," she sighed.

His hand somehow slid inside her own bodice to cup a breast through her chemise and squeeze it even as his lips took hers hard. She let out a yelp of surprise but it was swallowed within his mouth.

She pushed him away. "No. No–"

"Oh yes. Beautiful Abbie, this is the way I've dreamed it. Sweet Abbie. Abbie my dove."

It felt so right to arch against him when he collected another deep kiss. The room swirled around her, vibrating to both their hearts.

But he was pulling at her clothing.

"No," she said, and tried to blink the haze away. When he came closer she pushed at him. "No."

"But darling, these clothes are just getting in the way." He gave her an encouraging smile. "We can just lie here and touch, innocent as babes. As free as Adam and Eve were on the day they were created."

His eyes roved down to the décolletage he'd uncovered and then back up to her face. "You are certainly as beautiful as Eve. Let me see all of you. Now, lovely Abbie of my heart."

Abbie clutched the fallen edges of her bodice to her, her sleeves hanging awkwardly from it, partially undone. She couldn't bring herself to speak, but she shook her head.

"Please, sweetling. Dearest. A man can die for needs unfulfilled. Did you know that? You don't want me to die, do you?"

"D– die?" Abbie asked uncertainly.

"Absolutely." With a theatrical flourish, Jean-Marc threw himself back on the bed, his arms flung outward, his jerkin open to reveal his gaping undershirt– and oh my, what was happening under his hose!– and gave her such a look of deathly sorrow! "I will die without you, my lovely. Come to me now."

But Abbie edged away, finding the floor again with her feet. She backed to the door.

He rolled onto his side, watching her. More than anything else, Abbie wanted to obey those beckoning deep brown eyes, but something pushed her back to the door.

"I– I don't think you are going to die," Abbie said.

"Give me something to live for. Come to me, my Abbie."

"But… I am not your Abbie." She had crossed him off her list, remember? She tried to focus on that imaginary paper, tried to see the crossed-out lines she had penned over his name. And besides, besides–

"You want me for your brother," she recalled, "and yet you would… You would…"

Jean-Marc held out one arm, beseeching her. "We would only lie down together. All perfectly innocent."

"Perfectly…" Her hand found the latch behind her. Of all the room, it seemed the steadiest item. She held on to it and then released it, jerking the door open. She stumbled getting around it.

"Thank you for the necklace," she said as she slammed his door behind her.

10

Once Abbie's nerves had stopped jangling and her lips stopped tingling… and her cheeks cooled from their hot-as-the-fires-of-Perdition flush… and after she'd hit the mattress in her room twenty-five times and kicked the door twice… After all that she peeked out into the common area to ascertain that Jean-Marc was not there.

She gathered her writing materials and, lifting her chin high, strode to the table there and began to write.

First she added onto her letter to Christopher delineating her needs for a husband in specific and precise terms. Chris might not be good with the pinot noir, but otherwise he was a sensible and clear-thinking man. He would agree that the man with the talents she described would be good for the clos.

She also included pruning and mulching instructions so simple a child could understand them.

From inside Jean-Marc's room came a deathly groan.

Next she wrote to Uncle Gus and Aunt Danielle, a chatty letter outlining the wonders of Lyon. She did not tell them of Babette's perfidy, but neither did she mention her in her travel tales.

Two more groans. Then one louder than the rest, followed by a belch. That was certainly an inducement for romance. Abbie sniffed and went on.

She enclosed short notes to the young ones as well, with sketches of some of the things she remembered about the town. For little Francois she drew a scratchy juggler, for pious Guilliaume, the beautiful cathedral window depicting the Virgin. Abbie sat back to scrutinize her work and decided that though it was not all that perfect, it got its point across.

Abbie folded the letters and addressed them with directions so a traveler would know where to hand them off next. Needing some fresh air, she was relieved to find that Jean-Marc did not join her outside on deck either. He was sulking in his room. Or dead. She rather hoped he was; that would solve many problems.

She turned at a groan.

That was not Jean-Marc. That was one of the crewmembers in the back of the boat. She heard a watery splash and then another, and Abbie grimaced to herself. That had to be someone vomiting overboard.

Suddenly the door to the passengers' compartment crashed open and Jean-Marc ran out to throw himself onto the deck railing.

"Jean-Marc?" Abbie asked. He waved her off.

And then he threw up into the river.

"Jean-Marc, are you all right?" Abbie asked.

"Go away," he gasped before repeating his action.

He was trying to convince her that he was dying. Abbie put her fists on her hips.

"Be that way," she said. "It won't get you anywhere." And she sauntered back into quarters.

But she couldn't sleep. Groaning surrounded her. The eerie sounds came through the wall from the crew's quarters. She could hear the men being sick outside.

She was the only one who had not dined on the pork at supper.

Quickly she sorted through her bags and found some peppermint. That was a start; peppermint was good for upset stomachs. She brewed a big kettle of tea and handed a cup to Jean-Marc where he knelt on deck, haggard and distinctly green in her lantern's light.

"Drink it," she ordered, and he meekly nodded.

The way around back was narrow and treacherous in the dark for a woman wearing voluminous skirts, but she made it and insisted that the crew drink.

"We've never stopped here before, Miss," the captain managed to gasp to her just before he ran out of his cabin.

Jean-Marc and her lingering in Lyon had set the boat's schedule off, so they'd had to tie up here for the night.

While it sounded as if Jean-Marc were getting rid of the medicine he had just drunk, Abbie set her shoulders, gathered up her lantern and her skirts, and barely managed the rocking jump to the dock. The inn was at the top of the long bank that led down to the river.

Even as she braced herself to shove the heavy entry door open, a man burst out of it on a dead run, heading for the back of the inn and probably the privy there.

"Hello?" Abbie called into the public room. She heard murmurs from the kitchen and followed them, the feeble lantern light leading the way.

Two kitchen boys in just their long shirts sat on a preparation table in the good-sized kitchen, holding their heads in their hands in the light of two fluttering candles.

"You have it, too," Abbie accused them. One gave her a disinterested glance. He seemed otherwise oblivious to the world of the living.

"I need to get a doctor to our boat," Abbie insisted. "Where can I find one?"

"No doctor here," the boy managed to say.

A girl of ten or eleven pattered into the kitchen in her nightdress. Her braid was half-undone with brown hair sticking out, and her bare feet looked frightfully cold on the icy stone floor. She was all elbows and knees– and determined. "Where's the tea?" she demanded of the silent boy, who merely pointed at the bubbling pot on the fire.

"Stupid. You have to brew the tea, not just boil the water!" The girl set down her own candle and commenced doing just that. She sprinkled leaves and stems into a half-dozen individual kettles. Abbie went behind her to pour the water.

"You're the lady from the boat," the little girl said to her.

"They're all down with this," Abbie said.

"They've all got it here, too. But I sent for Grandmama. It's been a long time. She–"

"Here I am, here I am!" The back door opened for a little boy half the girl's age, and behind him stepped a slightly-stooped woman wearing three shawls and carrying a large covered basket.

"Grandmama!" The little girl burst into tears.

Her gray-haired grandmother set down her basket and gathered her close. "There, there," she said. "Suddenly you're the only one in charge, is that it? Well don't worry. I'm here now."

She peered at Abbie. "Who are you?"

"I'm Abbie Bourgogne. We've docked here for the night," Abbie said. "We all ate here. Everyone has it. Can they die?"

The woman shrugged and pulled her shawls closer around her spare body. "Perhaps. If it's just a bitty bit of food poisoning, it should go away after a day or two. In the meantime they'll just wish they was dead, that's all."

She shuffled around the room, taking stock of the cupboards and pantry. "I'm Marcy d'Auberge." Her granddaughter clung to her. "Boy," she told one of them at the table as the girl continued her hiccupping cries. "Let's get some more firewood in here. You can be sick in a few minutes, but we need that right now. We have some cooking to do."

"Cooking?" Abbie asked Marcie. "Isn't that what started this?"

"Oh aye, Franck has never been particular about the quality of meat that he gets from the Monettes, and this time he's paid for it for sure. Such a stupid boy, that Franck. Just like his father. Etta, I know you've been scared but you don't have to be now. Please stop that squalling. You're giving me the heebie-jeebies."

The older woman turned to Abbie and gave her a good up-and-down look. "Not one of those city women, are you, girl? Do you know how to kill and pluck a chicken?"

"Now? In the middle of the night?"

"Now is when everyone's sick. Boy, go show her where the chickens are. Get me a nice big one or two small ones, dearie. I'll start the water for it. Don't let her get Eudora, Michel; she's our best layer. We'll be making a vat of chicken broth for the sick ones, and we'll have some lovely chicken for breakfast for ourselves. Go on!" She waved Abbie and the child out the back door.

Abbie had to stop after she fulfilled her role of poultry executioner to fetch three bucketsful of water from the well. Grandmama Marcy soon had two huge kettles steaming over the fire. Abbie scalded the scrawny chickens in the smaller one, filled it up with new water afterward, and then settled down to the miserable job of plucking pinfeathers.

Marcy cut up onions and sautéed them before adding them to her brew. "No need in it being tasteless," she said as she nodded to Abbie.

Abbie minced garlic while the old woman chopped carrots and turnips and celery. Etta brandished a knife as big as her own head and quartered each chicken as best she could. The old woman showed Abbie and little Etta how to break the bones so the rich marrow could flavor the soup.

"And this will cure them?" Abbie asked as the concoction began to simmer.

"This will keep them alive once they've decided to go on living," the woman said.

Now that the task that would need most time to finish was simmering, they could work on more immediate matters. From her basket old Marcy drew packets of herbs to ponder.

"You gave them peppermint, eh?" she asked Abbie and nodded her head. "Good choice. A brew for the upset, but only a starter for a meal gone bad. Let's see… Let's see…"

She combined a number of packets while Abbie poured a fair-sized pot full of hot water into another with carrying handles made of rope. Marcy sprinkled a pile of herbs into the pot. The only things Abbie recognized were the coneflower and powdered almonds.

"By the time you get down to the boat, it will have brewed long enough. Tell them to keep it hot through the night. It will get stronger and more bitter, but unless they want to suffer their woes up here, this is what they get. After you're through delivering this, you come back here and help us."

"Yes, ma'am." Abbie said. "This will keep them alive? This will cure them?"

Marcy drew a now day-old loaf of bread from a bin and sliced it open. Reaching down to the edge of the fireplace with a large spoon, she gathered fine gray ash, which she sprinkled liberally over the bread. Then she spread a thick coat of butter over that.

"Only God can save a life, but this will help," she said, and handed Abbie the loaf. "The ash draws out the poison. It doesn't feel so good to chew, but it will work best of anything I know. Wood ash for poison, tea for vomiting and the runs. Unless they're sickly types, they should pull through."

Even Jean-Marc? As Abbie wended her way, lugging the heavy pot down to the dock with the greasy bread tucked under her arm, she felt feverish herself. She had to stop every twenty steps or so to rest from the burden, but it was the burden of her guilt that weighed heaviest.

She had turned down Jean-Marc's advances. He'd said he would die because of that. Was what he had just this food poisoning, which Marcy swore could be cured, or was it more? Had Abbie weakened him so he might– die?

She didn't know if she could bear that thought.

The board from the dock bent sharply under her weight. Abbie's kettle almost went into the river as she crossed to the boat, but she caught it at the last moment and heaved it aboard.

"I have medicine!" she called, and men looked up from where they'd been leaning overboard. Jean-Marc wasn't with them. As Abbie filled their cups and insisted that they eat the bread, she heard the sound of the door of the ship's privy in the back creak open and then shut. Then Jean-Marc's pale face appeared around the corner of the deckhouse.

This couldn't be her Jean-Marc, but she knew by the clothes and the long scruff of deep brown hair on his head that it must be. He dragged himself across the deck even as she hurried to him.

"Here." She pushed a cup at him. "This will make you feel batter. Marcy says the bread will sop up the poison. You must rest."

"If I rest I may never wake up." Jean-Marc's voice came out like a rasp on wood. "That might not be a bad thing."

He mustn't die! He couldn't. "Nonsense," she told him. "You drink this and rest all you can. Set this on the fire and keep drinking it even when you think you're not thirsty any more. Marcy says so."

Abbie saw Jean-Marc to his bed. She took the quilt off her own to add to the one on his shaking form. She tucked him in, then piled his furred gown upon him as well.

"You will get better," she told him and smoothed his sweaty hair back from his face.

He couldn't even summon the ghost of a smile. "Or else?"

"No 'or else.' You'll get better. Marcy says that by late tomorrow you'll be feeling much better." She pulled the gown higher on him, tucking its fur trim under his chin.

It would be her fault if he died. All her prideful fault!

"Promise me you won't die," she said.

"I'll try."

He closed his dark-circled eyes, and Abbie knelt down beside him. She pulled her new crucifix from her neck and held it between her palms as she prayed as hard as she'd ever prayed.

Then she got up, checked his covers, took his chamber pot out and emptied it into the river, cleaned up, donned her own cloak, and then returned to the inn to make more medicine.

When she returned well past midnight with chicken broth for the men, Jean-Marc looked worse than ever, though he bravely reported he felt might be able to drink some broth and eat a few more crumbs of ash-bread. He lost it soon enough, but they'd made enough broth that perhaps some of it might stay inside him to give him strength.

Abbie sat by his side listening to his groans as he doubled up under his covers. She kept the door to the common area open so that the warmth of the fire she stoked could penetrate.

Abbie brooked no nonsense with the rest of the crew, insisting that they share the warmth and quick availability of the broths and teas from this, the passenger side of the boat.

"Thank you, miss," they meekly told her before she returned to Jean-Marc.

She sat beside him and told him of summer days in Burgundy when the sun stayed up late to enjoy the world. She sang harvest songs for the grape and more songs about the first wine of the year. She even told him tales of Babette's more outlandish pranks when she had been a girl, and mentioned one of Chris's to prove that he had not always thought of responsibilities.

Should she write to Philippe Dellamer? "Your brother is dying," would be the only thing she could say at this point. No, don't worry the brother. Don't send him scurrying up here to miss a post telling him if his brother were alive… or dead.

Perhaps he would live. Sometimes people could be uncommonly strong, but Abbie had watched too many loved ones die. First her older brother. One afternoon he'd been laughing with her, and the next– cold and dead at God's unfathomable whim.

Then less than six months later the rest of her family had died as well. At least she'd had time to say goodbye to them, but she'd also seen them eaten away by the fever and turned horrible by the sores, weeping in their pain and terror. Guiltily, Abbie closed her eyes and thought perhaps it was for the best that they'd gone. At least they were at rest now. In Heaven, restored to their perfection and love, smiling down upon her.

But were they smiling now? She'd refused Jean-Marc when he said it would kill him. How far should she allow her own pride to carry her if it meant this? The death of a good man?

Or if it kept her from willingly fulfilling a contract that would uphold the family honor and increase its prosperity?

Jean-Marc stopped getting up to attend to his personal needs and began to rest a little easier. Or was he just exhausted from his climb to death? Abbie wasn't sure what she talked about, for she'd thought herself all talked out, and she heard herself tell him about her parents and brothers as they lived their golden days at the clos. She lay cool cloths on his forehead to ease his headache, and he held out his shaking hand to her.

"My angel of mercy," he said before he closed his eyes.

How thin he looked! His cheeks seemed drawn inside himself. Great dark bags under his eyes deformed what had been there a mere day before. His dark hair lay limp with sweat and dirt, and a day's growth of beard against his pale skin made him seem even more disreputable.

She had seen bodies laid out in their coffins who looked like this.

Abbie knelt down again, beseeching the saints to restore her Jean-Marc to health and to forgive her her dreadful sin. If God would only cure Jean-Marc, Abbie promised to be a better person. An upright woman, just as the priest had instructed her.

That was it. That was why Jean-Marc was so ill. He was being punished for her sins. Abbie wept bitterly as she clutched her cross.

Dear Lord, make him well. I promise I'll do anything. I will marry the man Dellamer if that's Your will. I'll be the most modest wife who ever lived. The most obedient. I'll give to the poor all the extra money that I am allowed. I will endure my time in Purgatory with a good will, if only if you will spare Jean-Marc!

Please, she begged the Creator of all things. *He is blameless in this.*

She woke with her forehead on Jean-Marc's blankets, pain shooting through her lower back from the position she'd collapsed into.

"Miss Abbie!" a small voice called from far away. It couldn't be a saint answering her, could it? "Miss Abbie!"

Abbie studied Jean-Marc for a long moment, making sure that he still breathed. Finally she hauled herself up and struggled to go outside, her joints complaining wildly for the first five steps before they realized she was awake. "I'm here," she told little Etta.

The girl with the lantern curtsied as Abbie drew close to the deck railing. The sky wasn't even lightening with imminent dawn yet. This terrible night was stretching far too long.

"Grandmama asks how they are?"

Abbie took a few minutes to check the crew. "They're sleeping," she said. She wiped the straggles of hair out of her eyes. "I think we all could use a little sleep."

Etta curtsied again. "Grandmama says you can sleep up at her house, that we must have better beds than they have down here. And afterwards perhaps you can help with dinner?" The little girl shook her head. "Though I don't think too many will be eating."

"I can't leave."

"Please, Miss. Grandmama could surely use some help. You can't do anything more here, can you?" Etta wrung her hands. "I don't think Grandmama will let me sleep if it's only going to be the two of us to help out."

The poor girl looked wretched indeed. How could they ask such an innocent young thing to work the night away?

Abbie sighed and nodded her head. Backed into a corner like always. She tried to form her mouth into a smile. "A comfortable bed, and a wholesome meal afterward? I'd be a fool indeed to turn that down."

"Oh, thank you, Miss! Thank you!"

Etta didn't make it back to the inn. Abbie had to pick her up and follow Marcy's instructions on where to tuck her in. Then it was a trudge back past the outbuildings and down a short path to a small, snug cottage. Even with Marcy snoring behind her, Abbie quickly dropped off into blessed slumber.

Morning came far too quickly. Together Abbie and Marcy began preparations for a quick meal for what patrons and family remained. "We'll let Etta sleep," Abbie insisted when Marcy suggested waking the girl. Marcy merely gave a grunt and returned to her work.

Through the morning Marcy filled her in with what she'd missed telling her during the long hours of the night. Marcy had come here as a young girl to marry a man with thoughts of taking over the inn. She had shared his dream and worked hard not only on her inn but on raising a family.

"Then one day he decided that managing an inn did not appeal to him," Marcy said as she checked the flat, unleavened quick bread on its griddle.

"Or maybe it was managing an inn with me by his side. He went off fishing. I expected him home for lunch and he never came.

"A few days later, with me all full of dread that he'd been murdered or drowned or just gathered in by the dreadful hand of God, I get word from two different folks about how they seen him up in Lyon with some girls. Partying. Me with five children, one of them sick, plus an inn full of customers wanting service, and he's off partying his nights away."

She scowled at the bread. "May his soul roast in Hell for eternity and a day," she muttered, and repositioned the pan to a cooler part of the fireplace. "Mark me well, girl, you can't trust a man. You think they'll stay with you forever and when you turn your back, they're gone."

Abbie frowned to herself. "They're gone," she echoed. "Off to see the world."

"Aye, a man can do that, can't he? But not a woman," Marcy said, "I was bound to stay where I was. I managed, and sometimes only by the grace of all the saints. It was my hard work what made this inn flourish, and now that I've turned it over to my oldest boy… Well."

She rolled her eyes at Abbie. "People never got sick off my cooking. Never as much as a flea in a bed, either, and I kept the rain from coming in the roof. Now, all that work is down the privy with our reputation that I worked so hard for."

She shook her head as Abbie stirred the stew. "I tell you, men be trouble. Find a husband you think will stay forever, wed him with vows that bind the two of you for eternity, and just when you think the river of life is running smooth at last– splat. He tips the boat over with you inside, and then swims off to party while leaving you to drown in your skirts."

"Even that seems better than staying married to the wrong man," Abbie murmured to herself.

"And have nothing but bile filling you for years afterward?" Marcy asked her. She sat down on a low stool by the fire, peering at Abbie. "You don't know anything about pain yet, dearie."

"But if my husband left me, I would only be happy," Abbie told her. "My cousin said he would take me back, back home."

The inner door to the kitchen swung open to let young Etta in. "People are starting to come down," she announced, rubbing her eyes.

"Good girl," Marcy told her, and the child beamed at the praise. "She's a fine girl. Takes after her grandmama, she does," Marcy purred.

Together Abbie and Marcy began to dish up plates of stew with the bread. Abbie took a place behind the bar in the public room to pour hearty mugs of beer. "It's not wine, but it's good for you," she said as she pushed a mug toward a pale-looking lady dressed in shades of russet and rose. "It will give you strength."

It did seem to do the job even better than the food, for soon the room buzzed with low conversation. Abbie looked over the small crowd of customers and the inn's family. She knew she was not catching them at their best, but the men who made up the majority did not seem attractive in any fashion. They hung over their plates, some with food dribbling from their lips. Belches punctuated brief, guttural remarks before another slug of beer went down the hatch.

Etta came up to lean against the bar and watch the crowd as well. "Hold down things here, would you?" Abbie asked her, and she cleaned up as best she could. Then she went down to see to the boat.

She met Jean-Marc and the crew stumbling up the rocky hill. "Praise God!" Abbie could have cried in relief. Jean-Marc was so much stronger than before! His face held a little color now.

"Here, let me help," she said quickly and offered her shoulder for support. He took it, letting the crew fend for themselves.

"Tell me if we're going too fast, if you want to stop," Abbie chattered. She wanted to laugh, to sing, to throw her arms around him in joy. Instead she encouraged him and the others with promises of fortifying food and drink and a comfortable, warm place to put up their feet afterward.

"You look so much better," she told Jean-Marc, and he gave her a wan smile. His bleary, red eyes watered. "Marcy says that by tomorrow morning this will all be like a bad dream."

"Let's hope so," he managed to say. "So far you're the only light within this nightmare."

Her heart bloomed as she half-dragged the rank-smelling man of adventure to his late luncheon.

Abbie made sure that her men were made comfortable and served. She poured great mugs of beer for them and refilled them whenever they seemed to be getting low.

Still, other people needed her attention, too, but now and then she was able to catch Jean-Marc's eye. He nodded at her, then went back to sitting over his dinner with his poor eyes half-closed.

Abbie wiped down one table as the diners went off either to the privy or back to bed. God had answered her prayers. She had promised something. What? To be a good wife. She'd promised to wed Philippe, hadn't she?

In horror, Abbie realized what she'd done. This wasn't like a contract between the Bourgognes and the Dellamers, she knew.

You didn't even think of tricking God.

She would wed Philippe Dellamer.

She would do it with good spirit and fulfill her duties toward him and her family. There would be no getting around this.

Would Philippe look like Jean-Marc, she wondered? Would he look like him on a good day or on a bad day? Would he be sullen or kind? Wise or foolish? Did he share his brother's dreams of freedom? Didn't everyone long to do what they dreamed?

Abbie carried a load of dishes back to the kitchens. Marcy peeked out through the door she'd just come through to study the crowd.

"Aye, they're coming around," she said with satisfaction. "There's nothing that the good Lord and a handful of the right herbs can't manage."

Abbie felt her life was teetering on some edge. If one thing changed, it could all fall into place. What could it be? She placed her hand over her crucifix. What was it? What–

"Can herbs make you fall in love?" Abbie asked. She sloshed the water in the wash basin as she suddenly turned to Marcy. "Do you know of any that would do such a thing? Oh, I wish someone would find an herb that could–"

"Oh, aye, there are herbs that will fill that need right enough," Marcy said. "I didn't know back when I needed them, but now I do. But I don't think a fine young girl like yourself needs herbs to attract a man's attention. You just do what comes naturally, dearie, and your man will come around quick enough."

"Not for him." Abbie stood bent over, up to her elbows in scrub water and dishes. Her heart had stopped with the news. With the possibilities. "For me." She stared at the bare wall in front of her. "Do you know of any herbs that will make me love someone?"

Marcy rubbed her mouth, eying the young woman. "You said you were on your way to Marseille," she said. "Someone chose you a man, did they? It's a fine thing, to want to love him. It shows you have a good heart, a willingness to live up to family responsibilities. You're a good girl, Abbie Bourgogne. I take it you two haven't met. Don't know nothing about him, do you?"

Abbie shook her head sharply.

"Afraid, are you? And how do you know you won't fall head over heels for him? How do you know he's not the man of your dreams, the man you want to devote the rest of your life to?"

"Because… Because–" The words stuck in Abbie's throat.

"Just as easy to love one man as it is to love another, isn't it?"

"No. No!" Abbie whirled. She scrubbed her guilty hands against her bodice, trying to rid herself of this terrible realization. "Oh, Marcy," she pleaded, "do you have an herb that will make me fall out of love? I mean, if I were in love. I mean–" Abbie clapped her hand to her mouth. When the pounding in her chest had lessened, she managed to whisper hoarsely, "Do you?"

"So you're in love, sweet?"

Abbie shook her head. "I don't know. I don't think so. But– It's just that– We're going to be together for so– I mean, he's so–"

The woman nodded and reached for her basket on the long table. She rummaged through it and drew out smaller, plain cloth bags before deciding on one.

She snapped it down on the table in front of Abbie. "A tea made of this, drunk for three nights in a row, will drive all thoughts of the man from your mind. Each time you must pray for ten minutes before and afterwards. You must be diligent in this."

The packet seemed to glow on the table as Abbie examined it like a rabbit does the wolf outside its warren. "It will work?"

Marcy clucked her tongue behind her teeth. "Someone told me about it long ago. I finally got over the ghost of Franck. It were because I still loved him that I hung on to the hate. Once I didn't care, it was gone forever. I was a woman reborn."

It was all Abbie could do to get her shaking fingers around the pouch.

"Think well before you use it, child," Marcy said.

11

They set off well into the next day. The crew was still unsteady on their feet, and Jean-Marc instructed them to find an early mooring for the night ahead.

Abbie had tearfully bade Marcy adieu, promising that she'd write, and Etta had hung onto Abbie's hand. A family heading north had taken Abbie's letters with them. She had paused before handing over the letter with husband instructions for Christopher, but reasoned that if he did come up with some suitable matches, he might also think of a way out of this contract for her.

Surely there was some honorable way out of this mess.

Abbie now had a contract with God, but He would arrange things as He saw fit. Did He truly wish this for the Bourgogne family? Did He will that the generations that had worked their lives to produce the burgundy were all for naught?

God's reasons were mysterious and not to be second-guessed by man. Wasn't that how she had consoled herself after Richard died so suddenly? God must have wanted him, but had He wanted him more than Abbie's family?

And then the sickness had claimed Mama and Papa and Andre— so quickly all of them taken, yet they lingered on their deathbeds in terrible distress. If God had wanted them, why did He make them suffer? They were good people. They hadn't deserved the pain and terror.

And now God expected Abbie to take up this contract left dangling by the traitorous Babette. Why should Abbie pay for the sins of another? Why should Abbie pile sins of duplicity upon herself to fulfill God's Will?

Abbie rubbed her forehead wearily. She didn't think she had the strength to do this. First her own family stripped from her. Then her foster family abandoning her. Now she was sent to be part of another family and wife to a stranger.

Worse than that, he was the brother of the man that she– that she–

She shook herself free of that train of thought. All she had to do was go into whatever awaited her with a good will and honest intentions. Could she rise to the occasion?

She thought of the Christian martyrs, tortured, burning at stakes, sent to the lions. Was she being sent to face the maw of a lion? Surely Philippe Dellamer could not offer her as grisly a fate as those early Christians.

She must do what she must do. She must fulfill her promise to God. Once again she felt duty and destiny closing in on her.

This time it closed in fast. She watched the river rush by on this blustery day, sweeping her farther from her clos. It was too powerful for her to stop. Some things in life were too strong to fight, like the Hand of God. She sat on the deck with her cheek pressed against the railing.

Now she began to understand how Jean-Marc must feel. How wonderful it must be to be free from family duties that would bind and constrict you for the rest of your life. That was a heady thing indeed to consider. Was this a lesson God had sent her to learn?

Babette had found her freedom. She was happy now. She had chosen her own fate, but at what cost? She had willfully given up the most important thing in the world: family. What could she look forward to? She'd sacrificed her roots and reputation for love of a man.

If Abbie had to, could she escape? Might she just jump off the boat at their next docking and run away to discover whatever life held for her that wasn't concerned with family?

Things were different for women.

And God would surely hate her for breaking her contract with Him.

"You're not coming down with it now, are you?" Jean-Marc asked from behind her.

She could tell from his light tone that he was joking. She should be so grateful that he was feeling better, but instead she felt her own life draining away into the Rhone. "I'm fine," she whispered.

Give me a sign, Lord, she prayed and then chastised herself for asking God instead of going through a saint. How vain He must think her! How blasphemously egocentric to assume that she could talk directly to Him! Perhaps this was what she was being punished for, her superior attitude.

She must be more modest. More obedient. She must offer more service to others. She must get up and do something or she would go mad.

It was all she could do to draw herself up and start ridding the boat of the foul odors lingering within the living quarters. She propped open the doors and scrubbed down the more offending areas. From there she gave a cursory touch-up to the sorry overall state of the place.

All along she pictured herself as a novitiate nun scrubbing down an abbey or perhaps a cathedral. Yes, the great cathedral in Lyon. That would take a lot of work, but it would benefit the many who came there. Even better, she imagined the nun had been assigned the work as punishment.

How she reveled in the messy job! Punishment would teach her her place. Punishment would make her a better person. This must be the reason behind it all. Her tears mixed with her wash water to sanctify the work. It was a holy misery she put herself through.

She sang hymns to herself to keep time to the long mopping strokes on the floor. While she scoured out the deep corners she repeated her rosary. By evening the health seemed restored to both the boat and all the people aboard her. Surprising herself, Abbie discovered that she was hungry.

Jean-Marc came up to her and stopped. He gave a long whistle. "This place looks marvelous," he said.

She looked up at him. How vigorous and bright he was compared to what he'd been! How confident and strong. Young and free and masculine, those lips that could kiss so well now turned into a warm smile for her.

How desirable he was!

Abbie bent over a metal cleat and scoured it with sheer self-fury.

The inn they supped in was one familiar to and trusted by the crew. Again they sat apart from Jean-Marc and her.

"I want to thank you for all you've done for me. And the crew," Jean-Marc added as they waited for their meal to arrive. He poured her a goblet of watered white wine. "I honestly don't think we'd have made it if not for you."

"Anyone would have done what I did," she said modestly. "We were lucky that Marcy knew what to do."

Jean-Marc shook his head with a smile. "You underestimate yourself. No one could have been kinder or sweeter than you."

"Jean-Marc."

He lifted her chin so she looked at him. "What?" he asked.

"The other night." A blush came to her cheeks despite herself. "You said… You said you'd die. Did you get so sick because… I mean, was it my fault that…?"

For some reason he seemed to deflate.

"Well, um…"

"Tell me. I must beg your forgiveness if—"

He took her hand and shook it softly. "No, I must beg yours," he said. "It was a pack of lies. I was trying to get you into my bed, that's all, and I know how easily good girls respond to guilt. You can't pull that with the bad girls. I know you aren't one of them."

His words sank in slowly. So she wasn't to blame for him almost dying! He could have died and she would have gone to her grave thinking herself a murderess!

How could he have been so cruel? So thoughtless? Because of him, she'd made a harsh contract with God!

"You tricked me," she hissed. "You tricked me!"

The remorse on his face was that of someone who was sorry he'd gotten caught. "I wouldn't call it a trick. I'd call it…" He searched for the proper word without success.

"You said you'd die," she accused him, but he merely shrugged his shoulders. "But you aren't dead." Such a shame!

He made a small noise, his eyes moving back and forth as if he were already working on another deception.

Abbie set her shoulders squarely. He had no idea of the agonies she had suffered that night. Men! "I am disappointed," she said, "but your brother will be pleased." His brother. Whom she had officially pledged herself to because of Jean-Marc's perfidy!

His voice came out low and sweet, drat him. "I am a walking corpse," he said.

"Then I'll call for a priest to give you last rites." Abbie snapped up her knife as a girl laid steaming platters in front of them. She proceeded to dig into her dinner with gusto. She was hungry. The righteous work had left her famished. She deserved this meal.

He sipped his almond-milk soup warily, though more bland food did get into him as the dinner progressed. He was still weak; good. Let him be ill for a time. Make him pay for his crime.

"More wine?" Abbie wiped her fingers on the tablecloth and then refilled his goblet from the pitcher. "This will indeed send you to an early grave. Whose wine is this? Whoever they are, they must not be French. Even a French dog can make better chablis than this after he's had a few long drinks from the river."

The faintest of smiles quirked Jean-Marc's lips. "I'm glad you're feeling better, too. It's Spanish. They call it *bastardo*."

"Ah, bastard Spanish dog chablis. That explains that."

When they returned to the ship Abbie seated herself primly beside a lantern with her book of psalms held up like a barrier to him. There would no hint of any bedroom shenanigans this night. Jean-Marc slunk to his cabin and stayed there.

Later she lay in the dark and wondered if a promise to God made under false circumstances was still binding. She wrapped her rosary through her fingers, trying not to pray as she did so, trying to escape God's notice as she pondered the problem.

She'd thought she was the cause of Jean-Marc's illness; therefore she had vowed to fulfill the contract if God would cure him. She had offered her life as the sacrifice.

But if Jean-Marc were only ill because he'd eaten some bad food and not because of anything she'd done...

Her temple throbbed as the dilemma lurched to and fro.

During that night she had made a hard-and-fast vow to God. There was no denying it.

Holy Virgin, show me what to do, she begged.

All that came to her were scraps of speech. Jean-Marc telling her that he meant her for his brother. Then Jean-Marc trying to talk her into his bed.

That night he'd had no excuse. He wasn't drunk. He knew precisely what he was doing.

Why would he try to double-cross his brother? Why spoil the bride? Why make things so much worse?

And why did Abbie still remember Jean-Marc's large, strong fingers entwined with hers as he led her through the sites of Lyon, the way his arms felt around her that afternoon on the deck? The way her body heated and came alive when his lips kissed hers? The way she wanted to run her hands all over him?

Oh, she was a sinful woman to think of such things when she was contracted to another! She trembled to recall his touch, and remembered the herbs in her bag.

Perhaps she should make the tea now.

But it was so late. By the time the tea finished brewing she could be asleep, and would have wasted the proper dose.

And why should she even consider the herbs when Jean-Marc was such a rapscallion? Trying to cheat his own brother. Trying to dishonor her. He might be a good man in many ways, but in too many small ways he was not.

No, she didn't need the tea tonight. But tomorrow, maybe. Tomorrow she would make the tea.

This new river was as different from the Saone as night from day. It rushed, nay, *hurled* its way to the sea, sending them at a frightening pace compared to the placid bobbing they'd managed on the Saone.

As misty, wooded cliffs gathered close, the river would pull itself up with a roar and thunder through the gap, dragging them with it. The crew used long oars and poles to keep them as best they could toward the calmer center of the maelstrom.

Then the land would ebb back and the river eased so that it could shift restlessly from side to side in its bed, plowing up dangerous shoals to catch a ship.

The experienced crew was keen to keep a watchful eye. Only rarely did the remains of a boat still stuck in its own doom provide a helpful beacon. Most times only the smallest of whitecaps marked dangerous obstructions below the waterline.

Jean-Marc assured Abbie, "This crew has been plying the river for near ten years now. They know it like the backs of their—"

The boat ran aground in midstream. It took them two hours of foul sweat and fouler language to push off again.

"No harm done to the boat," Jean-Marc reported later with a swipe to his grimy forehead. But Abbie felt that catastrophic harm had been done to the last of her nerves. How grateful she'd be to be back on dry land!

The next day dawned dim but cleared up as they set off again. The sun burned off the river mist, and a sharp, fierce wind rose to drive the clouds across the sky even as the river seemed determined to keep up, but in its own direction.

The captain signaled to Jean-Marc from above the deckhouse, and Jean-Marc joined him. They gazed downriver. Abbie peered over the railing trying to see.

It was a boat— not nearly as wide as theirs, but definitely of deeper draft, for she could see part of the hull jutting up at an angle from the water even as its sail tilted at an unlikely pitch. Whoever it was had run hard into a shoal. As they neared the wreck, a great hole just above the waterline came into view, admitting the occasional whipping wave.

Crew waved frantically at them from the ship's rigging but what caught Abbie's eye was the woman and two young children clinging to the railing, trying to stay upright at the awkward angle.

It called for tricky maneuvering. Abbie held her breath and clutched her cross, but their boat heaved up safely alongside the other, away from the deadly shoal. The two crews began to transfer the cargo of the one boat to theirs.

"We're loaded light enough," the captain assured Jean-Marc. "Now that we're on the Rhone we can afford to sit deeper." Still, part of the cargo remained in the second boat until another boat could be summoned or river pirates took it.

The stranded woman made sure that all her things were transferred first. She pointed out each of her many trunks, and then counted that all of her marked crates were saved. She rebuked the men when they grumbled that they had to carry the crates just so, but rewarded them with brilliant smiles and a batting of her eyelashes when they complied. Then she allowed her crew to do what they would with the rest of the cargo.

Abbie helped her and the children to the empty rooms of the deckhouse. The two young boys were chilled through and thoroughly terrified from the experience. Some warm wine and extra quilts saw them asleep in their small bed fast enough.

"Ah me," Nathalie Pelletier sighed in the communal room. Abbie handed her warmed wine and didn't water it much. Despite the bravado she'd displayed, the woman's delicate hands shook and her face was unnaturally pale under her dark brown hair.

Her traveling clothes had small ruffles at the hem, sleeves, and squared bodice, and her cloak had been lined with rich furs. A beautiful underskirt peeked through the split in the front of her dress, and delicate embroidery striped the sheer partlet that filled in her neckline.

Even so, she apologized for her appearance. "I am traveling without any maids," she said. "We would just have to send them back once we got to Marseille. Such a bother to do so! And my maids weren't the traveling sort, not at all."

"Oh?" Abbie said. "You're going to Marseille? So are we."

"How very fortunate! I'm afraid that now we shall have to beg you to take us all the way with you. Those bumbling louts have already been paid half for my passage. I will get my money returned or they'll regret it. This won't put you out, will it?"

"Nonsense," Abbie told her. "My mother told me there was no such thing as coincidence, that all things are ordained in Heaven. We must go on together."

"You're so kind! Perhaps we should be friends," Nathalie said. Her sweet, heart-shaped face dimpled as she smiled. "I should be very happy to travel with you. You remind me of my dear sister, so far away."

"Is she in Marseille?"

"Oh no, my father wanted to expand his business, so he married us girls off to the farthest reaches. Margot went to Spain while I got stuck in Paris."

"Paris!" Despite herself, Abbie boggled at the idea. "That must have been exciting. I mean, once you got used to being away from your family."

Nathalie drew her shawl around herself. "It is very cold and dark in winter," she said. "It's a fine place for fashion and society, but it's a false sort of society, I think, and not a good place to raise my boys. When my husband died–"

"Oh," Abbie said. "I'm so sorry."

Nathalie waved her regret off. "He had been sick a very long time. I was afraid one of the boys would catch it. Even so, Henri was a good provider," she crossed herself, "enough so that I can afford to take us back home. I have a comfortable living, and I'm still young enough to catch a good husband."

"Why, you can't be much older than I," Abbie said charitably.

That brought a definite look of pleasure to Nathalie's face. She patted Abbie's hand. "I must be near ten years older than you," she said. "Well, perhaps eight. But I will tell the gentlemen that it's only five years that separate us. A little smile, some praise for how well they have retained their own youth, and they'll think me a delightful young girl indeed."

Nathalie raised an eyebrow at Abbie. "And there's a delightful gentleman outside who is not a part of the crew," she said. "Is he your husband?"

"Jean-Marc? Oh no. He is my…" How to explain? Should she explain?

The hesitation piqued Nathalie's imagination. "He is your lover?" she whispered hopefully.

Abbie's hands jumped to guard her breast. "No!" she said. "He's my, well, he's the brother of the man I'm supposed to… that my cousin is supposed to–"

And abruptly it all came crashing in on her. All the deceit, all the horrible ties of family and responsibility that were strangling her. Suddenly she was confessing everything to Nathalie: Babette's treachery, the contract that was now hers to fulfill, the ailing vineyard waiting in vain for her to return to it.

Nathalie hugged her. "Poor thing!" she cooed. "Such a fate! We are women; we have no control in this world unless we can manage to control our husbands or our sons. It will not be so bad, poor Abbie. Jean-Marc is a handsome man. Surely his brother cannot be so different? What is his name?"

"Ph-Philippe Dellamer," Abbie said as she rubbed unshed tears from her eyes.

"Philippe Dellamer?" Nathalie sat back in her chair in shock. "Why, I've heard of him. Back when I lived in Marseille, everyone knew of Philippe Dellamer. I think I even met him once. But I do know he's a very respected man, a very rich man whose family has been in the area not quite forever, but long enough. Oh my dear, such matches don't come along often! You don't realize how lucky you are!"

"Fine," Abbie said. "You may have my luck. I give him to you instead. All I want is a vineyard far from Marseille."

"You don't have the choice," Nathalie told her sternly. "You must face the future with a good heart, willing to take what you're given and work with it. You must shape him like… like you would one of your grapevines."

Nathalie gave a little smile, obviously proud of the metaphor she had found. "Train him to be healthy and strong so that he can support your healthy, strong children and yourself. Picture your new household as your vineyard if you must. You can do this. It's a skill you as a woman must learn to use."

Abbie knew the woman was talking sense. She just didn't want to accept it into her heart. Not yet. Hold on to hope for a while more.

Nathalie tapped her chin thoughtfully. "Yes, yes, I remember Philippe Dellamer now. It was quite some time ago, you understand. He must have been… I must have been…" She counted on her fingers and shook her head. "We were both quite young," she finally surmised. "It must have been someone's wedding, for people were dancing and I turned around and suddenly there I was, face to face with Philippe Dellamer!"

12

Despite herself, Abbie asked, "What is he like?"

Nathalie let out a little huff of thought. "Well… You must remember, he was quite a young man back then. He might have been considered still a child if his parents hadn't been dead and left him in charge of the business."

"And?"

Nathalie gave her a crooked smile. "He was a googly boy. You know how boys get at a certain age. They hem and haw and can't form a straight sentence in their mouths, and they act like fools in front of the girls even as they're trying to seem so suave."

"Oh dear."

"Now, you absolutely cannot go by this, Abbie. It's been years, absolute years since then, and the man must have matured. And matured well. Why, every now and then we'd hear of him in Paris, so he's managed the business even better than his father had." She gave a little giggle. "And by now that little pimple on the end of his nose must be gone." She giggled again and said, "I'm sorry. Really, all I remember of him is the pimple and his stuttering. Surely he's outgrown that. Why, look at his brother– not googly at all. I'm sure Philippe turned out the same way."

Nathalie examined their little room. "And just look at this. This is a Dellamer boat, and a fine one, too, if it just had a little more pomp given it. Some embroidered pillows and a rug. An upholstered chair. A servant with a hot snack tray. Why, fix this up and it would be worthy of carrying the king himself. Of course, it wouldn't hold all a king's servants or cooks or guards or…" Nathalie glanced sharply at Abbie. "Where's your chaperone?" she asked.

"Chap–? I was supposed to be Babette's chaperone, and she mine."

"So you've been traveling for days now, alone with Jean-Marc and this crew?"

Abbie raised her hand to her throat. "I assure you," she said, heat rising to her cheeks because of what had almost happened, "that nothing untoward–"

"Tut tut." Nathalie waved her down. "We may be thankful of that. Young and lusty men– they don't often think with their heads." She tapped her forehead and glanced down to her lap significantly. "It is only a matter of time with them. Very well, I shall earn my fare by being your chaperone. Just let one of these men try to attack you, and I shall set my little Henri on him!" Nathalie snapped her teeth. "He bites. It's a nasty habit that I'm trying to break him of, but every once in a while it proves useful."

Abbie laughed and agreed, promising to protect Nathalie as well.

Avignon proved the longest tax stop yet. Jean-Marc usually knew just what combination of payment and bribe would get them past a guard point cheapest, but occasionally the bargaining took some time. It slowed them up anyway, having to dock and then for him and the captain to meet with men in bright army cloaks. Usually the taxmen's office was in a fine stone building on the river's banks, but here in Avignon it seemed more an armed fortress.

"This will take a while," Jean-Marc said before he left. He made sure that his back was turned from the soldier who'd come to collect him, and measured out some coins. He pressed them into Abbie's hands. "Take a couple of the crew," he instructed her, "and go out to see the town, get a good dinner. Some toys for the boys, perhaps; they seem bored. Buy any little trinket that you see, too. Leave enough of the men here to guard."

It was mid-morning. Abbie studied the soldier's fancy suit and jewelry and then nodded at Jean-Marc. Perhaps the richness she could see of the city came not by honest means.

She spent an hour examining the wine cargo while young Charles followed her around.

"What are you looking for?" he asked as she struggled with the heavy coverings laid over the section of wine casks.

"I'm trying to see how much wine we have lost," Abbie replied. "No matter how tight the barrel, some of the wine still leaks out." Even so, the clos's barrel makers knew what they were doing and losses were very light, she noted with satisfaction.

"Come away, Charles," Nathalie admonished even as she peered as the child did to watch Abbie.

"Maybe he wants to be a vintner or a shipper of wine when he grows up," Abbie said.

"Oh, I doubt that. Do you, Charles?" Nathalie didn't bother to wait for her son's answer. "Since his father's brothers took over the business he should have inherited– thank the saints I managed to sell the part we still held before those thieves could steal it from us– he'll go into my family's business instead."

Abbie turned, slapping the dirt from her hands and skirts. "And what is that?"

"Glass. We are glass makers."

Her mouth opened in wonder. "Glass? Your family must be famous indeed."

Nathalie wiped a smear of grease from her younger boy's face as he struggled against her, wanting to go to his brother. "Yes, we are. We've a factory in the hills above Marseille and specialize in wine glasses. I thought that might interest you."

"Babette's dowry includes wine glasses. I wonder if they came from your family?"

Nathalie patted the crate beside herself for Abbie to sit upon. "Perhaps they do. When we unpack I'll check the marks to see."

"I'm going to be a sailor!" little Henri insisted. He broke from his mother's hold and ran to the side of the boat, swinging on the railing.

"You are not running off to Portugal or Holland," Nathalie told him firmly. "I won't have you gallivanting around the world with some pirate ship while I worry about you night and day. Marseille is good enough for you, young man."

"Yes, Mama."

Abbie watched the two boys play amid the trunks and crates stacked on deck. "You have them well trained," she told Nathalie.

"That's what you have to do with a man."

She said it as if it were the most natural thing in the world. The woman was so amusing! "Did you have your husband trained?"

"Yes, both of them."

"Both?!"

Nathalie smiled at her small joke. "I am a widow twice over. Before I married the first time, my mother made sure I knew the importance of making my husband think he was in control when all the time he was really doing what I wanted."

"But–"

Nathalie tut-tutted her. "There is nothing sinful about it. It's merely payback. You know that women can't do what they wish. We are married to men we do not love, we are moved about the countryside with no regard as to our wishes, and we are made to bear children whether we want to or no."

Abbie didn't know how to answer that.

Nathalie took her hand and patted it. "My first marriage was over practically before it began. My husband fell sick of a summer fever during the third month, but not before he had moved me to Paris and left me pregnant with Charles. My second husband lived in Paris also, so my father thought it an easy and profitable match. Henri was a disagreeable-looking fellow with the worst breath you can imagine– like seven-day-old fish!– but he was not home too much to breathe on me, and when he did he made it quick."

Abbie blushed but Nathalie went on. "I made good use of our time together. I pointed out things he could be doing, but I coated my words with sugar and pampered him even as I told him what to do. He never suspected a thing. Most men are simpletons, dear Abbie. They never credit us with having minds of our own, and so it is easy to plant ideas in theirs."

"Plant ideas," Abbie said slowly.

"Like your grapes," Nathalie urged. "You plant the seed of an idea into your Philippe about living in Burgundy or buying a vineyard outside of Marseille or whatever it is you want, and if you water that seed and care for it, Philippe will come around soon enough. The best part is, if you do it right he'll think it was all his idea."

Nathalie cocked her head and looked off in the distance toward the wide, arched bridge that stretched across the river. Some large blocks of stone had fallen from it three-quarters of the way across. "You must be subtle, of course, but you can do it," she said. "You honey-coat it by telling them how manly they are and how much others look up to them. And then you smile and lean on them and tell them they are strong when it is really you holding them up."

Abbie sprang up and paced, wringing her hands. "It seems dishonest."

"Dishonest? Why, a male slave has more independence than a free woman. We not only get sold to men, but we pay them to take us." Nathalie's wave took in the barrels of dowry sitting on the deck. "We must sleep with men we do not love, we must bear them children at the risk of our own lives, we must nurse them and listen to them and shoulder the disgrace that they so often bring our families, and we must live far away from our own homes. And then they make things worse by telling us how we'll be confined for eternity with them in Heaven."

She crooked her finger at Abbie and leaned toward her. "I heard once of Muslim Heaven."

"Muslim? What's that?" Abbie drew near to hear the mystery.

"A Mussleman," Nathalie translated and was rewarded by a spark of recognition in Abbie's eyes. "My husband had a Moorish client, an ambassador from Morocco living in Paris. He had very dark skin and wore the most wonderful jewelry I have ever spied. I heard he had three living wives back in his homeland."

Abbie gasped.

Nathalie nodded conspiratorially at her. "I hid behind a door once as he described how in his Heaven, he would be granted seventy women to choose from to live with for eternity. There and then I determined that that was what I will find. I will not let some angel drag me off to live with either husband, but I will find a good man of my own, and him will I share eternity with. I figure that Paradise should not just be Paradise for men, but for women also."

"But that's–" Was it blasphemy? Abbie knew so little of the strange religion, except that it was not the True Church. Of course, it was less objectionable than that of the damned Huguenots, who deliberately rejected the Church whereas the people of Mahomet were too barbaric to have been introduced to Catholicism in the first place. But did that mean that some parts of their religion could be true?

Nathalie said, "Here on Earth we are granted a narrow path to fulfill our own desires. It's called marriage. How is convincing a man to do one or two things we wish for so dishonest?"

"I don't know," Abbie said slowly.

Nathalie pointed her index finger at her and shook it. "This is not your childhood home anymore," she declared. "This is the real world. This is your future. How are you to get home to your grapes if you don't connive a bit– for the greater good and for your happiness?"

Abbie sat back down, totally confused.

Nathalie slapped her own thighs. "Why, I've known many men who would have been living in a gutter if it hadn't been for them having strong, sensible wives guiding their businesses as well as their households behind their backs."

Abbie blinked in shock.

"You will understand," Nathalie told her.

As part of her continuing sisterly lecture, she explained to Abbie in detail what happened between a man and a woman on their wedding night. And then Abbie truly was shocked into speechlessness.

A small army of nuns walking along the city quay spurred the two women to pack up the children and requisition two of the crewmen to come with them. They hurried to catch up to the holy sisters.

The nuns moved at a brisk pace, their black cloaks billowing behind them, not from any wind but from the force of their own travels.

Nathalie called out. Three of the nuns broke from their formation while the others kept going. One turned around and scowled at the laggards a moment before returning to the business of her quick-march.

These sisters were friendly enough, especially when it came time to suggest some interesting parts of the city for the newcomers to while their time. The main cathedral, of course, was not to be missed, as was the papal palace. Sister Anne gave them the name of someone at the palace to mention so they'd be sure to get a thorough tour.

When they arrived Abbie gaped at the size of the edifice. Here was where the false popes had reigned, and it looked just as splendid as if the real pope could live here. White steps and fabulous architecture… This had been the home of some of the richest men in the world.

"They must have been very holy men to have owned things like these," Nathalie whispered as she held her boys close in front of a larger-than-life marble statue.

Through the halls of the palace stood statues of like size, all marvelously crafted so that they seemed to be real people made of stone. Between the statues paintings of rare beauty and splendor had been hung on the walls.

"But how could they be holy?" Abbie asked. "They were false popes."

Nathalie shook her head. "Did they know that? I always heard that they thought they were doing the right thing, avoiding the corruption that was then in Rome. Steering the church back to righteousness while our king helped them."

Abbie wasn't sure of the story at all, so she held silent. On their way out of the compound, she noticed once again the many beggars and badly-dressed commoners in the streets of the city. This city that had once been the hub of Christianity held all this opulence and yet all this poverty, too.

The thought clashed even as they marveled at the gilding of the great cathedral. Here was God's house, yes, but the poor outside were God's people as well. Why didn't the priests care for them better?

Though Abbie put a tidy sum in the cathedral's poor box under the approving eye of an old priest, she also saved a handful of copper coins to scatter among a small group of tattered children outside.

As soon as they saw she was handing out money, other ragamuffins began to surge toward her.

"All gone!" Nathalie called out. She spread her empty hands for all to see. "No more! Keep away!" From the side of her mouth she urged Abbie, "Hide the rest– quickly!"

Abbie did so. She drew her cloak's hood around her face and moved away from the crowd. Their two guards made some rude comments at the gathering people and gave some air blows with their fists as warning. Eventually the beggars backed off, and Abbie and Nathalie scurried away, herding the boys with them.

How fortunate to find the same nuns quick-stepping toward a nearby business district! The two women, boys, and their guards joined the nuns as they shopped. Shopkeepers left their regular customers to give precedence to the holy women. Sister Maria, their leader, ordered new settings for the convent tables as well as golden place settings to be delivered to the bishop.

Their trip through a glass shop allowed Nathalie to correct Sister Maria's assumption that one pattern of gold-tipped goblets was of a high quality. "The gold has been used to cover the imperfections," Nathalie pointed out. She showed them the thickness of the glass and compared it to a thinner kind, more cunningly crafted. The owner agreed with her over its quality, and Sister Maria changed her order accordingly.

"My family's glass is even better than this," Nathalie told them. She gave one of her brothers' names to the glass seller to contact, knowing that the sister would also hear. There were many convents in the country, all of which needed something for their sisters to drink from. Nathalie's brothers would enjoy an increase in their business.

The choices the sisters made elsewhere surprised Abbie. Gold and silver candleholders, a few rich rugs, blankets of surpassing quality...

"Our people deserve to enjoy life, too," Sister Anne insisted. "We have given our lives to God. Our house should reflect the majesty that is His, so as to inspire the common folk to follow in the righteous path."

And yet Abbie wondered how many meals– perhaps even homes– for the poor could have been bought with what it took to buy four golden candlesticks.

Five of the younger sisters kept giggling as the others conducted business. One lifted her skirt slightly to effect a twirl as if she were dancing.

"It's our turn to attend the cardinal's dinner tonight," she said.

Abbie's eyes widened. "What an honor."

The girl giggled again. "Oh," she said, "these dinners are not nearly as serious as you'd imagine. They're great fun. And afterward there are the cleverest games!"

"Sometimes the priests get very rowdy." Her companion grinned. "I see them in church and they're so serious. It almost makes me laugh then to know how silly they can be!"

"Why, I don't think I've ever seen anyone who could drink as much as Father Claudius and still be able to walk," the first confided.

Abbie pulled Nathalie away from an earnest conversation she was having with Sister Maria about the quality of silks and some cottons from Egypt. The boys were bored, as were their guards.

Instead they investigated the more modest stores of the neighborhood until they found one with a large selection of toys. That kept the boys busy, trying out one and then another. It was all Nathalie could do to keep them from accidentally breaking some of the other items in the shop.

A hearty supper slowed them down, and by the time they returned to the boat with the last of the sunlight barely illuminating the sky, the boys' eyelids were heavy. Nathalie tucked them in.

Jean-Marc and the captain still had not returned.

Abbie and Nathalie spent the evening cleaning what they could of their clothing.

"Once you get these boats in shape for upper-class clientele," Nathalie told her, "I'd hire a competent washer-woman for on-board service. If you fill these rooms with passengers and crew, there'd be more than enough work for her."

Abbie actually considered it. She would be wife to Philippe, and thus own this boat through him. "Chris and Jean-Marc do think that these would make good transports," she mused.

"You should suggest your husband polish up this boat and put it to good use," Nathalie said as she vigorously brushed her sons' boots. "Perhaps you can even make a separate income from it. A woman should be entitled to an income as much as a man, if she does the planning and supervision of it."

"Money should go into the family's coffers," Abbie countered. "Those who need it can get what they need."

"And if your husband dies?" Nathalie asked. "Does his money go to you or to his brother? Does it go to your children? Are they allowed to be rich as they grow up while you languish in some poor women's home, unable to share in their inheritance? Or can you manage their money for them while keeping some for yourself to live on?" She shook her brush at Abbie. "You must think of these things. Get your worst-case provision plans set down in writing with your husband's permission. Then get your priest to witness it. There are too many starving widows in this world as it is."

Abbie laughed to break the tension. "Perhaps I'll just come back here to Avignon and take my vows with the nuns. They seem to live a comfortable enough life."

Nathalie joined in her laughter. "Don't they! Why, Sister Maria was telling me things that made me think that they might be queens setting up their courts. Have you ever heard of such a thing!"

Loud voices from outside made them freeze. "The crew is on guard," Nathalie said.

"It's Jean-Marc," Abbie replied.

He was in a foul mood, muttering about the amount of bribes it had taken to clear them of this port. The Dellamer name and its wealth were well-known here.

Abbie and Nathalie quickly served him and the captain what they'd brought back with them from the restaurant, including some fine Malvasian wine that Abbie had picked for them to sample. It was all Abbie could do not to stare at Jean-Marc with her new-found knowledge of marital duties. Would a man really do that? Would a woman truly allow him to?

By morning his anger had disappeared. He looked forward to another city to explore.

"I paid for it; I should get my money's worth out of Avignon," he declared.

Choosing a different direction from the one the women had taken the day before, he escorted them and the boys into the town where the false papacy had left its mark with astounding cathedrals and princely palaces for cardinals– though the grand marketplace was the site that impressed the boys most. Here they could run like bandits as they had not been able to do for weeks.

Of course when they stopped for a rest Jean-Marc found travelers with the most outrageous stories of distance places, and even Nathalie seemed quite interested.

"He's a curious fellow," she whispered to Abbie. "That bodes well for the brother. Intelligence is a quality you rarely find in a man, but it does run in families."

Nathalie joined Abbie in watching Jean-Marc chase down the boys. Abbie jumped when Nathalie suddenly said, "This is a man who cares for children. It means that wife-beating and violence does not run in the family. That's very good indeed."

But Abbie hadn't noticed that. All she'd seen was the wild grin on Jean-Marc's face, like that of a boy. His brown curly hair tousled even more in the wind he whipped up, and when he herded the boys back to their mother, his step was fine and strong, his carriage cocky. The very cut of his clothing, the jaunty feather in his cap, marked him as a modern man of fortune. The boys looked up to him in admiration even as he made jokes for them.

Abbie didn't care if Jean-Marc's qualities bode well for Philippe; all she knew was that Jean-Marc was the most wonderful man she'd ever met. His shortcomings could be easily forgotten. He was kindness and curiosity. He was recklessness and cutting the apron strings. He was freedom.

Jean-Marc tucked Abbie's arm under his and then reached for Nathalie for his other side. He made a laughing comment about being the envy of the entire city with his two beautiful ladies. As Nathalie tittered and winked at Abbie, Abbie miserably knew that she herself was lost.

13

Nathalie rested on a bench next to a small park while Abbie attended to the boys' play. Jean-Marc studied the younger woman.

The square neckline of her sapphire blue gown bared a neck that begged to be nibbled. She wore his gift. The crucifix with its bit of vine circled her neck and then looped down to dangle in a spot that he longed to explore.

Such a beautiful girl. He admired the way she moved, the way her skirts flowed around her tantalizingly, the occasional peek of ankle. The afternoon sun behind her gave her a golden halo like the angel she was.

Such a pure and caring heart. And such unplumbed passion.

Jean-Marc blinked as Nathalie called out to her boys. It was a good thing that Nathalie traveled with them. Without her, he might be tempted too far again.

How could he have let his control lapse like that? Abbie in his arms that day, soft and sweet. Her gaze had melted into his, her lips parting in invitation.

A saint could not have resisted her. He'd known his gift would please her, but hadn't realized the joy that it gave him to see her so delighted. He wanted to give her more gifts. He wanted to see her smile and hear her magical laugh. He wanted her to kiss him forever.

Damn his selfish heart anyway!

She was for Philippe. Wasn't it bad enough that Jean-Marc was going to abandon his brother's ventures to strike out on his own? Did he have to play with his brother's wife's heart as well?

Jean-Marc determined that he would keep his distance from Abbie. She must still hate him for what he'd done, what he'd tried to do.

"Monsieur Dellamer?"

Jean-Marc turned to the unfamiliar male voice. A young priest stood behind him uncertainly.

"Yes."

"Monsieur Dellamer? Of Marseille?"

"That is I."

The priest nodded and then reached inside his cloak. He produced a letter and handed it to Jean-Marc.

Jean-Marc had had a few pointed things to say to the Cardinal of Avignon about how business in his city was handled, so he'd sent a report of yesterday's problems to the man early this morn. Here was a note from the cardinal's secretary. It apologized for the trouble and invited Jean-Marc to come and dine with the cardinal himself this evening. Perhaps there they could work out a more equitable arrangement, particularly if the Dellamers planned to come back through the area often. The cardinal was a man of exotic tastes, and the range of goods handled by the Dellamers was well-known.

Jean-Marc smiled to himself, sensing a round of sharp dealing ahead. "Very well," he told the priest. "We shall be honored to dine with Cardinal Guesclin tonight: Mme. Pelletier, Mademoiselle Bourgogne, and I."

The priest didn't flinch at the additions to the guest list. Perhaps it was expected. "The honor is ours," he said, and then gave Jean-Marc instructions on where to go.

A thousand candles must have lit the spectacular dining room at the cardinal's palace. Eighty people at least were seated at the long, elegant tables, elevated above a central area.

Abbie stood with the others as the cardinal and his aides entered in a parade of red velvet, silks and satins, and astonishing jewel-encrusted gold jewelry. The cardinal's table stood another three steps higher than the others. The man of God sat on a wide cushioned chair that would put many thrones to shame.

Under the high ceiling ornately painted with Bible scenes and legions of angelical hierarchies, priests, nuns, merchants, and pilgrims alike feasted on savory meats and sumptuous dishes brought in by a parade of young monks. Laughter rang through the hall in great peals.

Abbie found herself seated next to a bishop. "Not an archbishop," he modestly told her, "but I'm hoping that by this time next year, I may serve in that position."

Bishop Sierck was not as old as she'd imagined archbishops to be. Gray wings above his ears betrayed his age, but his face wore only the signs of years that a mature man might have. His cassock was beautifully embroidered primarily in gold, a design of crosses with tiny red roses twining up them.

It made her very glad to have new clothing to wear for such an august occasion. She loved this shade of blue and knew it fit her well. Nathalie had loaned her one of her beautiful partlets, cunningly embroidered to cover her décolletage modestly. "I'm just a simple country girl," she told the bishop as if the cut of her dress didn't proclaim that to the world.

"Nonsense! There's no such thing as simple country anything," he told her. He had a rare energy about him, a concentrated focus in his attention that riveted her. No wonder he'd risen to be a bishop. "People don't value the countryside enough. That's where we get our heart from, where we can go to replenish our souls. So, you say you're on your way to meet your fiancé?"

She told him of her family, especially her Uncle Gus, and he nodded.

"Sounds like a fine man. We need more like him. Perhaps I could meet him one day." He winked at her. "I do love my mustard."

After dinner he explained the Mediterranean style of dancing that a small troupe put on for their amusement in the central area. The same large band remained afterward so that the diners could move out into the spacious room and dance as well.

The bishop clapped to encourage the dancers' rhythm, and applauded them as well as the band when the dance was over. They reminded Abbie of the dancers at the Lyonnaise restaurant… and then she remembered what had come after that. Jean-Marc had kissed her. And the next day he'd kissed her some more and lied to her so that she'd made a holy contract with God under false pretenses.

Bishop Sierck turned to Abbie and frowned. "My daughter, aren't you enjoying this?" he asked.

"Of course I am."

"You don't look it."

Abbie apologized. "I've just had to face something these past few days." She summoned a wan smile for his sake. "I've done a lot of praying on it, but I'm afraid I don't understand what is being said to me in return."

"How long since your last confession?"

Abbie told him: Lyon.

"Come, child," the bishop told her. He quick-rubbed her knee in a fatherly way, stood up from his chair and held out his hand for her. "Let us attend to the important things first."

Holding her hand tightly, he led her through wide but dim hallways of the palatial building until a doorway opened to the interior of a private chapel. It was small by Avignon standards, but as large as the village church back home. Both knelt before the altar before taking their places within the confessionals.

There Abbie poured out her story, especially the part about how she had bargained with God. "But Jean-Marc misled me," she told the priest in the next cubicle. "Does that mean that I still must do as I'd promised? This marriage will be a lie."

"Do you love this Jean-Marc?"

Abbie tried to consider honestly. She couldn't love him. Either she was to marry his brother, or she'd return to her vineyard. Neither scenario could end with her together with Jean-Marc.

"No," she decided, though the word was difficult to form. She waited.

It was a long time coming, punctuated by two heavy sighs on the other side of the barrier between her and the bishop.

"Yes," he finally said softly. "I believe it could work."

"What?" she asked. "The priest in Lyon mentioned indulgences, but Jean-Marc said–"

"No, indulgences would not work in this case," the bishop told her. "The sin hasn't been committed yet. Come with me."

They left the chapel and Bishop Sierck led her down narrow halls that were lined with doors along one side and a few open windows on the other.

"We're in the monasterial annex," he told her.

Abbie put her arms around herself and shivered in the night chill.

"Down here."

A steep, circular stair led into shadows. The light of the torch at the top and one at the bottom of the long stairway provided the only light, but the air seemed to warm as they descended.

"The remains of an old Roman bathhouse lie down here," the bishop explained. "We keep the fires stoked for recreation, but we also use the pool for some very important private ceremonies."

Sure enough, at the bottom of the staircase was a door that opened into a large lit room, almost entirely filled with a marble-lined pool. The white walls held streaks of greenish-brown mold in hard-to-reach spots. A narrow walkway on the side passed fluted columns.

They proceeded beyond this pool to an even warmer, though smaller room. Here was adequate passage on both sides of a pool, with benches and cushioned lounges. The room was empty, though torches kept it well-illumined.

The walls were set with thousands of large, brightly-colored ceramic tiles. They formed pictures of people dancing and… something. In places it was difficult to make our what they were doing. Many of the tiles had fallen due to the ancient age of the place. There the walls had been painted a flat blue-green.

The bishop went to a cabinet and retrieved an ivory box with golden hinges. He set it on the intricate abstract mosaic that formed the floor. Two square pillows from a chair went next to it. Bishop Sierck motioned for her to kneel on one while he knelt on the other.

"We must pray," he said, and Abbie shut her eyes tightly while he communicated directly with God. He said his prayer in French and punctuated it with Latin to seal it.

"We ask Thee to rechristen this woman," he said, "so that her heart is reborn pure and without deceit to fulfill this holy contract."

He turned to Abbie, taking her hand so she'd open her eyes. "There is an ancient ritual of the Church," he told her. "First you must be prepared, and then I will re-baptize you in the old way, by immersion."

Abbie eyed the pool. At least it looked warm enough.

"Do you remember your catechism?" the bishop asked her.

"Of course I d-do." Another baptism?

"Don't be afraid." He unlatched the lid of the box and opened it. Inside was a dark velvet lining that held various flasks. He lifted one, loosened its top and sniffed, then nodded.

"Great holy Father," the bishop intoned. "I anoint this servant that she might do your work without taint of sin."

He lifted the flask over Abbie's head and drizzled a thin stream of oil into her hair. When he was done, he put his hand on her head and then frowned.

"Here," he said. He set his flask down and reached to unpin her hair. It fell in thick, unbraided ropes around her shoulders as he twined his fingers through it, distributing the oil.

"Better," he pronounced, and set the flask carefully back into the box. Then he produced a jar and worked its lid off. A musky perfume wafted toward Abbie.

"This is myrrh from the Holy Land," the bishop explained. "You must be prepared with this. It has been blessed by the Pope, and its properties are for purification of the body just as the water is to purify the spirit."

He put his finger into the jar and dug out an almost honey-like substance, using it to draw on Abbie's forehead and then down either side of her cheeks. He chanted in Latin as he did so.

"Now do I get re-baptized?" Abbie asked.

He shook his head. "The entire body needs to be purified," he explained.

"Entire...?" Abbie's lower lip shook. "Your Excellency–"

The bishop patted her hand. "Yes, I know," he told her kindly. "It must be frightening for a pure girl such as yourself. Here, I know of something that will help."

He rose and went to another cabinet, returning with a jar of wine and two large glasses. He poured one to its brim and handed it to her.

"Drink," he said. "This is the same type of wine that Jesus made as His first miracle at the wedding of Cana."

Abbie was shocked that the wine held a sharp vinegar aftertaste. It was one of those awful Rocquemaure wines. Still, she did as Bishop Sierck said.

He refilled her glass and set it down within reach. "Bear with me in this," he told her firmly, "for it means the life of your soul."

She nodded, eyes wide.

He unlaced her sleeves, drawing them off her slowly and placing them with care a length away from them. Then he unlaced the back of her dress.

"I am a bishop and a priest," he whispered to her as he drew her dress off her. "I do not come to you as a mortal man, but as God's own servant."

With her kneeling in her chemise, he ran more lines of myrrh down her bare arms and across her shoulders. He chanted and crossed himself, then reached for the straps of her chemise.

Delicately he drew them down, and then pulled the delicate garment off her breasts, down to her waist.

"Drink," he instructed.

Abbie didn't think she could get the wine down her constricted throat, but it did warm her. She had started to shiver, but it wasn't from the room's chill. She was only aware of Sierck as a man, not a bishop. Sternly she instructed herself to be still and not disturb the holy ceremony. This was so much more important than her modesty!

His long fingers traced lines down from her shoulder blades, between her breasts. Then he circled the myrrh around her nipples, then down her stomach. A tug on her chemise and he circled her navel.

A special chant was required as he took her breasts in his hands and squeezed. Abbie sucked in her breath, ashamed that she could become so aware of herself as a woman and him as a man during her re-baptizing. She turned her face from him.

"The body must be purified," the bishop whispered in her ear.

He pulled the chemise completely off, then her caleçons followed. She could hear the name "Eve" mentioned in the Latin prayer that he offered up, and she drank full this time, grateful for the numbing effect of the wine.

For this chant he started at her feet with his lines of myrrh, then proceeded up to circle her knees and pay attention to her naked thighs.

"Open your legs, child," he whispered huskily. "I apologize for the embarrassment, but it must be done."

He offered her another glass and she took it. She almost didn't notice when he slipped his cassock off, leaving himself in just his linen undershirt. "It's hot in here," he explained ruefully. "Please excuse me."

She gave a start when he rubbed the myrrh over her–

"You're doing well," he told her, but his breath came out quick and heavy. He placed his hand there and closed his eyes to intone a prayer, crossing himself at the end with the other.

"You are advancing into marriage," he whispered, tipping the newly-filled glass to her lips. "You must be purified from within as well."

When he set down the half-empty glass, he lifted the bottom of his undershirt to reveal…

Abbie's eyes couldn't get any wider. This was what Nathalie had told her about. It was so different from what she'd seen on her brothers.

And he was pouring the oil from before onto himself, reddish-purple with full erection. He still knelt between her legs, still chanted as he worked the slippery liquid.

Abbie let out a shriek and scrambled away on hands, feet and butt. Her voice echoed through the pool room.

He glanced up at her with a questioning look. "This is the purification," he told her. He patted the pillow in front of him. "Come back. This will only take a few minutes more, and then I will baptize and bless you in the pool. You can go with heart and soul reborn."

She shook her head wildly as she scooted farther from him, running into her discarded chemise.

"Come, my dove," he purred. "It does not hurt when a priest does it. You will feel the angels themselves blessing you."

With a movement so fast she couldn't believe it came from a priest, he sprang upon her. "Let's get this over with," he whispered in her ear as he fondled her hip. "It's as uncomfortable for you to be in this position as it is for me."

When she screamed as loud as she could, he silenced her with a savage, thrusting kiss, He held her by the hair so she couldn't pull away.

She lurched under him.

He cried out and clutched where he'd just been anointing himself.

Abbie gave him another, stronger kick and he groaned to curl up in a tight ball.

She snatched her chemise and what clothing she could reach. Her shoes, stockings… She wadded them into a ball and ran.

14

U p the stairway she flew.

"Help!" she cried. "Oh, help! Help!"

A door opened at her push, and she found herself in a monk's bedchamber, thankfully empty. She managed to pull her chemise on, her shoes tied quickly but loosely. She shivered into the main part of her dress, letting it hang open in back for she couldn't bother with the lacing now. The separate sleeves she gathered in her arms.

Abbie checked the corridor in both directions before venturing out, then ran like the very demons of Hell were after her. She didn't take any particular direction. *Away* was good enough. After her mind returned to her, she tried to zig-zag her way through the maze that was the palace… or was she still in the monastery part? She met no one, her ragged breath thundering through the hallways until–

"Abbie!"

She whirled.

"Jean-Marc!"

She threw herself into his arms.

"Abbie, are you all right?"

"Jean-Marc, Jean-Marc, Jean-Marc," she babbled.

He clasped her close, thanking the heavens. "What's happened? Tell me, sweet. Has someone hurt you?"

"The bishop. He– He tried to–"

She wept against his shoulder and he held her tight.

"I'll kill him," he swore into her ear. "So help me. I will. What was his name? Let me talk to the cardinal. I'll see him thrown–"

"I want to go home," Abbie sobbed. "Now. Please, Jean-Marc."

Jean-Marc held her for a moment more and then put her at arm's length to examine her for injuries. He helped her into her sleeves, helped her with the back laces. Then with her tucked tightly next to him, he hurried her through the corridors.

"I saw you leave," he told her. "I thought you'd been gone too long. I came looking." He was lost, too, so it took them some time before they found a familiar corridor. When they arrived back at the great dining hall, he hid her behind an arras. "Stay here," he ordered. "I'll be back in a few minutes."

He was as good as his word, returning with Nathalie and their cloaks. "Now," he told them both, "I'll see if they can rouse the cardinal. He passed out a while ago."

"He's probably as crooked as his bishop," Nathalie said. "We had the same problem in some of the cathedrals of Paris. The rot goes all the way to the top. The priests aren't blind; they know what's going on. It's sanctioned."

Jean-Marc's eyes narrowed as he regarded the throne-like seat where the cardinal now snored.

"I want to go home," Abbie moaned.

"Take her home," Nathalie urged.

Instead Jean-Marc marched up to the upper seating area where the cardinal sprawled. A guard stepped in his way.

"I need to talk to His Eminence," Jean-Marc said, his voice steely. It would have carried farther if the orchestra hadn't been playing so loudly and the revelers laughing so loud.

The guard glanced back over his shoulder. "As you can see," he said and then shrugged.

"I need to see someone. Someone in charge!"

An aging, thin man in a much-padded ruby-red cleric's gown eased himself out of his chair and stepped forward. He wore a velvet cap to match his gown. "I am Archbishop Cartier," he said. "This had better be important, to interrupt the cardinal's–"

"Your Excellency, one of your bishops has assaulted a young woman. A young maiden I am conducting to her future husband."

"One of my–? Who makes these claims?" The Archbishop's eyes narrowed and swept the room. It didn't take him long to find the pale faces of Abbie and Nathalie anxiously staring up at him from the furthest corner. Nathalie tried to push Abbie back into the arras and out of view.

"A girl," he murmured to himself. "A mere girl wants to sully the reputation of one of my bishops. What proof have you?"

"Her word. She is of sterling reputation, of one of the most prominent houses north of the Rhone," Jean-Marc said. "This man is not worthy of–"

"And who are you to tell me who is worthy or not?" The archbishop's keen gaze targeted Jean-Marc. His withered jowls shook as he said, "Who are you to try to take a holy bishop's name and drag it through the mud? Are you his enemy?"

"I don't even know his name yet," Jean-Marc protested. "The cardinal should speak with the girl. She's terrified after what she's been through."

The archbishop ground his teeth as he looked past Jean-Marc and then back to pin him in his gaze. "Are you a Protestant?" he accused.

"No! No, your Excellency, I am a good Catholic."

"Your name!"

Dainty hands clasped Jean-Marc's shoulders from behind. "This is F-Franck d'Auberge from L-Lyon," Abbie's voice said.

"Yes."

Jean-Marc turned to see that both women stood behind him. Abbie so pale and disheveled, but standing straight and strong. Nathalie with her lower lip pushed out defiantly.

"Franck d'Auberge," she repeated Abbie's claim. "A well-respected man and supporter of his home church."

Jean-Marc turned to face the archbishop, not quite knowing what to do. Guards had come up to flank Cartier, looking ready to take prisoners.

"I would speak to His Eminence in this matter," Jean-Marc said, surprised his voice came out so evenly. "I was his guest this evening. Personally invited by him. He would not care to see his hospitality impugned."

"We can return to our hotel to wait," Nathalie interrupted. "Clearly the cardinal is not to be spoken to tonight, and in the morning he must have many appointments. He is a busy man."

The archbishop said, "Too busy to handle false accusations."

"False! How can–" Abbie blurted, but Nathalie hushed her.

"Not too busy to hear charges from a righteous victim about an unrighteous man," Jean-Marc said.

"We can leave our address," Nathalie said quickly. "He can summon us at his pleasure. We will stay in town until we hear from him." Then she gave the name of a hotel they had passed just yesterday, one looking like it housed only the rich and influential.

"My name is–" Jean-Marc began, but again Nathalie stopped him.

"Franck d'Auberge," she supplied. "Come, Franck. Come, Babette. There's been far too much excitement tonight. Babette needs to rest after her ordeal." Nathalie curtseyed sweetly to the archbishop and dug her fingers into Jean-Marc's gown, pulling him back.

"Now!" she hissed into Jean-Marc's ear.

They gathered up their things.

"Slowly!" was Nathalie's order now. "Don't make it seem as if we're fleeing. But we must make haste."

Jean-Marc grimaced. "I feel like a coward," he said.

Nathalie thwacked him on his shoulder. "Better a live coward than thrown in the dungeons and tortured under a false accusation. It'll be her word against that of a bishop. Who do you suppose will win?"

Jean-Marc regarded Abbie.

"Home," she whispered desperately.

Finally he nodded. "Yes."

They caught a carriage and, after conferring with each other, Jean-Marc directed it to the hotel Nathalie had mentioned. There they pretended to the management to have come in only for a warm midnight drink. After they had paid, they bribed a maid to show them out a back exit.

From there they scurried through the night streets. Nathalie held a single lantern to light their way.

Through the shadows they flitted, their cloaks billowing behind them. Nathalie hid the light of her lantern when they heard horses coming closer, and they huddled in alleyways to hide.

"In Paris I heard of people taken away in the dead of night, never to be heard of again," Nathalie told them after the danger had passed.

Suddenly a shadow leaped out at them, lunging for Jean-Marc. Abbie let out a shriek before she could clamp her own hand over her mouth.

Whoever it was attacked Jean-Marc, but he fought back. Nathalie's lantern caught the flash of a knife blade as the opponents grunted and cursed low at each other. Jean-Marc got in a heavy punch, then another. He quickly wrapped a fold of his thick cloak around his arm and blocked the knife. A sharp but well-aimed kick– a battering punch to the nose, followed by another to the chin– and Jean-Marc finished their attacker off with a hard blow to the midsection.

Jean-Marc raised the thug up by his collar and knocked him against the cold stone of the stoop they'd fought on.

"Go!" Jean-Marc told them, and they ran as quickly as they could toward the river.

It was tricky navigating on a moonless night, but they eased the barge two quays downriver before seeking their beds, in case someone were to send unwelcome visitors. They departed Avignon at first light.

Abbie scrubbed hard at her skin until the brush left crosshatched red marks. A few raw spots bled into the bathwater. She let out a shriek when hot water cascaded over her head.

Nathalie set the large pitcher down and put her hands on her hips. "Time to get out," she said.

"I want to scrub my skin off," Abbie growled. "I want to get rid of everywhere he touched me!"

"And kill yourself in the bargain. It's all in your mind, not your skin, and you can't reach into your head to scrub him out."

Nathalie reached for the drying cloths and held one expectantly out to Abbie. "I'd like to have my turn before it gets cold," she hinted. "And the boys could use a good cleaning as long as we've paid for this."

Reluctantly Abbie got out and helped Nathalie with her bath. Then both wrestled the boys into the tub and managed to get the first layer of filth off them before the breeze coming through the thin-paned window cooled the water to unbearable levels.

"Good enough," declared Nathalie.

Jean-Marc had begun his luncheon without them. "What?" he demanded when he saw their glares. "I'm not stopping you from eating, and I'll join you at your meal. I was hungry." He rubbed his skinned knuckles. "I'm healing. Now, if you'd gone to the Roman baths I'd have come along, just to see what they're like."

"Men," Nathalie sighed as she hustled Charles and Henri onto the table benches.

"He was hungry," Abbie defended Jean-Marc. Strong Jean-Marc who had been the one to search for her, the one to find her. Magnificent hero Jean-Marc who had fought so bravely for the two of them. She could hide in his arms and he would protect her.

It scared her that she needed protecting. When she was in her vineyard, she was in control. Now on this journey she'd discovered that she did not hold the reins of her life. And last night she'd found out that some people wished her harm.

How much worse was it that it was an impersonal kind of harm. It wasn't because someone disliked Abbie Bourgogne or even her wine, but because some evil man in the disguise of a priest wanted to use whomever he could for his own pleasure and profit.

Even after the bath she still felt dirty.

Jean-Marc placed his hand over hers. "How are you doing, sweetheart?" he asked, searching her eyes.

She managed a small smile for him. "Better," she lied. "Though I gave false witness to an archbishop. It was in a good cause, don't you think?" Abbie looked at both of them anxiously. "We couldn't have them arresting us when we were innocent."

"Of course not," Jean-Marc soothed. "For a moment there I thought we might get an unbiased trial, but thankfully–" he nodded to Nathalie, who half-closed her eyes in self-satisfaction– "someone reminded me that I was a stranger in a strange land. Tell me, is there really a Franck… what was his name?"

"Franck d'Auberge, I think," Nathalie said. She turned to Abbie with a questioning look.

Abbie's face took on a curtain of guilt. "Marcy's husband," she explained. "Kind Marcy who saved us from the bad food." She licked her lips. "I thought that if Franck hadn't yet been punished for what he did to his poor wife and children, that perhaps it wouldn't be too evil if I directed some earthly punishment– no matter how unwarranted– in his direction. Was that terribly sinful?"

Nathalie and Jean-Marc laughed. "At least you'll have something interesting for your next confession," Jean-Marc told her.

Abbie said miserably, "I'm in sore need of confession, but to tell you the truth, I think I'll wait for more distance between us and Avignon before I'll feel safe going inside a church again. May all the saints forgive me."

Jean-Marc patted her hand and then rested his hand again on hers. "You're just being the sensible girl you are, Abbie Bourgogne."

Nathalie reached over and removed his hand. "Yes, she is," she said. "And a good walk will help clear her mind of this. I take it you wish to act the tourist, Jean-Marc?"

They did indeed look over this new town of Arles. "The crew is becoming restless," Jean-Marc admitted, "but since I'm paying them by the day they can't really complain that we're taking too much time to reach the ocean."

It was diverting to see the local colors. Abbie couldn't have imagined that a place within her own country could be so different from her home, but here it was. People built their houses of a lighter stone, and sometimes they would use curved tiles to roof, making their houses seem peculiar. They said their words differently, more languorously, and they spoke of the Mediterranean as familiarly as did the people at home of Beaune or Dijon.

The familiarity of the basics calmed her after last night's strangeness. Stalls filled with new kinds of bright-colored fruits showed up at the market, and some offered flats of still-blooming flowers. Mustards were in short supply, as were burgundies and chablis.

They passed a small church that was just as lovely as the ones back home, but Abbie drew back from it. She and Jean-Marc waited outside as Nathalie and the boys went in for their prayers.

To while the time, Abbie and Jean-Marc browsed the shelves at a sculptor's atelier. Jean-Marc guided Abbie with a hand around her waist and she didn't argue. She felt so safe with him around.

He had to take back his hand to pick up various pieces, so instead Abbie slipped her hand inside the crook of his elbow, completing the circle with her other. As Jean-Marc examined one small sculpture of a lion, she examined his face. So familiar now, so kind and clever.

"Philippe would like this," Jean-Marc said. He held it up and twisted it so he could see it from all sides. "Don't you think so?" he asked.

"I wouldn't know," Abbie said softly. She rubbed his solid arm. A layer of tension rolled off herself.

He set the lion down. Then he looked at her, directly into her eyes.

She smiled at him.

He smiled back, then brushed a stray lock of her hair ever so slowly off her forehead, tucking it back into the mass she had pinned upon the crown of her head.

"Have I ever told you how beautiful your hair is?" he murmured.

She shook her head and lowered her eyelids coquettishly. "I don't believe you have."

"Not even to compare it to honey? Or the sun itself?" At her blush, he dared to ask, "And have I told you your eyes are like the sea at dawn? And your lips like—"

"Ah, monsieur! Madame!" a bold voice came from behind them. "Are you interested in anything you see here?"

They turned to find a slender, dust-covered man of middle years anxiously awaiting them. He wore a long apron over his clothing, both equally covered in layers of whitish dirt that powdered off in bits as he moved.

Abbie turned a burgundy red. She opened her mouth to correct the man that she was a "mademoiselle" and not a "madame," but he would never see them again. What would be the point?

Instead she brazenly kept her hands around Jean-Marc's arm even as he dropped his own to his side.

"Ah," he said, the silver-tongued charmer. "Ah—"

"We were wondering," Abbie chimed in and pointed with a sure finger, "how much would you ask for the lion there?"

Jean-Marc watched her from some far-off place within himself. Could she truly have changed her attitude so much toward him? The lightness of his being, songs sung that only he could hear, said *Yes! Yes!*

She was the most beautiful of women in body and spirit, the most desirable of her sex since Eve. And she was smiling at him. She was leaning into him, rubbing his arm until his mind whirled at the distraction. He reveled in it until something pulled him from this most blissful of moments:

The memory of Philippe's voice.

"See if you can get us the Bourgogne account," he'd told him. Philippe had glanced at the miniature portrait he'd been sent. "The girl seems presentable enough. Unless she's totally bereft of mind or unhealthy, she'll do to cement the deal."

Jean-Marc had been ecstatic. "High time you settled down, Phil," he said.

Philippe raised an eyebrow and the corner of his mouth at his brother. "I don't remember ever leaving Marseille," he said.

"With a *wife*, numbskull. Wife, kids, grandkids... You'll have a happy home at last."

There had been a sadness in the way Philippe picked up the portrait again. "You have such new ideas, Jean-Marc," he said. "I'll marry to help the business. I'll produce heirs to build the family to what it should be."

"I see many busy nights ahead of you, Philippe."

"So when are you going to settle down?"

Jean-Marc barked a laugh. "Never!" he declared. "It's up to you to do all this family stuff."

Philippe sighed. "So soon?"

"You aren't getting any younger. And your children will take their time growing old enough to start in the company." Jean-Marc shook his finger at Philippe. "You've been working too hard too long taking care of it and me as well. I want to see you settled with a good wife who'll take care of you since you won't do so yourself. Children who'll make you laugh. A woman who'll get your blood hot and bothered."

Philippe rolled his eyes.

"That's why I've done all this." Jean-Marc spread his hands over the many miniatures on the white-laid table, a display of the finest of the young women from France, Spain, and Italy. "It's time you got to enjoy life, Philippe. It's been hard for you. You need to take it easy every now and then."

"You worry too much about me," Philippe said with a little smile.

"I owe you everything."

"You're my brother."

"You didn't have to keep me here with you. You didn't have to do half or even a tenth of the things you've done." Jean-Marc leaned on the table. "I love you. I want you to find someone who'll take care of you when I'm gone."

"You're not going to leave."

Lightly Jean-Marc slapped the table with one hand. "I don't know how I can get it through your thick head. Someday I will leave. I'll go crazy if I spend my whole life here! I'm just not cut out for a desk, Philippe. You know that. You've always known that. I've done what I could, but the day will come when I won't be able to stand it anymore. I want you cared for when that happens."

Philippe pursed his lips together. "Perhaps we can find a way for you to get out more often. Will that please you? Will that satisfy these travel urges? I can't lose you, Jean-Marc. You're my brother, the only family I have." He had reached out to squeeze Jean-Marc's hand.

Jean-Marc had grimaced. "We can try that," he said. "I don't guarantee anything. Let's get you that bride. You need a wife more than you need a brother."

"Perhaps I need both?"

With Abbie hanging onto his arm, Jean-Marc sighed. She was for Philippe. She would be his salvation, but the feelings Jean-Marc had for her were anything but brotherly. He tried to pat her hand in a brotherly way, but his blood roared through his veins to touch her. He was aware of her every movement, and his imagination often sent him into sweet, erotic territories with her as its focus.

Somehow he would have to overcome himself. Either that, or desert his brother before his own plan could come to fruition, leaving the company to fall apart in his absence. Better the company than his brother's life.

15

Transferring their cargo from the river-faring barge to the ocean-voyaging cog took much more time than Abbie would have suspected. It had only taken a few hours to load the barge originally, but now the cargo not only had to be unloaded but carted down four docks and then loaded up a gangway that looked too flimsy to hold both handcart and porter.

She stared in amazement at the Mediterranean. So this was an ocean. It seemed to stretch out forever, farther than any water ever should. In the distance she could see lines of white rhythmically lunging to the shore, though here within the bay the water seemed only a little rougher than the river.

The mild, sour smell of riverside was amplified a thousand times here as the stench of ripe fish clung to the air. An army of seagulls screamed in the wind. Men of many colors crowded the docks, shouting above the din. They used shocking profanities, and sometimes spoke in tongues that Abbie could not decipher.

They leered at her and Nathalie, and the two women both held close to Jean-Marc.

The boys broke out of Nathalie's grasp. Abbie automatically ran off to capture Charles while Nathalie took after her younger son.

A dirty man suddenly appeared at her side. "Here now, I'll get him for you, missy. And then you'll owe me, won't you?"

He tried to grab her arm, but she whirled away from him, just in time to see him stagger from Jean-Marc's blow. He caught him just under the jaw, then again in the gut.

But the man reared up again. Abbie took two unwilling steps backwards, aghast and terrified that he might hurt Jean-Marc. But a cartman and the Dellamer captain stood at Jean-Marc's side.

"I wouldn't," the captain told the man.

He rubbed his jaw and considered the situation as Jean-Marc said, "Go about your business. This is a good woman, promised to my brother." He glanced down the docks. "Charles!" He shouted at the boy, who'd paused to watch. "Get back here! Now! Or there'll be hell to pay!"

The boy immediately ran back to them, fear and respect in his eyes for Jean-Marc.

A new hubbub attracted their attention. Even as Nathalie and Henri rejoined them, a crowd of people clamored not far from them. A short dock led to a small boat, and the crowd shouted their derision at it. Many waved their fists in the air. Someone threw a stone that rattled against the boat's cabin.

"Protestants, sir," the cartman explained to the captain. "There was a roundup of them last night. Some of the last are being shown the quick way out of town." He spat on the weather-beaten wooden walkway. "Me, I'd show them an even quicker way out." And he made a slashing motion across his neck.

Someone of his ilk had similar ideas. A flaming torch arced its way across the space between dock and boat, landing on the deck. One of the men aboard who'd been hurriedly casting off stopped to grab a bucket of water to quench the flame before he went back to his work.

Abbie could see women and children peeking out of the cabin's door and windows. She knew that they were making the same kind of bargain with God that she'd made just the other night.

Somehow, even though they were Protestants and thus had turned their faces from the rightful Church, she wished them well. Perhaps some of them had run into priests who wanted them for unpriestly purposes, or to cheat them out of money that would never see its way into true church coffers.

She wished for them that God granted their prayers.

As God had granted hers.

Guiltily, she glanced at Jean-Marc. He was alive, whole, and vigorous enough to cower a swarthy sailor for her honor. How different from the night when he lay so deathly ill!

That had been when she'd prayed to God to save him and God had blessed her by relenting.

It didn't matter that Jean-Marc had lied to her about whose fault it was. All that mattered was that she'd made a promise to God, and God had fulfilled his side of it.

Right?

As they approached their cog, Abbie eyed the way the giant, sturdy structure bobbed like a seed in a storm-tossed lake. They expected her to ride on that? Yes, she realized that this maze of docks represented the hundreds and thousands of ships that had made successful ocean voyages through the years, but this seemed to her an unreliable means of travel.

If she was going to get through this alive, she'd need God on her side.

Realization dawned in her that if she was to live for eternity in Heaven after she'd departed this life, she would need God on her side forever. And to do that she needed to walk on the path He blazed for her.

He'd caused Jean-Marc to be sick so she would learn that it was up to her to fulfill the marriage contract. Even more, God would expect her to fulfill it with good will to the best of her ability. She must happily put Philippe's ring upon her finger and make the best of her life, even though it meant she would never see her vineyard again, never care for her precious grapes.

Perhaps there was something better waiting for her within Philippe's house, but she couldn't imagine what it could be.

Perhaps… Perhaps this marriage was to lead her back to her own vineyard. She'd met Nathalie, and Nathalie was teaching her how to convince a man to do her will. Was this what God had in mind? To cement her to a marriage that would lead her home forever?

That bishop had been a sign for her that she'd been unable to see until now. There he'd been, a man supposedly of God but who'd strayed so far from his true path that he must sully life for those around him. He was a plague who passed his evil from person to person.

She must not be like that. She must not mope or complain, but set upon her task with good heart. She must have faith. Faith would get her home to her grapes.

Jean-Marc turned to take her hand, smiling his special smile at her.

He was a test. He was sweet temptation. She must not give in to him and thus make God proud of her.

She held her head high and did not look at him as she boarded the boat.

There was great rejoicing at the Venise Glass Works when Nathalie Venise Pelletier and her sons arrived home. At their lumbering wagon's approach on the hills above Marseille, sunburned men wearing leather aprons appeared at the stone pillars that marked the entrance to the Venises' holdings. They squinted at Jean-Marc, but Nathalie's excited wave and halloo caught their attention. Soon people of all sizes were swarming over the wagon, laughing and hugging.

Even Abbie got hugged several times, and she could have sworn that two men hugged her more than once even after she'd pointed out their mistake.

Jean-Marc helped unload until the Venise men insisted on taking over. Instead Jean-Marc, Abbie, and Nathalie all received a tour of the factory.

"You do amazing work," Jean-Marc remarked as they stopped at a storage rack filled with glass bottles and jars. Right outside the factory door stood one of the mammoth mountains of firewood it took to keep the glass furnaces going.

"It's so beautiful," Abbie added in wonder. "The glass is like a crystallized breeze. It seems a miracle that a man can make such things."

That pleased Nathalie's oldest brother, Paul. "We make miracles every day," he said and then hastily crossed himself for his slight blasphemy. He picked up a bottle, tossing it to spin in mid-air before he held it out to them. "Here, look at this."

It was beautiful, dark glass that might hold a pint or more of liquid. Abbie oohed over it and he let her hold it.

"Very pretty," Jean-Marc agreed. "I'm sure you make a good business with this."

Paul nodded. "We can turn these out very quickly. Even a common man can afford these. Plus they're sturdier than most bottles. My brother Vince just got back from Germany through all the unrest there last summer. He brought their secrets of strong glass. If it's packed right, you can stack these on top of each other and they will rarely break."

"Too bad we didn't ship the wine down here in these," Abbie said as she returned the bottle to Paul. "We would have suffered less loss. I take it they don't leak?"

"Not with a good seal at the top. You don't lose a drop."

She nodded. "We usually have to ship an extra barrel for every twenty to replace what leaks during shipment," she said.

"In that case I should order five hundred bottles straight off," Jean-Marc said, and Paul laughed. "No, seriously," Jean-Marc told him. "We plan our first large shipment in February."

Jean-Marc turned to Abbie. "If the wine doesn't leak, will it also store longer in glass? Like that pottery your uncle kept the six-year wine in? Could we ship it any time?"

For once a wine question had stumped her. "I have no idea," she said. "I suppose we could experiment."

Jean-Marc took an open-mouthed glass out of the pile of products next to him. "The mustards would look very nice in this, too. These are sturdy, you say? Do you suppose the mustard would last longer in these as well?"

Both Paul and Abbie shrugged their ignorance at him.

Jean-Marc nodded. "You'll need to meet with my brother," he told Paul. "All of you should come down to town for a few days to talk. Now show me these magnificent wine glasses of yours, Paul."

Nathalie left her children with her family while Paul accompanied her, Jean-Marc, and Abbie to *chez* Dellamer. Nathalie told the both of them that it would look more seemly if she rode up with them as if she'd been with them the entire journey.

"We can say that I've been your chaperone since you first took to the river," she said, "or we can say nothing and let them suppose."

From the hills where the Venise holdings sat, Marseille stretched out below them. A skinny island housing a mighty fort paralleled the long, concave shore.

And the ocean–! When she had first glimpsed it at the mouth of the Rhone, it had terrified Abbie. A half-day of rolling on its expanse was still something that she and her stomach would rather avoid if possible. But from the steady hills of Marseille it lay placid and impossibly crystal blue, stretching out forever to south and west. Clusters of white marked sails of the ships coming into port for the evening.

As they rode through the city, Abbie saw wondrous constructions and scaffolding surrounding an immense cathedral. Modern, balconied buildings of timber as well as of stone bespoke the prosperity of the huge seaport.

Everywhere were trees and flowers still bedecked with green. Pink and red blossoms peeked out from trellised south-facing walls, a remainder of summer that lingered on the land.

After they passed through the heart of the city, Jean-Marc pointed out a long stone building near the primary docks that was his family's warehouse. Men shouted there as loudly as the careening seagulls above them.

Jean-Marc slipped his arm around Abbie's shoulders to turn her to where she could see it to best advantage. Abbie glanced at him, and his eyes met hers warmly. "It's the finest in the region," he told her proudly, using his chin to point. His hand dropped to linger a sweet moment at her waist, but she shifted away.

A rise took the warehouse out of their sight. Stately blocks of family homes sprawled before their wagon.

"Isn't that the Beaumondais's residence?" Nathalie asked Paul. "I remember this. It's been too long, but I do remember. And that is where Marie duGarm lived, and back beyond there is where my good friend Rachel lived. I wonder where they are now? All married off far from here, I suppose."

"Not at all," Paul replied. "Rachel and Marie both live not far from here, on the north side of center ville. We'll send for them tomorrow or you can visit. I think one of the girls mentioned that Marie was talking about you just last week at mass."

Nathalie clapped her hands. "It's so good to be home. You can't imagine."

Home. How Abbie longed for home! But now… She looked at Jean-Marc out of the corner of her eye. He lounged back in their seat, content to be where his home was. Even the world traveler could value a resting place.

"Here we are," he said.

Abbie tried to swallow, her mouth suddenly dry.

The Dellamer estate wrapped around an enormous, rolling block that took up an entire hill unto itself. It was situated so that the vulgarity of the waterfront could never hope to penetrate through the lush greenery that surrounded the house, both outside and within its expansive courtyard.

Jean-Marc brought the wagon up within that yard so that they were surrounded on four sides by two stories of very old stone walls climbed by flowering vines. An iron gate swung securely shut behind them.

Despite her dread, Abbie couldn't block her curiosity of the ancient grounds. Home had always felt like it had been there forever, but this was much older. The courtyard was terraced into herb and ornamental gardens, then an open area, perfect for children at play, and a broad graveled section for workers separated an area for chickens and pigs from the rest.

A long, low wall guarded the estate's expansive gardens in the distance, large enough to feed the family, its workers, and guests.

Here, closer to the house, two white marble statues of noble-looking people sat in a circle of flowers, and a group of what Jean-Marc assured her were lemon and orange trees added a fantastical element to it all.

The house itself was clearly Roman in design, which Abbie surprised herself by recognizing with her new worldly knowledge. Rounded arches were cunningly worked into the walls, echoing the arched carriage entryway and the other doors around the courtyard. The darker stone of the house was set off with white granite trimwork, which also outlined all the archways and windows. Wide stone staircases ambled out of doors every so often, shaded by trellised vines, and here and there a servant worked slowly in the warmth of the afternoon.

"It's beautiful," Abbie breathed. "Babette will be sorry for the rest of her life that she missed this."

Jean-Marc's squadron of servants and employees swarmed to their wagon to help unload. They brought flat, low wheelbarrows to carry the wine casks and mustard jars that Jean-Marc had selected from the dowry, while others hefted trunks between themselves.

"Set Mademoiselle Bourgogne up in one of the guest rooms," Jean-Marc ordered. "It can't yet be appropriate to put her in the room for the mistress of the house."

Abbie and Nathalie wandered in behind the servants, in awe of the house and its comfortable if dusty furnishings.

"This will be yours," Nathalie whispered to her.

But it couldn't. She didn't deserve this. It all came down to this, didn't it? This mansion was the reward for an honest contract, to be fulfilled by the correct woman so as to conduct a righteous marriage that would last into Heaven.

All Abbie wanted was a sweet old stone house in Burgundy, her vineyard and winery, and… and…

She forced herself to look away from Jean-Marc.

Abbie would inform Monsieur Philippe Dellamer exactly what was what and who was who, and he would send her back home. Perhaps she should tell these people to keep everything on the wagon. Perhaps she should–

"There he is," Jean-Marc said, leaning to peer out a window.

From the far side of the court, a tall, dark-haired man strode up the terraces toward all the commotion. He did not have Jean-Marc's easy stride, but rather marched straight as a soldier.

Every scrap of clothing he wore was perfectly laced and arranged. His deep blue gown was not like Jean-Marc's short one but so long that it reached to his toes and flowed behind him in the breeze he kicked up, a gown of authority and power. Its shoulders puffed out to narrow only at the wrist. The upper band of his shirt was wide and white against his throat, and a four-corned blue hat gave him a studious air.

Abbie blinked when she saw that his clothes contained no slashes at all. When had she become used to expecting them?

Philippe's hair was shorter than Jean-Marc's. It looked of the same curly nature, and if he'd worn it longer it would have fallen into his face as it did into Jean-Marc's. But this man's hair followed his commands.

His face was longer than Jean-Marc's but of a kind. He seemed much older. That could have been due to his dark, well-trimmed beard or to his expression: pinched and unsmiling. Concerned, perhaps.

Yes, perhaps it was only worry for his brother's welfare, for when he caught sight of Jean-Marc, a smile appeared on his face and he looked ten years younger than he had. Abbie gaped at the change. It was an extremely handsome man that Jean-Marc hugged in welcome.

"Not so googly anymore," Nathalie whispered to her.

But when he turned to her, his face slid into a neutrally pleasant expression. He allowed the slightest of polite smiles as he bowed.

"Mademoiselle Bourgogne," he said to her. "Your portrait does not do you justice. I am glad to see you arrived safely. And here we have…?"

Nathalie curtsied as Jean-Marc introduced her. "Madame Pelletier was kind enough to step in as chaperone along our trip when our original one became ill. I brought her brother, Paul Venise, along today too, because I think we should be interested in doing business with them," he said. "You've heard of their glass, of course. Let's schedule them for long talks as soon as possible, Philippe. They brought some interesting products to my attention."

Abbie curtsied the way she'd seen Nathalie do. "I am so pleased to meet you, Monsieur Dellamer. I need to explain–"

"Yes. I'm sure I will see you at dinner. Monsieur Venise?"

With that Dellamer drew Paul and Jean-Marc aside and turned his back on the women. They walked away and all Abbie could hear of the conversation included crates and dowries and schedules to be met.

"He must be very busy," Nathalie said to her. "He might need a little training, but perhaps not that much. He has fairly good manners for a man.

And he's just as handsome as his brother but in a more refined way." She caught Abbie's eye and gave her a little encouraging smile. "His breath was sweet," she said.

But Philippe did not attend dinner. Jean-Marc slipped in midway through to explain that reports of some of their returning ships had arrived, but one ship was missing. Philippe had sent runners to discover more if they could. Adding to all this was that another of their ships had arrived just the day before, and that would entail hubbub for a week and more as the cargo was unloaded and buyers found for it, inventories triple checked, crew was paid, and repairs to the ship were made even as its next voyage was being proposed.

"It seems an exciting life," Nathalie told Jean-Marc, and he shrugged.

"If you like that kind of thing."

"I should think you'd enjoy the gamble of the enterprise," Paul said.

Abbie said, "I should think you'd enjoy overseeing the men and helping them. Listening to their stories of distant ports."

Jean-Marc glanced at her with surprise. "Yes, that's the one part of this that I do like. How did you know?"

"It's what you've always done," Abbie told him. "You've been friendly with everyone you've met. Except– you know– with Michel Fichaud. You didn't lift a finger to help him."

Jean-Marc reached for the wine. "I didn't feel that Fichaud needed any more help than he already possessed. May God have mercy on his blighted soul. I believe he has a wife I wouldn't wish on anyone."

"I was going to tell your brother about her when he got back," Abbie said. "When will that be?"

The wine glass paused halfway to Jean-Marc's mouth. "I couldn't say. Too many things happening, and Philippe is very dedicated to the business. He might not come up for air for a few days. I have to send someone round with his meals, or he will forget to eat." He shook his head. "Sweet Jesu, how he loves the business."

"He seems to have done quite well," Nathalie said. She looked up as her brother eased his chair back.

"Are we going so soon?"

"Perhaps we have already overstayed our welcome," Paul hinted.

"Nonsense," Jean-Marc said quickly. "We can have rooms made up. Stay the night."

"No, no, we should be going. I've finished discussing business with Philippe. Now I need to take his offers back to the family. We don't wish to impose."

Two maids brought in bowls of honeyed fruit for dessert.

"At least stay for this, Paul," Jean-Marc said.

"Well…"

Paul managed some fruit and some cheese besides, and was curious enough about a rare Turkish drink called *coffee* that he stayed long enough to taste. He shook his head vigorously after a few sips.

"No, this stuff will never catch on," he declared. "An infidel brew. I prefer a more civilized wine."

"My brother swears by it," Jean-Marc said.

Paul made their excuses before any more delights could be found. "Besides, I'm sure my sister's children will want to see her before they sleep."

"That's true enough," Nathalie said and dabbed at the corners of her mouth. "I need to see to the boys. They're in a strange house for them and they might be scared. Such a lovely dinner and good companionship. Good night, Abbie. Jean-Marc." She promised to stop by again within the next few days.

It was all Abbie could do to rouse herself from a sleep of pure exhaustion after the trip and the tension of meeting her false fiancé, but she attended mass the next morning alongside Jean-Marc. The cathedral was crowded enough that no individual priest would approach her. Besides, Jean-Marc was with her. He'd protect her.

Still, it was too soon for her to go to confession.

"Where is Philippe?" she hissed to him between prayers.

"Probably still in the office. I don't think he came back last night."

"He doesn't attend mass?"

"Not when he's busy. Shh."

Sure enough, it was not until that afternoon that a very haggard-looking Philippe dragged himself into the dining room as they finished their luncheon.

"Good news," he told Jean-Marc without any other greeting. "All three cogs have been spotted. They're riding well in the water."

"Excellent. Sit down and eat, Philippe. You don't look well."

Philippe gave him a bleary smile. "All I need is about a day's measure of sleep." Only then did he spot Abbie. "Mademoiselle Bourgogne. My apologies for running off as I did yesterday. It has been a busy week with little time for proper courtesies. I trust you have settled in? Jean-Marc has been taking good care of you?"

Abbie immediately set down her spoon. "There is pressing business I need to discuss with you as soon as possible, Monsieur Dellamer. It concerns the wedding contract."

Philippe rubbed one eye, leaving the other hand to accept the bowls and plates of food the servants offered him. "Then I must apologize again, Mademoiselle. I haven't had the first moment yet to read the contract. Please give me a chance to rest and then review the document, will you? Then we can discuss it."

He sat back and the length of time it took to blink his eyes, the way he opened his mouth as if to say something but instead shook his head, told Abbie he must be tired indeed.

Still he had the presence of mind to say, "You must call me Philippe. And your name was Bar– no, Babette, was it not?"

"Abbie."

"They call her Abbie," Jean-Marc said quickly. "It's really Babette. There are a lot of Babettes in the family, all named after a grandmother."

"Abbie," Philippe murmured, already in a dream of sleep.

Jean-Marc waved the servants off. "Let's see how much he eats," he quietly told Abbie, "and then I'll put him to bed."

Watching Jean-Marc care for his older brother touched Abbie's heart. He dabbed the slight bit of food that had stuck to the edge of Philippe's beard even as Philippe apologized and tried unsuccessfully to swipe at it himself. By now Philippe couldn't put his words together coherently.

"Here, let's get you to bed," Jean-Marc told him, pulling him out of his seat. "If you wake up you can ring for some food and then sleep some more after that. When are you going to learn that regular hours are more efficient than these all-night, all-week work binges of yours?"

Philippe muttered something, and Jean-Marc laughed.

"What would you do without me?" he asked his brother and then turned to a manservant. "Give me a hand here, will you?"

A chance to talk to Monsieur Dellamer and Abbie had missed it. What kind of man wouldn't spare the time to get to know his betrothed?

A man who was more interested in business than marriage.

Abbie rubbed her lower lip as she sat in her luxurious bed. This house was a castle. Its furnishings displayed great riches. Monsieur Dellamer– no, Philippe– must put great stock in such things, or in a society that did.

She couldn't care less about such. A good, bug-free bed was important, to let you sleep the night through so you'd be ready the next day to work. Out in the country, company was usually of the same social position as their hosts. There were no airs to be put upon, no pretense to be held. Guests were treated like family, not royalty. Respect was the highest honor you could give someone, not a chair padded in velvet.

Perhaps this was a way to conduct business, Abbie mused. Impress people and make them customers. That fit in with what little she'd seen of her intended.

No, of Babette's intended. Poor man to have been betrothed to Babette. Poor man to have been betrayed by her!

And poor man to have to live unknowingly with a cheat, especially when everyone else was in on the plot!

Abbie got out of bed and knelt down next to it in front of the crucifix on the wall. She crossed herself.

Holy Mother Mary, what do I do now? she asked. She'd come to realize that Jean-Marc was Temptation. As such he must serve a purpose to her, a way for her to prove her righteousness to the saints. But there was no way around it: this contract was a false one. Philippe seemed an honest man, concerned with the people he worked with if not the people he would be living with.

It would be a horrible sin to cheat an honest man.

And yet it would also be horrible if the consequences ricocheted back to Uncle Gus. Uncle was also the most honest of men.

What should I do? What?

She wiped the sweat from her brow. Even going thrice as many times to confession, even if she bought some of those Indulgence things– that was not going to save her from Heavenly Punishment. How many years, decades of Purgatory would she have to endure because of this?

What was Purgatory like, anyway? As a young girl, she'd pictured it as a long, wide hallway that linked Heaven and Hell. It had an uncomfortable bench along one side that stretched off into the distance in both directions. All the sinners would sit on the bench for their duration while angels lectured them on how to overcome their sins, doling out punishment when it was due.

Now as an adult she wondered if that vision were right. Would one be able to hear the shrieks and screams from Hell echoing through Purgatory? Would some of the infernal heat reach there? Were people well-treated, or were they half-starved and sickly during their sentence? Would she suffer or would she just be expected to be patient and learn, until the saints approved of her?

How long would it take to rub a sin like this off her immortal soul?

A shudder of horror swept over her body. This sin was not just hers. It would be Jean-Marc's as well. Nathalie's? Perhaps a little. Uncle Gus's? If he never found out?

Regardless of the others, Jean-Marc's soul was definitely in jeopardy just as hers was.

She shook her head at the thought, trying to chase it away. She could do nothing about Jean-Marc's soul; that was for him to worry about. But as for her... If she was a good wife, a hard-working wife who bore Philippe the sons he needed...

But how could she guarantee that? How could she be an honest wife if she lived under the shadow of such a lie? Would her sin reflect upon her sinless husband?

She hit the mattress in front of her, growling in her anger. She didn't want to do this! She wanted– no, she *needed* to be at home, at the clos, saving her family's honor by producing the best wine in all France. She could do so much more for her family there than here, in a loveless marriage to some stranger who was more interested in his work than in her.

She had to get back home. How? How? She clutched the bedclothes and rocked back and forth on her knees as she tried to sort things out.

A voice inside her said, *Tell the truth.*

Was that you, Holy Mother? she asked but heard no answer. Was it a divine order, or just her talking to herself? Had she received the Holy Word or was it just her common sense?

She set her jaw. Either way, it seemed right to her. Get out of the lie with honesty. Hand the truth to Philippe and see what his decision was. Then decide if that decision was one she could live with.

Sleep came easy to her lightened heart.

Abbie paced the main room, a comfortable place with bright light from two tall windows. "Is he getting up sometime today?" she asked.

"Probably not," Jean-Marc said. He'd just come in from the office and had settled down on a padded bench against the wall, putting his feet up on the exquisite table next to it. He pulled his hat down over his eyes and feigned a posture of sleep. "He does this all the time, work for three or four days straight through, then sleep for a day, a day and a half. I didn't worry about it when he was nineteen, but he's not so young anymore. He refuses to believe that."

"And what will he do when you take off and leave him?" Abbie demanded.

Jean-Marc pulled up one corner of the hat so he could look at her. "Why, by then he'll have a loving wife who will insist that he keep normal hours like everyone else. She will feed him deathly hangover cures and when he's sick she'll tell him sweet stories of her childhood. Then when he's well again she'll complain about the Spanish *bastardo*."

"I am not going to marry him."

"You'll be the best thing that's ever happened to him." The hat fell back to cover his face.

Abbie plopped down beside him. "Perhaps you haven't been listening," she said. "I am not going to marry him. I've decided."

Again he crooked the edge of the hat. "You got someone else in mind, hm?" He said it with a flirt in his voice, but something in his eyes was hard on hers, examining her response minutely.

"I am handling it," Abbie replied curtly. She crossed her arms over her chest, and his eyes traveled down to rest there. Hurriedly she uncrossed her arms.

He settled the hat back on his face. "I know what I'd like to handle. Ah, I remember a quite pleasant afternoon with a lovely young lady. A very warm and friendly young lady, as I recall."

"You are a cad. A liar and a bounder."

"And apparently not in your plans. Who is, *chérie*? I've been keeping my eye out for any rivals, but I have yet to see or hear of any. I think we've narrowed it down to Philippe."

"You don't remember. I sent my cousin Chris a letter."

That brought him up to attention.

"You what?"

"I asked him to compile the names of available non-landholders around the clos. He's going to list them in order of suitability."

"And you'll choose the top three and then let your uncle decide."

"Yes."

Jean-Marc seized her hand. "Listen," he said. "You're going to marry my brother. The deal has been made. A priest has witnessed it."

"We'll just ask that priest who exactly he was witnessing for."

"You were the one talking scandal and how everyone's reputations would be ruined."

"From the five minutes I've seen of your brother, he seems sensible to me. We can keep this quiet and there will be no scandal for anyone. Then I can marry whoever it is that Chris recommends and I get control of the clos."

He shook her hand in his powerful one. "And you listen to me. You're going to marry my brother. And if you don't marry him, then–" His jaw worked and he scowled at her.

Abbie's heart stopped. "Then what? Who will I marry?"

He dropped her hand as if it were fire. Her pulse beat hard in her throat. She couldn't look away.

"You will marry my brother," he growled at her. "That is that. No more discussion. I will tell Philippe that you made a mistake and don't have any questions about the contract, that it suits you perfectly. Do you hear me?"

With that he took her in his arms and kissed her hard.

Abbie gasped as he leaped up off the couch and stormed out of the room.

16

Abbie nosed about the house, investigating dusty rooms, linens with encrusted grime. She supposed one must expect such in a household ruled by two brothers. She should get Nathalie to teach her how to command a house staff.

That thought brought her to a halt. She didn't need to know that, because she was only staying long enough to set things aright with Philippe. Then she would be gone. He would surely send her home.

She knew Philippe was awake now, because she'd caught sight of his back walking briskly across the courtyard toward the family offices. Abbie wasn't sure how business was done here in the big city, whether acquaintances could barge in and confront someone with personal business. Probably not.

Well, Philippe would show up for dinner unless he chose to work through it again. She frowned at her situation and, unthinking, reached for the latch to this next door.

It opened to the street– and a sudden revelation of sunlight cascading around a huge, bearish silhouette that hulked just outside. Abbie scrambled back, grabbing for the door handle.

"Abbie!"

With a gasp she cried, "Uncle Gus!"

Before she could say anything else, he'd taken her in one of his great hugs. It lifted her off the floor. Finally he set her down, patting her shoulders as he examined her general state and she caught her breath again.

Then he peered about the room behind her. "Well, where is she? Is she here?" he asked. "Invite me in, girl. Let me look around."

Abbie couldn't remember needing to invite Uncle Gus anywhere, but she stood aside and he bustled in, taking in the lavish furnishings. A boy stood on the walkway behind him, two large traveling bags beside him.

"Fancy place," Uncle Gus rumbled. "Boy! Bring my bags!"

The boy jumped to obey. As soon as the bags had been deposited, Gus paid the boy and sent him on his way. He shut the door decisively and turned to Abbie.

"Now, girl," he said. "Tell me."

Abbie backed away. "I– Um… Is this a visit, Uncle? It's so soon. You'd think you left–"

"Almost as soon as I found out that something had happened on your way to the river. Had a devil of a time making connections. You wouldn't believe the condition of some of the things they have the nerve to call 'boats,'" he told her as he scooted around the room, rooting through curtains and peering through doorways. "The wagon boy comes back and says that Babette was 'taking a long way to Marseille.' What does that mean, Abbie? Is she here? Tell me she is. I've had far too long to sit and think about possibilities."

"Did you get my letter?" Abbie hedged.

"No, I did not get any letter. I went to town and questioned folk and found out that only two people got on the barge to Marseille. Two, not three. I so pray that the second one was Babette. Tell me it was."

"I, ah…"

"The second was me."

Abbie whirled to find Jean-Marc just inside the neighboring hallway, a half-eaten apple in his hand.

"I don't think that–" Abbie began.

"Do you mean to say–" Auguste said.

Jean-Marc held up his index finger while hanging on to the apple. "We have had to make a little substitution," he told Uncle Gus.

The older man sat down right on top of his travel-dusted bags. "That girl…" Auguste growled, low in his throat.

"That girl would not have made a good wife to my brother," Jean-Marc said.

Auguste blinked at him. "Brother? I signed no contract for your–"

"His real name is Dellamer," Abbie told her uncle. "Jean-Marc is Philippe Dellamer's brother."

Uncle Gus's shoulders slumped. "Brother," he said softly. He set his palms firmly on his knees. "So. My daughter is not here, you are Dellamer's brother, and there is the matter of an invalid contract. And where my daughter is. And who she is with. And why you didn't send Abbie back home as soon as whatever it was happened."

Jean-Marc chewed thoughtfully on his apple. Then he said, "I found a better Babette Bourgogne to fulfill the contract. Come, let me help you to your room, and I can fill you in on the rest." He handed the apple to Abbie and reached for one of the bags. Auguste stood up to allow him access.

"The boy said she got off the wagon and took many crates with her."

Jean-Marc led them down the hall, then upstairs to the bedroom level. "She did manage to take an extraordinary lot. I have compiled an inventory of the stolen goods. She also bribed me with a fair amount of jewelry, which I have added to the list under a subsection." He gave Auguste a bow and a smile. "In case you did not truly want me to keep it. And in addition to all that, she stole Abbie's mother's crucifix. I believe that that piece is completely irreplaceable, priceless, and a part of Abbie's dowry, not Babette's."

Auguste beat on his head with his fists. "That girl! She will be the death of me yet!"

"Stop it, Uncle Gus! You'll hurt yourself." Abbie tried to pull his arms down, but she held the apple. She offered it to him instead, and after glancing at it, he decided to finish it off fiercely.

Above his bushy beard his face almost glowed with redness. "How did this happen? How did you get here on your own, Abbie?" Auguste stopped and glared at Jean-Marc. "Without a chaperone?"

"Nothing happened, Uncle Gus. In fact, we met a very nice woman with two children who decided to accompany us. She lives here in Marseille."

"Well. Well and good, then," Auguste said. His teeth ground against each other. "That's one less man I have to kill. She went with Fichaud, then?"

"Didn't Chris tell you any of this?"

"I didn't have time to stop and visit Chris, not when I was trying to play catch-up with the two who had gone on downriver. I lost much time in Avignon with people who wanted bribes to let me pass." Auguste glared around at his room as Jean-Marc dumped his bags on the big bed. Abbie opened the curtains to the two tall windows that flanked the bed.

"Fichaud. I will fire him before I kill him."

"He's gone to work with a cousin or someone in Dijon," Abbie said. "I believe that if he tries to return to his job he will find it no longer available."

"Good. No one of his family will ever work with a Bourgogne again, not as long as I or my sons live."

Jean-Marc settled on the bed, watching Auguste pace the room. "Interesting that you mention his family," he said. "Our contract was for me to deliver one virgin to my brother, and I fear I must inform you that your daughter no longer fits that description."

Auguste stopped and flexed his fists. "I will kill him with my own hands. And I will not ask for forgiveness afterward. God would not require that of me."

"By now they are married, Uncle Gus. They were going to stop and see the priest that very night."

Auguste looked hard at her at that, and then turned to Jean-Marc. "My niece is a very trusting soul," he said. "Tell me what your impression was."

"I doubt they would have thought of a priest for at least a few days," Jean-Marc said. "When they came up for air, perhaps they would remember it was time for a priest. Perhaps when her belly was rounding, they might think to visit a church."

"No!" Abbie gasped.

Jean-Marc raised an eyebrow at her and glanced at Auguste, who shook his head, covering it with his hands.

"Ah, Babette, Babette…"

His hands slid down over his eyes, then over his bearded cheeks. "Tell me what Master Dellamer has decided."

"Philippe thinks his bride has arrived in good condition." Jean-Marc nodded at Abbie. "He has not checked the inventory of the dowry yet. In fact, I don't think he's had a chance to check the contract, unless he's finally gotten to it this morning."

"He's a very busy man, Uncle. I've been trying to–"

"She's been trying to tumble the beanpot in the kitchen," Jean-Marc accused. "People's reputations will crumble if the beans are spilled."

"Scandal," Auguste whispered. "Dishonor."

"No, no, Uncle." Abbie hugged him from behind. "From what I've seen, Monsieur Dellamer is a very sensible man who will see that the blame lies only on Babette's shoulders. Not yours. He will send me home and perhaps he will demand some kind of reimbursement when he finds out, but that is all."

Auguste met Jean-Marc's eyes with the slightest of smiles. "A trusting soul, Jean-Marc."

"I've noticed. No sir, Auguste, my brother is a sensible but businesslike man. He knows a contract signed is a contract that must be fulfilled. If it is not, then others must be made aware so they do not deal with the reneger, the thief, who has tried to steal from my brother. He will offer your name far and wide as a kindness to others, that they should not find themselves in the same position when they bargain with you."

"No."

"Or…" Jean-Marc stood up in a move that seemed half-stretch. He held out his hand to Abbie. "We can make a little substitution."

Auguste turned slowly. "Abbie," he said.

"I believe her Christian name is Babette. Babette Bourgogne, the same as the name on the contract," Jean-Marc said. "Beautiful, kind, trusting, honorable Abbie. A perfect wife for my brother. Do you wish the dowry returned, sir?"

"Abbie…" Auguste's eyes narrowed as he considered her.

"The dowry, sir?"

"What? Oh. No, not yet. Not until I think this through."

"It's such a dishonest plot, Uncle," Abbie said quickly. "Surely you won't agree to trickery. At the very least God will see through it and–"

"Perhaps this is the way God wants it," Jean-Marc said. "My brother has need of a good and caring wife."

Abbie set her hands on her hips in defiance. "And you are just in this to secure your own future. Don't listen to him, Uncle Gus. He's merely after any excuse to quit his brother. He needs someone to leave him with, that's all. Anyone will do.

"Get out," Abbie hissed at Jean-Marc.

He raised an eyebrow at her and stood firm. "My house."

"Please get out." She stood glaring at him and crossed her arms in front of her chest. Finally he bowed and exited.

"What is it, child?" Uncle Gus asked.

"It's obvious, isn't it? We can't allow this charade to continue. Dellamer has to be told the truth."

"Life isn't always so black and white, Abbie."

"In this case it is. I can't lie the rest of my life to this man. My soul could not bear it. I cannot marry this man."

Uncle Gus frowned at the floor and sighed. "I should have trussed Babette up as soon as I found out about her fancy with Fichaud. I should have had her shipped here to Marseille encased in a barrel along with the wine!"

"Uncle–"

He gathered her hands in his and gazed into her eyes. "Believe me," he said, "I will come up with something. I will find a solution to this just as soon as I can think of one. Trust me, Abbie. You always trust everyone; how is it you can't trust me?"

"But…" Looking into his eyes Abbie saw only kindness and concern for her. She was lucky to have such an uncle. She sighed. "I will trust you on this."

"Good. Now let me get some rest. When is dinner around here?"

Abbie paced the house restlessly. She spied the housekeeper and told her of the state of Uncle Gus's room. It would be cleaned right after he emerged from his nap. Reassured by that a little, she walked in the gardens of the courtyard, clasping her cross with its precious splinter of the clos.

What could Uncle Gus do? Things seemed so desperate. There were no villains here– except Babette. For some reason Abbie could understand how desperate love could make one.

Abbie sat down with a thump on one of the garden benches.

Oh dear saints, she knew exactly how Babette felt. Every time Babette looked at Fichaud, was she seized with speechlessness? Did her heart thunder in her veins when his hand brushed hers? Did the sun suddenly appear whenever she caught sight of her lover?

Abbie slapped her hand over her mouth so she wouldn't cry out in horror. She couldn't be in love. She couldn't.

No. This was unacceptable. She couldn't marry Philippe, of course. Anyone could see that, because it was all deception. God had warned her of the great sin of deception with that evil bishop.

Equally of course she'd be a fool to wish to marry Jean-Marc. Jean-Marc would be gone soon. When she was sent home, he'd be out of her life. If they made her marry Philippe, Jean-Marc would be gone as soon as the first babe arrived.

No, she could not, would not be in love with Jean-Marc!

She took her cross in a steely grip. Clos Bourgogne was the reality here. That was where her life must be focused.

How long would it take for that letter to reach Chris? How long for the response to reach her? If she even had a name she could learn to love it. She could learn to make it her life.

A name to share the Clos Bourgogne with her. They could live in the neighboring village, and each day she could walk to the clos and work its precious ground. She could be useful in bringing the grapes along, in overseeing their pressing, then the fermentation and the racking. Every day she'd tread the sacred ground that her family had trod for generations.

She clasped the cross between her hands and prayed fiercely.

Was it an answer to her prayers that when she opened her eyes the first thing she saw was Uncle Gus and Jean-Marc– how the sunlight flashed upon his manly shoulders!– walking companionably across the graveled terrace toward the Dellamer offices?

So she paced and paced, even as the sun sank lower in the sky. What could they be doing that was taking so long? Why wasn't she, at the center of this entire mess, invited to their meeting? Had Jean-Marc eaten more than that apple for lunch? He looked tired today. Penned up. What would Uncle Gus come up with? Could he send up to Dijon to fetch Babette and force her to come here? Would Philippe accept her?

Certainly Philippe would never accept a pretender.

Abbie clung to her cross though it bit deep into her palm. Clos Bourgogne. Clos Bourgogne. Somehow she had to come out of this with permission to marry a man who lived near the vineyard.

Would he have Jean-Marc's laugh? Would he walk the way Jean-Marc did, so regally yet in an honorable way, too– and ofttimes with that swagger he had. Would he have the same insulting little grin of Jean-Marc's? That grin that made her want to slap it off his face sometimes… but sometimes she just wanted to blush and tingle under it.

And when he kissed… Would her senses swim the way they did with Jean-Marc? Would his voice linger along her cheek the same way?

It was almost twilight when the two reappeared. Philippe came with them. He strode next to Uncle Gus and read a long piece of paper as they talked. Jean-Marc walked quickly behind them.

He spotted Abbie and swerved to her as Philippe and Auguste kept to their course.

Abbie hopped in place, wringing her hands. "What has happened? What? Is he very angry? Is he angry at me?"

Jean-Marc put his arm around her and steered her back toward the main house. "No, he's not angry, not at all. Not at anyone."

"Not at all?"

"You worry too much. Everything is proceeding very well. I like your uncle very much, Abbie. He's a good man."

"But I don't see how—"

He turned her toward her and all she could take in was the way his eyes caught the glow of light from the sky, how warm they were under his eyelashes.

He said nothing for a moment, just looking at her face, and she waited for him. Finally he said hoarsely, "We fixed everything. Leave it to us."

It was the way he said it, his hand holding her shoulders. She could trust him. Abbie breathed a sigh of relief and smiled at him. "At last," she said.

"At last." He turned her back to the house where dinner should be served soon.

Uncle Gus and Philippe stood in the drawing room. Philippe held the paper steady on a desk and tapped excess ink from his pen back into its pot.

"It all seems in order," he said.

"We'll send the final items in time for the February run," Uncle Gus said. He looked up to see Abbie. "Ah, here's my lovely daughter now," he said as Philippe scrawled his signature verifying the marriage contract.

17

Abbie excused herself from dinner by claiming illness. Philippe politely hoped she would sleep well. He never noticed the fleets of poisoned arrows Abbie sent with her glare toward Uncle Gus and Jean-Marc before she turned on her heel and left the room.

Uncle Gus came up later and sat on her bed. "It's for the best," he told her without introduction. "This way no one's reputation is hurt and you get a fine, wealthy husband."

"I don't want a wealthy husband. I don't want Babette's hand-me-downs. I don't want Philippe. Chris is going to send me a list of eligible men who live near the clos. I'm going to live there and work in the vineyard." Abbie lifted her chin defiantly. "I could probably find a good man to take me even without a dowry. I know the grape. My skill is my dowry."

Uncle Gus sat silently, rubbing the stripes on his sleeves. Finally he heaved a great sigh. "Yes," he said, "you probably could, and you would wind up with someone, perhaps, who saw you as a way to get into the Grand Cru by our family. Do you hear what I'm saying? That they would only be interested in the wine, and not in you."

"At least they'd be interested in something Bourgogne. I don't think Philippe has actually looked at me the entire time I've been here."

"He is not one to beat his wife. There are many men out there who think nothing of returning home after work and spending a good fifteen minutes hitting their pregnant wives. He's wealthy. The marriage contract specifies that if something happens to him, you will be provided for."

"Chris says that he will take me in if something happens to Philippe."

Uncle Gus nodded thoughtfully. "Yes, that would be the best. But will you hasten Philippe's trip to the grave, Abbie?"

"What?"

"Would you… speed the natural order to send him to his death just so you could go home?"

"What!"

He gave her a hug even as her mouth hung open in shock. "No. Because you're a good and righteous girl. You wish no harm to others. You think the best of all."

A murderer! He could even consider such a thing! "If you must know the truth," Abbie said, "I don't think too much of certain people right now. You were outside all this. You were kept innocent of the sin, and now you've dug yourself neck-deep into it."

"It's for the good of the family."

"You're cheating an honest man!" Abbie pulled her fingers down the sides of her face. "You were the best of men and now you've deliberately sinned against another. How could you do this?"

Uncle clucked at her, shaking his head and grinding his palms into his knees. "Sometimes, child, the end justifies the means. He'll have a different wife but otherwise things will work out well for everyone."

"It's a lie. And it's my life, not Babette's!" Abbie's lower chin quivered. "Why does she get what she wants and I have to suffer until I die with this awful situation? And then after I die– how much longer will I suffer because of this?"

Uncle put his arm around her shoulder and squeezed her. "We'll go to church tomorrow," he promised. "You can tell the father everything in confession–"

Abbie shrank away from him. "No! No confession!"

"No confession? Abbie, you need to–"

"No!" She pushed him away. She didn't want the comfort he offered. "I refuse to confess to any priest. Not now."

Uncle Gus sucked his cheek as he regarded her. "Why don't you want to confess? You always said it made you feel so much better afterward, like you had a new soul."

She flinched at that. "Not a new soul," she said abruptly. "Never a new soul! I like the one I have. I'll keep it." With a fierce grimace she looked up at her uncle. "Say I don't have to go to confession!"

"What's happened to you?"

"Nothing's–" Abbie stopped. Uncle was innocent of the bishop's crime at least. "Something happened. At confession. In Avignon."

"At confession?" His frown told her he was trying to understand.

"An evil priest. A man of the devil and not of God."

He reached to take her into his arms. "Child," he said. "My precious Abbie, are you all right? What did he do? Where was Jean-Marc? Where was your chaperone? Ah, why wasn't I there to protect you?"

She shook her head against his beard. "I want you to tell Philippe the truth, Uncle. Tonight. He can't go on believing a lie. We shame ourselves when we do this, even more so than backing out of the contract."

"It's for the good of the family, girl. Not only for the family as it is, but for the next generation, perhaps even the generation after that. We'll strengthen our reach."

"While our foundation rots from under us!"

He tapped his forehead. "You think too much. That's something that Babette, may the saints pinch her every morning, never had to worry about. What we're talking here is practical matters. Come down from your heavenly heights and see the position we're in here on Earth. This is our chance for fame, for a reputation that will stand through the ages."

"A reputation for inferior wine."

He winced at that.

"Find a way, Uncle Gus," she pleaded. "I need to go home and work the grapes. I can make us great by giving the world a great wine with our name on it. I'll train the next generation. The Dellamers and their rivals will come beating on our doors, begging for the honor of shipping our wines. They won't need to enslave one of us to force us into the deal."

Uncle Gus rose to slowly pace the room. "This is the best way, child. In the grand scheme of things it's the smallest of lies. It's best for you and it's best for both Philippe and me. In a while you will look around and find yourself happy and wonder how you could ever have objected to this. You will deem yourself a fortunate woman."

"I will not!"

"Marriage is a most wonderful institution, Abbie," he told her. "My first marriage contract sent me shaking to the altar, but we worked it out. She was a good partner, my Bernadetta. She raised the children well– although I think now that perhaps I spoiled Babette. Well, that was my fault and not Bernadetta's. I grieved when she passed. But here I am married again and I couldn't be happier."

He raised Abbie's hands to his lips and kissed them tenderly. "You are frightened of all this. Frightened of a false contract, but also as a maiden approaching her wedding bed. You will find that it all works out if you keep your warm heart, dear Abbie. You have the kindest heart of all. I could see the good influence you had on my Babette once you came to live with us. I only wish that you'd had more time to teach her your ways."

He set her hands back down and gave her an apologetic smile before turning to the door. "Good night. Think on it tonight and you'll discover how right I am."

With that, he closed the door to her room behind him.

Several minutes passed before Abbie stood up. Then she went about the room and carefully kicked each and every piece of furniture.

The only thing it accomplished was to make her toes throb.

She opened the window to the too-cool night air and leaned out, examining the layout of the street in front of the house. Three very long blocks that way was the church, she knew. Those might be its lights in the windows that she saw. Just beyond it was an abbey.

Briskly she closed the window again and found her traveling bag. She began to pack, and when she filled it, she started loading a small trunk with the new gowns that Uncle had ordered for her. These were hers. Everything else would remain here.

Creeping downstairs, she ascertained that lights came only from deeper within the Dellamer house. She deposited her traveling bag behind the draperies of the front room and returned to her room for the trunk.

It was heavier than she'd thought. She could drag it a few steps, but then she had to stop and rest. She couldn't chance going down the main stairway; someone might come upon her there. Instead she chose the longer route by the back stairs. That might be better anyway. She could borrow a wheelbarrow from the yard and load everything in it.

A runner rug under the trunk allowed her to slide it with great difficulty to the head of the stairs. Then she had to return the rug to its proper place and then crouch in front of the trunk as it angled down the stairs: *ka-chunk. Ka-chunk. Ka-chunk.*

Did it make as much noise as it seemed? *Ka-chunk.*

No! Her skirt caught underneath it. She tried moving the trunk down one more step, easing the material out of the way, but she seemed caught even tighter.

"Let me try."

She turned to see a blacker shadow against the darkness. "Go away," she hissed.

But Jean-Marc came up behind her to heft the edge of the trunk. "What in God's teeth do you have in this thing?" he huffed quietly.

"None of your business." Hurriedly she freed herself. "Give me that."

"And where do you think you're going with it all by yourself? At this time of night? How far did you think you'd get?"

"Go! Away!"

He grabbed the chest and hoisted it, carrying it back upstairs. They spoke in whispers. "This— uff— isn't your Burgundy country. Strangers walk these streets at night, and some of them can be rough. Uncivilized men from barbarian countries comb the town with their own unspeakable notions of how to treat a woman."

She tried to let what he said slide off her. "Give me my things! Those are mine!"

He had to set the chest down to open her bedroom door. When he'd lugged his load inside, he pulled her in, too, and shut the door with his foot.

"Now," he said as he lit a candle, "tell me you weren't running away."

"I was. I was going home."

"And how were you going to afford that? You don't own any jewelry except–"

She clutched her cross to herself.

"No, I didn't think you'd sell that. Sit." He pointed to the bed.

She made no move toward it, so he grabbed her hands and pulled her as well as himself to it.

"What happened to your plan not to dishonor anyone?"

She regarded him stonily. "If that phony contract of yours states that I am the daughter of Uncle Gus–"

"It does. And it also states that only part of the dowry is to be delivered before the wedding. The rest will be sent in February." Jean-Marc shrugged. "Auguste agreed that the remainder will be considered your dowry alone."

"While the rest is Babette's, so we are still misleading your brother. I can't believe what you've done! You've made my innocent uncle into a willing sinner. Well, if your contract is a cheat and yet legal, then that must mean that I am the cheat here. So I remove myself from the deal. I leave and good riddance. Everyone will know it was my fault and not Uncle Gus's."

"But your uncle will have to pay a penalty for breaking the contract."

"He can do so with my dowry. I don't want it. I only want one thing."

Jean-Marc could clearly see how tightly she held her cross, but she held it up to him anyway. He frowned at it before he closed his hand over hers, forcing the cross back against her breast.

"My brother needs a good wife," he said.

"Your brother needs a nursemaid. Go buy him one. He couldn't tell the difference between wife and nurse anyway. He may be an excellent businessman and a wonderful brother, but he is lacking in the skills that a husband must have."

"And what skills like that would you know about?"

"A husband should be able to pick out his wife's face in a crowd. I doubt if Philippe has glanced at me twice since I've come here. We have only been together a few minutes, and never alone."

"Good," Jean-Marc said under his breath.

"No. A husband should love his wife, or at least respect her. And a husband should be there for the children. Children are supposed to look up to their father. What will they do when there's no father around because he's in his office or in bed from exhaustion?"

Jean-Marc shrugged. "If he's not here, then I'll play with them."

"You will be gone." She gazed at his dear face. "Where will you be? Where will you go? Will you go to China or just to Switzerland? Will you take passage aboard one of those ships that sail around the world? Can you really leave in one direction and return from the opposite? Would you write? Would you ever come back?"

He leaned to her so close that his breath intermingled with hers. "Would you be here?"

She whispered, "Would you dishonor your brother's wife?"

"You are not his wife yet," Jean-Marc said and pulled her to him.

Such heaven to kiss his lips again! Abbie wrapped one arm around his neck and the other firmly behind his back to secure him, but she had to release to let him kiss a burning trail along her jaw. He fondled her breasts through the thick material of her gown and kissed them the same way, but when he eased her skirt up, his fingernails dusting the bare skin behind her knee, she said,

"No. Please, Jean-Marc. Just this much."

"Abbie, Abbie, I can't sleep for thinking of you." He kissed her feverishly. "Philippe asked me if I were ill. What could I tell him? What could I say?"

She fell on him with more kisses for that. How she wanted to caress him, but the thick padding of his jerkin hindered her.

"Just this much," she panted as she scratched at the laces on it. "Just this and no more." Clumsily he tried to help her as she pulled it off.

"And for you." He reached for her laces. "Just a little and then we stop."

Her bodice followed his jerkin, and then only thin linen covered their upper torsos. It was enough. They fell into each other's arms, twisting on the bed as they explored each other with fingers and tongues and lips.

His palm was full on the cheek of her butt under her caleçons when she called a halt. They lay panting on her bed, side by side in the candlelight.

"What will you do with your freedom?" Abbie asked him.

A smile came to him as he played with her now-unbound hair. "I'll be free. I'll do anything except sit in a dark office and write figure after figure into books. I'll travel everywhere to begin with, just to see where I want to go. And then I'll build a house with my own hands and I'll start a business with them, too. I'll do everything myself and I'll never have to depend on anyone else, nor have them depend on me." He gazed at her in triumph. "I'll be free."

"I am a woman," Abbie told him. "Women are never free, not for anything in life."

"You are beautiful…"

"Which will get me the husband I want?"

"Your husband will shower you with jewels and silks. You will have this fine house."

"All I want is dirt and a grapevine to start me. I would willingly live in rags, squat with just the trees to shelter me, and be the ugliest woman on Earth." She lay against his chest and played with the lacing of his undertunic. "Wine is my freedom. They have taken that from me. All gone. All gone."

With a start, she sat up. She combed her hair back with her fingers and looked around. "I must be out of here before dawn. They'll find me in the day."

"No, no, come back here with me." Jean-Marc pulled at her arms.

"You will be gone, too, before long and in another direction. I must get home before they suck all the life from me. Let me go, Jean-Marc."

He pulled harder and she fell against him. "Hush. Hush. You can go tomorrow night. Just tonight, rest you here with me."

She put her arms around his neck and said something against his skin. He stroked her long, golden-brown hair.

Soon her breathing was deep and regular against him.

"You must marry Philippe, Abbie," he whispered before he, too, closed his eyes.

18

Jean-Marc dusted his hands as he came downstairs. He'd found Abbie's hidden bag and returned it to her room even as she still slumbered.

"Ah. Jean-Marc," Philippe said as he rounded a corner into the library. Philippe was thumbing through a great book, part of a pile he had stacked upon his desk. "You're up early this morning, considering."

"Things to do," Jean-Marc replied. What he wanted to do was return upstairs, to climb back into bed with the delectable Abbie and… His imagination fired up even as his body did, and he realized again that what he truly wanted to do would betray his brother.

But she was still asleep, her honey hair strewn across the pillow and her face smooth with innocent dreams. That chemise of hers bared tantalizing areas of flesh blushing with youth, and unveiled curves that he'd been dreaming of for weeks now. It still kept too many parts of her secret from him. Perhaps this morning would reveal all.

He wanted her in the morning light. He wouldn't take her all the way. Captain Giralbini of the Dellamers' *Fair Weather* had once bragged to him of techniques that would make even too-experienced women of the world scream with desire, and some of them would not deprive his sweet Abbie of her virginity.

How he wanted her to pant, to moan, to shout with desire for him!

"Do you remember where I put those reports from Arnaud's voyage in fall of last year?" Philippe was saying.

"It was in here last time I looked," Jean-Marc said hurriedly. "Now, if you don't need me, I'll just—"

A knock at the front door interrupted him. Jean-Marc and Philippe looked at each other before turning in the direction of the door.

"Who would be coming here at this hour?" Jean-Marc wondered as they walked down the hall to answer. "Here, and not the office?"

Their houseman had already answered. In the doorway stood Father Gaston from the cathedral and Nathalie Pelletier. The priest's gloomy black and gold-embroidered robes seemed particularly severe next to Nathalie's excessive burgundy gown. It was worked with pink roses, twining vines, and a chic translucent partlet with ruffled collar. A gauzy pink balzo in her hair completed the charming but luxurious picture.

"Hello!" she called out around the doorman before the priest could express his greetings. "Look who I found!"

"Messieurs Dellamer," the good father nodded a greeting. "I thought it was I who brought the lovely young lady along."

Nathalie tittered at his flattery while twining her arm around his, cementing it with her other hand. "We met at early mass this morning," she said. "I told him I was a friend of Abbie's. He showed me where he'd just posted the banns for the marriage, and then said he'd accompany me here while my brother makes some deliveries."

"Madame Pelletier, a pleasure to see you once again." Philippe bowed. Jean-Marc couldn't perform quite as grand a gesture; he hadn't had the *coffee* that clearly energized Philippe.

Philippe had the presence of mind to inquire, "May we offer you breakfast? Come in; make yourselves comfortable. I'm sure Cook has something prepared by now. We were up late last night with business."

The priest nodded his gray head. "Yes, I'm sure the marriage preparations are keeping you busy." He patted Nathalie's hand on his arm. "I've seen so many couples acting as if it were the ceremony that was the ultimate act, and not the eternal commitment that it serves to usher in."

"But the ceremony is quite important," Nathalie insisted with a teasing smile. "It's possibly the only day in a woman's life when she is treated with some measure of importance."

The bishop clucked disparagingly at her comment and then looked around eagerly. "You say there might be something to break my fast?"

"Where's Abbie this morning?" Nathalie asked Philippe.

"Abbie?" He looked blank for a moment and then said, "Oh."

"I think she had a late night as well," Jean-Marc said. Nathalie glanced sharply at him, her eyes squinting accusation as she assessed his body. He tried to gaze evenly at her, feigning a non-committal innocence, but she frowned.

"Have you a chaperone for her yet?" Nathalie asked. Before either brother could answer, she said, "It could be a scandal, even with the betrothal in place. She needs a chaperone. And I'd wager– if I ever wagered, Father–" she gave the priest a pretty smile, but in his eagerness to find the dining room he didn't notice, "that you haven't arranged a lady's maid for her as well. Has she been dressing herself?"

"I'm quite used to dressing myself."

Jean-Marc turned at the melodic voice. Abbie descended the stairs, her golden skirts adding even more grace to her movements. She held her chin high– such a strong woman, certain of what she wanted– but did not look at him.

Did the sun darken when he realized that? He smiled at her, ducked his head this way and that to attract her attention, but she studiously ignored him.

He blinked when Nathalie grabbed his arm and whirled him around to face the backs of the retreating bishop being led by the houseman. She gave him a little push to urge him to follow, but stayed where she was.

Philippe bowed his head to Abbie. "Good morning," he said.

"Good morning. Don't bother worrying about me. I've been dressing myself and my cousin for quite some years now."

Jean-Marc noticed Nathalie jerking her head toward Philippe even as she stared Abbie down. Abbie raised an eyebrow at her and Nathalie jerked her chin again along with a wavelike scrunching of her eyebrows that seemed some kind of code to him. Then he distinctly heard her say, "Hmmf!" under her breath so softly that Philippe could not have overheard.

She went to Philippe and wrapped her arm around his as she'd done the bishop. "Surely you don't want your marriage steeped in scandal," she urged. She wiggled her eyebrows at Abbie in such a way that Philippe couldn't see her action.

What was she doing? Jean-Marc scowled at the scene. He was missing something.

"I don't see how it–" Philippe began.

"I'm sure that with your sterling reputation, Philippe, no one would ever suspect you of doing anything inappropriate," Nathalie purred to him.

"Ah…"

"But this is an inappropriate situation," Nathalie declared. "A young lady kept alone in a house with not one, but two single gentlemen present. Some people might find that something to take advantage of."

"Surely not," Philippe declared.

"Abbie's father has arrived," Jean-Marc announced.

Nathalie stared at him, open-mouthed. "Father? I thought her father–"

"Was in Burgundy?" Jean-Marc finished smoothly for her. "Auguste Bourgogne decided to come here for the wedding."

"Auguste…" Nathalie looked from him to Abbie and back. "Oh. Ah. Oh, Abbie, you must be so happy that your father is here to look after you." Without waiting for response, she added, "But still, as the future lady of this household you simply must arrange to have a maid. Or two, I'd say. A woman of the illustrious house of Dellamer needs two maids."

"A maid," Philippe murmured.

"At least one." Nathalie leaned on his arm, looking up into his face. She batted her eyes as she smiled winningly. "But a man of your renown should have at least two ladies to wait upon his wife. She will have need of that many."

"Two maids," Philippe repeated. "I suppose I could ask around. I can see where a maid is–"

Nathalie squeezed his arm. "Two." She tilted her head as if knowing the sweet angle played up the playfulness of her expression.

Philippe sighed. "Two," he agreed.

Nathalie laughed lightly. "You are quite the wise man," she declared. "You'll discover that once you are married your social circles will expand like high tide coming in with a storm. You'll be invited everywhere– simply everywhere!– and the both of you must be prepared for it." She rubbed her hand up and down his arm. "You look so fine this morning. I assume that you have at least two servants to help you."

Philippe swallowed. "Actually, I've been awake and at work for quite some time. And I dress myself. No reason to rouse the servants with my odd hours."

Nathalie let out an injured squeal. "How you do abuse yourself! First with your long work hours and now with no help. A man of your station, Philippe Dellamer, should have all the help he needs and deserves."

With that, she glanced again at Abbie, and again made the chin-jerk. "Here," she told Philippe, "your fiancée should be on your arm, not me."

With that she pointedly crossed to Abbie. "Like puppies and babies," Jean-Marc heard her say as she dragged her over to Philippe, then placed his arm firmly around Abbie's.

"There," she declared. "What a pretty picture you two make."

Philippe's eyes switched back and forth with discomfort that Jean-Marc might ordinarily have seen, but a haze filled his sight, dark and focused on where Philippe and Abbie's bodies met.

This is what they would do once they were married. And on their wedding night…

Jean-Marc pictured Philippe as turning back the linens from Abbie's body. Of Philippe burying his face in Abbie's hair, tasting her neck, fondling her body… Of his skin sliding over her nakedness. Him sinking into her and taking her with all the power of their holy marriage behind him.

Of her moaning Philippe's name.

Of him enjoying her. Any time he wished.

Of her curled up against him afterward, her honeyed hair splayed upon his chest.

"Jean-Marc?"

Philippe was asking him something. Jean-Marc had to force his jaws to unclench. "I'm sorry," he said in a voice that sounded angry even to him. "Must have been daydreaming for a moment. What was that again?"

"I was telling Abbie that Father Gaston works at the boys' orphanage across town. You've spent quite some time there teaching, haven't you?"

"Yes." It was still difficult to talk. "Yes," he repeated, "sometimes I teach them their numbers, and sometimes geography."

"Why, how kind of you, Jean-Marc," Nathalie said.

"If not for the kindness of my brother," and Jean-Marc nodded toward Philippe, "I would have been raised there."

"Nonsense," Philippe said.

"Oh no, it's true. I was motherless, fatherless, and Philippe was left with the business to run. Uncle Leo was in little shape to help him. Phil had no time or need to raise a young brother."

The sight of Abbie's arm on Philippe pained him to the core. She was his gift to Philippe. "But he did," Jean-Marc said. "He has been as loving a brother to me as there has ever been in this world, and somewhat of a father besides."

"We are family," Philippe replied gravely, though the smile he held for Jean-Marc was sentimental. "We are the only ones left to carry on."

"So you are the last of your line as well," Abbie said as if caught in a remote daydream of her own. "You have survived, Philippe, and not only that, but prospered as well."

"I have done very well, these past ten years especially. I have devoted myself to the company."

Abbie nodded. "And it's paid off. You believe in working to one's own strengths, don't you?" She glanced quickly at Nathalie and then lifted her face to Philippe's with a glorious smile.

Jean-Marc's fingernails bit into his own palms.

Leaning into Philippe's arm, Abbie continued, "Sometimes a woman has strengths that lie outside the household. For instance, I am a vintner. Everyone back home knows that. Don't you think that a family as…as fine and… grand as this one should have a vineyard in its holdings? I could run it for you. I mean, as your wife." She flashed him another smile.

But he'd hardly looked at her. He shook his head. "I don't think so," he said. "A wife should be head of the household. It's what wives do."

The smile disappeared from Abbie's face. "I know almost nothing about running households. As little as you do, I'd guess."

Jean-Marc glanced around his familiar home. Perhaps the place was a little dusty, with dirt showing on the wall hangings and furniture. He rubbed a thumb over the arm of a wooden chair. It was dull, old-looking, the carved grooves embedded with the leavings of the years.

"Philippe spends his time on the company," Jean-Marc said. "He has no time to keep up with the house."

Nathalie bustled over to Abbie. First she patted Abbie, then Philippe's arm. "Not to worry," she declared. "I know everything about household management. It is a rare and exciting art form; you'll see, Abbie. I'll teach you everything that I know."

"And in return shall I teach you everything I know about the grape?" Abbie asked archly.

"I know," Jean-Marc interrupted. He must keep Abbie happy. He must keep her here with Philippe. "I'll send for your cousins. They can come here and learn from you."

Abbie turned her green eyes to his– finally, finally!– and listened to his offer.

"We'll plant grapes in the gardens," Jean-Marc babbled. "No, we'll buy a small vineyard in the hills, just a short ride away. Yes, that will do. And you can teach your cousins there, Abbie. You'll be able to care for your own grapes and you'll be able to help your own family as well."

How pleased he was at his cleverness! He stood there and grinned at his sweet Abbie and was rewarded when her face changed from sullen to considering. Her eyes brightened to gaze in interest upon him.

Jean-Marc swam in happiness. He was in Abbie's good graces again.

At this time of year it seemed strange to Abbie to sit in the gardens and work while wearing only a shawl over her dress. But the sun shone bright and clear, and the courtyard cut off the cool breeze blowing from the north. Flowers of frilly yellow and orange still bloomed, including the one that had been set outside her door this morning.

She knew it was not from Philippe.

She attacked her sewing with renewed determination. Her bodice and a sleeve had ripped slightly last night when they came off so quickly, and her chemise held several tears, easy enough to repair.

Again and again she replayed within her mind the night's conversation. Twice– twice she had told Jean-Marc that she loved him and not once had he ever returned the sentiment.

Not once.

She stabbed at the material in front of her and vowed that she would not cry.

Jean-Marc had his mind on other climes. Perhaps he looked forward to more casual dalliances with other foolish girls. How many times had he told her he would never marry? She could not lower herself to become a man's throw-away lover.

And neither would she ever relent to be a throw-away wife, just to be used to bed and begat heirs for a stranger. She would not have her own soul consigned to Purgatory because she had conspired to deceive an honest man.

Uncle Gus snored peacefully in the chair next to her. It was difficult to think of him sitting in Purgatory with her, but there he would be. That brought a small smile to her face. At least Purgatory wouldn't be too boring. And perhaps… perhaps Jean-Marc would be there as well. Her heart beat faster to think that they might be enchained in Purgatory together for a century or two. Could Purgatory be Heaven in disguise?

Uncle's snores cut painfully through her thoughts, and she returned to the material world with decisions to be made.

If she split the contents of her small trunk into two bags, she could more easily maneuver them in her escape to freedom. Uncle Gus had bags she could borrow. She had unpacked them for him yesterday evening; she knew where they were.

Part of that breeze found its way to her now, along with male voices. As she looked up, she gathered the shawl around her shoulders more closely. Far across the courtyard Philippe and Jean-Marc emerged from the stone offices. Then a squeal of poorly-lubricated hinges caught her attention from the opposite side of the yard: someone was opening the iron gates.

Two horses and a small, neat carriage entered the courtyard. Abbie stood up, squinting against the high sun. A woman sat behind the driver, a wide hat throwing her face into shadow. It must be Nathalie again– how nice! A private visit with her friend was precisely what Abbie needed.

Nathalie might have some ideas. Why, Nathalie's house might be a good place to hide until she could cement her plans.

"Here, Uncle, wake up," she urged him with a nudge. With a sput he roused himself. "I want you to meet my friend Nathalie."

She walked ahead to let him waken at his own rate, and the carriage turned in the driveway to stop in front of the main entry to the house. The driver dismounted and reached up a hand to help his passenger descend.

"Nathalie!" Abbie called, and the woman's head swung around to her.

Abbie stopped in her tracks.

"Babette," she whispered to herself.

19

Babette let out a shriek and then ran down the walkway to embrace her cousin. "Oh, Abbie! Abbie! There you are! For a while I thought I should never see you again!"

"Babette." Abbie stood paralyzed.

"Is this the Dellamer house? Oh my, it's an estate. It's magnificent. He must be very rich, this Dellamer. Very rich."

"Babette." Abbie tried to get her mouth to say something more. "Why are you here?"

"Oh, do get someone to take my bags and trunks," she said. "What does this man want? A gratuity? Everywhere I went, there were men wanting things called tips. Bribes, I call them. I mean, they can't be bothered to do something out of common courtesy. I believe I've gone through most of my money just in getting here."

She flounced back to the carriage and deposited a single coin into the driver's hand. As soon as she'd turned away he gave her a rude gesture, and once the last of the boxes and bags had been unloaded, fairly galloped his team out of the courtyard. A boy swung the squealing gates closed behind him.

"Babette!" Uncle Gus shouted from behind Abbie. "It is! You ungrateful little girl! You wanton snip of a–"

Abbie caught him by his shoulders. "Philippe is coming," she said quietly and nodded to the curious men across the courtyard.

Uncle Gus followed her gaze and set his jaw. Then he turned to put his back to the Dellamers and pointed at Babette so his hand would be hidden from their view. "You will be quiet during this," he said. "You will listen and play along. No questions. I won't have you messing up this contract again."

"What are you–?"

"You be quiet. I don't want to hear a word from you until I tell you to say something. You hear your father, girl?"

Babette's lower lip protruded in a pretty pout. "Yes, Papa."

Gus turned with a smile as Philippe and Jean-Marc came closer. "Look here, it is little cousin Babette, come to see my daughter wed!"

"Babette," Philippe murmured as if the name rang a bell.

"I told you, they are all named Babette," Jean-Marc assured him. "What a surprise to see you, Babette. The last I saw you I could have sworn you were setting off to Dijon."

Babette glanced at her father and then merely smiled, offering them a small curtsy.

"Well, more relatives." Philippe scratched the back of his head. "Will there be more to arrive?"

"Actually, we weren't expecting my niece," Uncle Gus said. "She won't impose on your hospitality but for a few days. Long enough to arrange travel home for her."

"Ah. Well." Philippe bowed to Babette. "Welcome to our house. Since you'll be here for so short a time, perhaps we should move the wedding up, eh? Perhaps this Saturday. Get it over with. I wonder if the bishop could be persuaded."

Abbie squeaked in spite of herself, but the sound was covered up by Babette's declaration.

"You must be Philippe Dellamer." The young woman and her wide-brimmed hat stepped forward so far that Philippe had to ease backward. "No one said you were so handsome a man."

She thrust her face into his, and he made another backstep. "Thank you," he murmured. "You are a cousin of, ah, Abbie's?"

"She's my brother's girl," Uncle Gus said quickly.

Babette reached to take the edge of Philippe's gown between her fingers to test its quality. "And not at all old. They all said you were an old man."

Jean-Marc stepped between the two. "I don't believe the subject of Philippe's age ever came up," he said. "But then, what would it matter to you? You were about to be married to a local boy, weren't you? Or didn't you go through with it?"

Reluctantly, Babette drew her gaze away from Philippe and regarded Jean-Marc coolly. "You were mistaken," she said. "The man actually expected me to clean for him. And cook. And he lived in the smallest hovel I've ever seen. It was even stone, not timber– can you imagine? I've heard it gets very cold in those old stone country houses. Burgundy gets very cold in winter."

Jean-Marc met Uncle Gus's eyes.

"Come along, girl," Gus said abruptly. "Let's get you settled in a room. In Abbie's room. I'll tell you all about this place."

Abbie almost protested against the arrangement that had been theirs for the past four years. Babette in her room. There would be no chance of meeting Jean-Marc there again. There would be little chance of sneaking out in the middle of the night, unless Babette were truly so tired she wouldn't hear.

Perhaps Abbie could slip something into her drink at dinner to make her sleep soundly.

"I'll see to her, Unc– unless you would like to help," she finished lamely.

"We will both see to her. Family is family." Uncle Gus grabbed Babette's arm with such force that she almost cried out. He led her by it all the way to the house.

Abbie scrambled behind them to get Babette's remaining baggage. She could handle the one smaller bag, but the larger one– Jean-Marc reached for it, lifting it easily, and settled it onto one arm.

"I'll just deliver this and return," he told his brother over his shoulder. Philippe nodded and turned to the study entrance. Quietly to Abbie, Jean-Marc added, "You can sleep in my room tonight if she snores." He gave her a light squeeze on her butt and she jumped.

He laughed at her.

Abbie swung her bag in a full circle that would have caught him squarely in the chest if Babette's other bag hadn't protected him. "You can take this up as well," she huffed. With steely gaze she held the door open for him, and he had the audacity to grin at her.

As soon as he was inside, he dropped his burdens and whirled on her, pinning her against the wall just inside the partially-open door that shielded them from view.

"I liked last night," he whispered in her ear. His tongue swept down over her neck, and she shivered despite herself. "The cold sometimes descends here, too. We'll keep warm under the covers together. Tonight. After she falls asleep. I'll be waiting for you, *chérie*."

"I am not some kind of, of…"

"Tart, like your cousin?"

"She is not– She isn't…"

"I'm afraid she is, cabbage."

"Cabbage." Abbie spat the word back at him. "How can you call me that?"

He tweaked her collar and grinned at her anew. "What would you prefer me to call you?"

"Last night I told you I loved you, and you didn't say a word."

"Last night I was busy doing other things." His hand rose to cup her breast as he leaned down for a kiss. She didn't kiss back.

Instead, she pushed at him. "You are a cad."

"A bounder, yes, yes, we've been through all that before. I didn't hear you complaining last night. In fact… What was it you said? 'Oooo, Jean-Marc,'" he whispered in falsetto. "'Oh, Jean-Marc. Oh darling, do that again.'"

Abbie flushed red and pushed with all her might, sending him stumbling back. She stomped off.

"Tonight," he said with a laugh.

"My cousin is here," she replied. "I'm sure that everything can be straightened out now."

That sent him running to catch up, leaving the luggage behind. He whirled her around. "No," he told her. "Things may be confused, but they are not to that point. That girl is never going to set foot in this house again. She's a tramp and a gold-digging thief. She would spend all my brother's money and then ignore him once he'd finished supplying her with what she wanted."

"She's a tramp," Abbie huffed. "And yet you give me an invitation for tonight. That would make me a tramp, wouldn't it?"

Jean-Marc gathered her to himself, despite her struggles to get away. "You could never be dishonorable," he told her fiercely. "You are my Abbie, and you are all I can think about. Tonight– Tonight I will not dishonor you. We will only go as far as we did last night. But I must have you again, Abbie. Please."

The look she gave him held ice. "And tonight I'll tell you that I love you and again you'll be silent."

"I can never marry, *chérie*. I must be free. But I can give you to my dear brother. He is the best I can give to you."

That ice settled in Abbie's heart. "So be it," she said. "Enjoy your freedom, Jean-Marc. And get Babette's luggage."

Uncle Gus looked up long enough to see who was entering the room and then continued laying down the new rules for Babette: "You will not approach Monsieur Dellamer that way! For shame, Babette. You gave him up. He is yours no longer. You will do nothing to embarrass Abbie before the wedding, either. Close the door, Jean-Marc."

Jean-Marc hurried in, dropping the bags next to the bed.

Uncle Gus pointed at Jean-Marc. "This is the brother of Dellamer," he said.

"Oh ho, so we're not the only ones to have kept a secret," Babette smirked from where she sprawled across the pillows.

"I will tell you another secret," Jean-Marc told her. "I don't like you."

She stuck out her tongue at him. "And I don't like you. He stole extra jewelry from me, Papa. Make him give it back."

"The jewelry he took was from what you stole from me, girl," Gus growled. "You've cost me far more than I bargained for."

Now Abbie spoke. From the shadowed corner where she'd been sitting, she rose and drew up to her full height. "I'm afraid I will cost a little more, Uncle," she said. "You two revised the marriage contract when you tried to pass me off with a lie. Now you will have to rewrite it again."

Uncle Gus glanced at her and saw the steel in her eyes. "What do you mean, Abbie?"

"I need to serve the family in a way that makes sense. I want the clos and the winery. I want access to it in some form. I want to be able to work there. I want to be able to live in a room or a barn or a shed somewhere near it, whenever I wish. Take back what you added to the contract and add that instead."

"Your husband will not let you live somewhere else."

"Philippe doesn't even know I'm alive. All he wants is someone to make babies with. I will drop two babies for him, enough to fulfill anyone's idea of a contract, and then I shall be off. No doubt he will be the happier for my absence. Who wants a stranger living in one's home?"

"No woman would ever demand such a thing!"

"Uncle, I am a fury, not a woman. I am a trapped animal with teeth bared, ready to do anything to get what I need. I am an Amazon willing to battle to save my home. Alter the contract or I will tell Philippe exactly what is going on. He will have Babette, and I will stay with Chris to find a husband near the clos."

"You think you're funny," Jean-Marc growled.

"I am deadly serious."

Uncle Gus stared. Finally he pointed at her and said, "This is your mother in you. She was always stubborn."

"Yes, she was," Abbie said proudly.

"Once she got her head set on something, she wouldn't budge." Uncle Gus looked at Jean-Marc. "Could we do it?"

Babette picked at her bowl. "What is this stuff?" she asked.

Nathalie nodded at Babette. "It's bouillabaisse, dear," she said. "And Cook has done a fine job with it. It's been years since I've had some. How I've missed it! Monsieur Dellamer, I for one truly appreciate your superb hospitality."

Philippe gave her a little bow over his own setting. "I am pleased that you approve, Mme. Pelletier."

Abbie watched as the others at the table– Uncle, Jean-Marc, Nathalie, Paul and another brother, as well as the bishop who was to perform their wedding, and two assistant priests, one of whom was Father Gaston– went at their dinner.

"Ew," Babette groaned, and Abbie kicked her hard under the table.

Philippe leaned to Uncle Gus. "How old did you say she was?"

"Oh, younger than she looks, Philippe. Much younger. She is still a child. I'm afraid we spoil our children in the country."

Babette gave him a nasty look.

The bishop smiled benevolently at them. "The banns need to be posted a full six weeks before the wedding," he told Philippe.

His tonsured colleague gave a thoughtful look that almost seemed unrehearsed. "If they wish to speed up the wedding, perhaps we can bend the rules," the rotund man offered. "A gift to the new wing of the monks' dormitories would please the cardinal enough that he could overlook the impropriety, hm?"

"Why, yes," the bishop said too quickly. "A generous gift. If you are that eager to be wed, Monsieur Dellamer, it won't be that much of an encumbrance to you to–"

Philippe waved his hand as if swiping the thought away from himself. "Yes," he said. "Whatever. Tell me what you need and I'll consider the sum."

"Excellent. A ceremony at the end of the week; I believe we can gain license from the cardinal for that."

Jean-Marc cleared his throat. "Now, about that contract, Philippe. Auguste and I have been talking, and I did speak at length with Christopher– he's the son who runs the Clos Bourgogne– when we were there. It seems that Abbie has a real feel for the grape. She's the family's leading expert on horticulture and fermentation. It's a shame to waste those talents. Clos Bourgogne is a Grand Cru, and the way it's going to remain that way is if she can give the family some pointers every now and then about the place."

"Then that should have been written into the contract in the beginning, shouldn't it?" Philippe dabbed the corner of his mouth with his finger. He lifted a plate of fresh bread and handed it to his right. "Some bread, Madame?" he asked Nathalie.

"Do call me Nathalie."

"But if Clos Bourgogne remains a Grand Cru," Uncle Gus said, "it will make more money for you when you ship it."

"Hm. That's true enough. I shall think about it."

Abbie grimaced at Uncle Gus significantly.

"Please try to think about it before the wedding," Uncle Gus said.

The bishop picked up his wineglass. "This chablis certainly is a fine one," he said. "And you say the Bourgogne Grand Cru is even better?"

"Burgundy is a wine for the most educated of palates," Philippe said to all around the table, nodding last to Nathalie. "And Clos Bourgogne Grand Cru is the best of the burgundies. I was saving it for dessert."

"I look forward to it," Father Gaston said with a contented smile. "We can make the final decisions for the wedding. Shall we set three days from now as the date?"

In the tense darkness of that night, as Babette lay breathing deep and regularly beside her, Abbie heard someone approach her bedroom door. She thought she heard her name whispered through the crack, but she made no move to investigate. Again she heard her name, and then something large and bulky slid to the floor in the hallway.

After a long time whoever it was finally left.

20

With the wedding being in two days, there were things to be done this morn– though what, Abbie had no idea. She wasn't about to wake up that lay-a-bed, Babette, to ask her. Abbie hoped she slept the next three days away at least so she'd miss witnessing Abbie's shame. At least she'd slept through Abbie's search through her bags, seeking her mother's crucifix.

Abbie had found it at last, and wore it now in triumph along with the other. Its presence gave her a feeling of determination such as if her mother were beside her, giving her advice to stand up for herself. Her mother had indeed been a strong woman.

But "We must prepare for the reception," was all that occurred to her as the family finished a breakfast that Philippe actually attended.

He waved his fingers off-handed at her. "Do whatever you wish," he said.

"But how many guests are there to be? What time of day will this be held? How much food do we need to serve? How long will the reception go on?" Abbie asked.

"I suppose you can decide all that."

Abbie glanced at her uncle, then at Jean-Marc, who did not seem to be in a good mood for he kept scowling at her. She scowled back at the uncaring lout.

"Do we need to provide anything special for the ceremony?" Abbie asked Philippe. "And how about– afterward? Do we need anything here to… Ah…"

Philippe sipped the last of his *coffee*. "Whatever you wish should be good enough, so long as you are not too extravagant. We do not have to put together a spectacle to amuse the entire city, as I have seen far too many people do." He wiped his fingers on the tablecloth and rose.

"I will be in the office most of the day. Please inform me of anything I will need to know."

Abbie pushed back in her chair, scraping it loudly, and also stood up. "Would you be so kind as to tell me if you're planning to attend the wedding? Or will you be conducting business in your office during that as well?" she said sweetly, belying the thrust of her jaw and the fists on her hips.

Jean-Marc choked. Uncle Gus cried, "Abbie!" And Philippe actually paused to turn around to fully gaze at her.

"Of course I will attend," he said slowly. He looked at his brother, who now included him in his scowl. "Have I missed something?"

"Yoo hoo!" a familiar voice called from the outer door.

"Nathalie!" Abbie breathed a sigh of relief. Help at last. Perhaps even an escape route.

With two burly brothers behind her, Nathalie swept into the dining room all smiles. She halted as she surveyed the scene. "Whatever has happened?" she asked.

Abbie pointed at Philippe. "He is going to work all day today and doesn't offer a hint as to what I should do to prepare for a wedding or inviting people or a reception or… afterward. Not anything!"

Nathalie covered her mouth with a shocked hand as Philippe bit his lip.

"He will go work all day and probably all night as well," Abbie accused, "and tomorrow he will be too tired to do anything of any import. If indeed he decides to show up at the wedding, he will probably collapse from exhaustion in the aisle!"

Nathalie cluck-clucked. "We can't have that. No, not at all."

"The lady exaggerates," Philippe said quickly.

Propped on his elbows at the table, Jean-Marc settled his chin upon his palm. "No, I'm afraid Abbie has you pegged right, Philippe. You can't work today. Or tomorrow or the next."

"But there's work to be done."

"There is always work to be done," Jean-Marc countered. "It will wait a day or three. Perhaps even four without the world coming to an end. I'll talk to Gerard to see what he can do."

"Just for today you can put it off," Abbie said. "I really have no idea what to do. Back home the families provided a meal outside the church or inside the inn just down the road if the weather wasn't good."

"Musicians," Uncle Gus put in. "Some of the boys get together and play for everyone. Jean Cowherd's middle boy– he's a clever one with the pipe, he is. You can't sit still when he plays."

"Some of the boys down on the docks can make a good tune," Jean-Marc said. "I'll see if they'll play for us."

Nathalie said, "There are better musicians available, I'm sure. Professional ones. We can't have just anyone playing at a Dellamer wedding. Paul, Luke– you can think of someone, can't you?"

Her two brothers stood there scratching their heads and muttering possibilities, uncomfortable to be caught in such a domestic upset of another family.

Abbie nodded. "All right. Back home some guests bring extra food in case there isn't enough, and everyone dances and eats until they're all too tired or drunk and go home. I don't know how people in Marseille get married. I know no one outside of Nathalie here. What I need is some guidance."

She centered Philippe in the target of her gaze. "If you wish to go back to work immediately after the reception, please feel free to do so. But we all require your advice until then."

Philippe looked around the room at the anxious faces aimed in his direction. From his own expression it was obvious he'd caught the consequences of no wedding night from his bride-to-be.

Nathalie waved her hands in the air to wipe all the negative emotions out of it and bustled to Philippe's side. "Tut-tut, Abbie," she said. "Men get wedding jitters, too. Philippe just wants to hide himself in his work instead of facing the reality that he, too, is getting married. He knows how great a step this is even for such an important man of industry as he."

Subtly, she motioned from Abbie to Philippe with her chin, wiggling her eyebrows at her.

"If we could get a list of your friends, Philippe," Abbie said quickly, "we could start writing some invitations. And, and–"

"And your favorite foods," Nathalie put in. "We'll have them served at the reception. There won't be any need for others to bring food because a good host supplies more than enough for all. Oh, it will be here, won't it? You have such a lovely home. We'll need to get the staff to make sure the public areas at least are in top shape, and the gardens, too, if the weather holds. And the valuables put away in case pilferers sneak in with the crowd. Your cook staff will need some temporary help, Philippe."

"You need to finish working on the marriage contract," Abbie insisted. "That comes first."

"Bed linens," Nathalie countered. "A new marriage requires new ones. Come, let's see your rooms, Philippe, so we can figure what is needed."

The Venise brothers and Uncle Gus took turns writing short, scratchy invitations from the list Jean-Marc came up with as Nathalie led Abbie and Philippe through each room of the house, taking inventory. Her hold was firm and uncompromising on both their upper arms.

Their tour woke Babette from her sleep. Nathalie riffled through Abbie's gowns, clucking to herself. "This will do," she finally decided, "but it needs some adjustments. We'll take it along." She stuffed the voluminous material into Philippe's unquestioning arms and then trotted down the hall to go through his own selection of clothing.

She tsked there as well. "You look very nice in these long gowns, Philippe," she declared, "but they give you such a serious air! Why, look at your brother. He's wearing trunk hose today– such a fine choice for a man who still has some life in him, don't you think?"

"I, ah, don't own any trunk hose." Philippe muttered.

"Easily enough taken care of. Now come along!" Nathalie snapped her fingers and the two fell into place behind her command.

Jean-Marc returned to the house from a quick reconnoiter with a small mob of neat-looking peasants, followed by rough dock-workers. "We're hiring these for three days to help," he announced before handing them over the housekeeper.

Nathalie took fifteen full minutes to address matters of housekeeping with the woman, then another twenty detailing the menu for the next day even as Abbie quizzed Philippe about the dishes he preferred.

"Is this going to cost a lot?" he finally asked weakly. Perhaps it was the description of a swan to be roasted and then presented with all its feathers pasted back on that seemed a questionable expenditure.

Jean-Marc grabbed him by the front of his gown and swung him around so they met face-to-face. "God's teeth, this is your wedding, man!" he yelled jovially. "Be thankful she's not calling for it to wear a gold crown with sweetmeats as jewels." But when he turned away again from his brother, the smile slid from his face.

"I'll need a new dress," Babette hinted as they all rode into center ville in the Dellamer's splendid, spacious carriage.

"You have a trunk full of new dresses," Uncle Gus said. "Sit and be quiet, girl."

Nathalie patted Abbie's hand as the younger girl fretted. This was going much too fast. They were missing the important things.

"The contract," she said again and again between stops. "Home. Clos Bourgogne."

At least Philippe nodded at her when she said that. But the day was long.

Nathalie dragged the two of them into the finest tailor's shop Abbie had ever imagined. She held up the offending outfits from both of them.

"Slashing," she announced, and both Abbie and Philippe cried out, reaching for their garments.

Nathalie swept the clothing out of their reach. "You two must keep up with the times," she told them.

"But that's a perfectly good—" Abbie and Philippe said at the same time. They looked at each other, then frowned at Nathalie.

"I will not stand to have my best clothes destroyed," Philippe said. His tone was not neutral. In fact, it held a definite threat.

Nathalie shifted the clothes to one arm and waved the other arm in the air, snapping her fingers. Three tailors scurried to her side. The owner of the shop, Master Ganse, held a handful of what looked like long fritters done in cloth.

"Appliqués," Ganse explained. "We can sew a few to your clothing–"

"To make it appear as if you both had paid some attention in the past ten years to fashion trends," Nathalie inserted.

Master Ganse bobbed his head, as if beseeching Philippe not to include him as agreeing with Nathalie's opinion. He said, "Later if you find that people have not exclaimed over the beauty of your clothing, we can remove them and no harm done. But this will look very good, very good indeed."

With a raise of her eyebrow in Philippe's direction and a toss of her head, Nathalie said, "And Master Dellamer must have a set of trunk hose made up. Several sets, in fact. It's his new look."

The tailor fingered the fine material of Philippe's only short gown and the pretty, if not so expensive, fabric of Abbie's dress. "Yes," he murmured, "I can work well with this." With a sudden roar he shouted, "Wife!"

Who was this mouse who scampered out of the back room? She hunched and held her arms over her chest, ducking her head as if expecting a blow.

"Wife," Master Ganse ordered, "get the needles and thread. Our finest silk thread, of course," he nodded a bow to Philippe.

The woman quick-shuffled to the back while the assistant tailors began to spread the garments out on their long wooden tables.

In moments the woman reappeared. She held the thread and implements out like an offering to her husband.

Instead he slapped it all from her hands.

"Does that thread look to you like it remotely matches these outfits?" Master Ganse shouted at her. She cowered. "Have you not a lick of sense in that stupid head of yours?" He held up Philippe's gown. "Burgundy cloth– burgundy thread!"

She cowered even more, winding up on the floor in a heap. Silent tears streamed down her face.

Master Ganse heaved her up with one hand and slapped her hard with the other.

"Here, here!" Philippe cried. "There's no need to–"

"With all respect, Master Dellamer," Ganse said between gritted teeth that he tried to form into a polite smile. "This is my wife, and she has not a brain in her ugly little head. This is the only way to keep her under control." He gave his wife a push and she ran to the back storeroom. "Hurry! And get it right this time!" he shouted at her.

He turned to see the horror on the group of faces. Now he became all smiles. He spread his arms out in supplication. "Thank Heaven the good Lord has given husbands all rights over our wives," he said. "Women are too stupid and simple to survive without a strong man in their lives. I have to be stronger than most, for my wife is far stupider than most."

Jean-Marc muttered something to Philippe that sounded like, "In the future take your business elsewhere," but Ganse did not hear.

The correct thread was brought, and the tailors fell to their task with great speed, urged on by Ganse's low threats that he thought he'd hidden from his clients.

Faux slashing. Abbie watched the first piece applied onto her dress sleeves and indeed, it did give the illusion of a slash with fine underlinen pulled through.

"All right," Philippe said uncertainly as he viewed the result. "I suppose I can live with that. The clothing must be finished by tomorrow."

"See?" Nathalie whispered to Abbie. "Philippe's quite trainable under a clever woman's tutelage. The truly intelligent ones always are. But like a dog, you must remember to reward them afterwards." And she gave her a lascivious wink.

Just a few weeks ago Abbie wouldn't have known what that wink implied. Now she did. Her… and Philippe? Her stomach tightened and she tried to hide her trembling.

Think of the clos, she told herself firmly. *Only this way can you get home!* Would the torture of having to do… *that* with Philippe be worth the clos?

The master tailor's mouse-wife scurried anew through the shop to fulfill her husband's order.

No, *that* was torture. That was Hell on Earth. Philippe wouldn't be like that. A husband who ignored her was to be desired far more than one who delighted in such personal cruelty.

Was this marriage compromise one to be fought so dearly? "The contract," she reminded Philippe, and he nodded.

"I will consider it as soon as we return home," he told her.

Exotic spices, bed linens, pillows for the public rooms, special dishes for the reception, a band arranged, two jugglers hired, cut flowers ordered, the delivery of a hefty payment to the bishop for the quickening of the banns… After all their emergency errands, they still had to deliver their invitations throughout the city. After that even Philippe insisted that due to Nathalie's great kindness it was merely fitting that they see her and her brothers safely home.

It wasn't until the exhausted crowd returned home to a light supper and a madhouse of cleaning that they finally got around to revisiting the subject of the marriage contract.

This time when the men adjourned to Philippe's office across the courtyard, Abbie invited herself and followed.

"You say she needs to advise?" Philippe asked his brother.

But it was Abbie who answered. "I need to be there to oversee the pruning, the mulching, the harvest and pressing, and the racking at the very least. I need to keep the books."

"Books?" Philippe perked up at that. His own account books were stacked all around his tall-ceilinged office.

"We keep records of experiments," Abbie said. Her eyes sparked with life now. At the very least, she had the clos within her grasp, if only for a short while every now and then.

Uncle Gus nodded. "My great-great… How many is it, Abbie?… great grand-father was a Cistercian monk," he said. "They experimented with the grape and kept notes of what worked and what did not. Our last vineyard master was an ex-Cistercian. Though we are not a monastery," he gave a little smile, "we keep up the experiments so we can produce the finest wine."

"Experiments?" Philippe frowned at that. "I prefer the safe, conservative route."

Abbie shrugged. "If we want to be conservative and always produce a fair wine, we can grow five or six types of grapes and combine them all. But if we want to grow a great wine, we grow the best version of the pinot noir we can find."

He looked unconvinced.

"My f– uncle was about to experiment with Dutch candles when he died," Abbie said. "The Dutch have a way of treating the barrels so the wine keeps longer."

"And if the wine keeps longer, we can ship it farther," Jean-Marc urged.

Why did he even bother to endorse her arguments? He would be gone soon as if he'd never existed. "I can show you our books," Abbie said. That hollow space that was eating at her heart could be filled again by going home and working the vines. "You come back with me and you can read all the improvements we've made. That's why the Clos Bourgogne is the best, and it will stay that way if we keep experimenting."

Philippe twirled his quill slowly between his fingers as his gaze focused far away. "I don't know," he said slowly. "There's something in this that bothers me. It doesn't seem such a marriage contract as a business contract."

"When was that ever different? Are we not marrying the two businesses?" Abbie asked. "We want them both to thrive."

The night wore on and the lights in the main house went out even as decisions were made in the office.

"Back to the clos at harvest for two and a half to three months, then one month in spring to oversee the pruning," Philippe finally read from the document. "Otherwise, Christopher Bourgogne is in charge of the vineyard."

Jean-Marc leaned over the desk, reading the contract upside-down. "I would not allow my wife to be gone from me a third of each year," he said softly to his brother.

"Philippe is a busy man," Abbie said briskly. "He will never even notice I am gone. Now, where do I sign?" She pushed Jean-Marc's arm out of the way as she reached for the quill. She knew there was no space for her in the contract, but she made one anyway.

The next day three letters came, all bundled together. They were from Aunt Danielle, directed to the two girls and her husband. The formal handwriting told Abbie that they'd been dictated to a church cleric.

Abbie took hers to a sunny corner to read. Aunt Danielle had no clue of Babette's perfidy. To her Abbie was still uncontracted and free to choose her future husband from the entire city of Marseille.

"Make sure you choose for love, dear Abbie," she wrote. "Marrying for the family's wishes can lead only to a lifetime and beyond of misery. Be aware that what you do now affects how you will live the rest of eternity in Heaven."

Abbie was still lost in thought considering her aunt's situation when the Venise carriage pulled up with Nathalie and one unlucky brother as passengers, as well as young Charles and Henri.

"It seems my sons both saved up energy from their long trip," she apologized. "Having them around all our family's glass…" She made a face, shuddered to herself, and put the two on the cleaning crew.

Nathalie inspected the progress within the house with approval. "You have good staff, Philippe," she said. "All they need is the proper supervision." Then it was time to sally forth to pick up the items they had ordered the previous day, everything but the food and flowers.

Philippe gracefully bowed out, since there were no decisions to be made, and promised he'd work hard so that he could take a couple days from the business.

So it was Nathalie, brother Matteo, Jean-Marc, and Abbie who set off with a Dellamer wagon following. The goods soon piled high on the wagon. Matteo came in handy, since his burly bulk and the snarl he could summon up when he wasn't joking kept would-be thieves at bay while the others went into various shops and stalls.

When they went to collect their wedding finery, it met Nathalie's high standards. Abbie would have congratulated the master tailor profusely but for his wife cowering in a corner, her face badly bruised.

Instead she turned to Jean-Marc and said conversationally if not a bit too loud, "Is it true, Jean-Marc, that the Dellamer household has an open position for a live-in assistant for the housekeeper?"

"It does?" he asked.

"I suppose most girls wouldn't apply for the job," Abbie continued as she played with the sleeves of her redone dress, "because the quarters are so remote from anything else within the Dellamer compound. Why, it took me forever to find them! I'd wager– if I ever wagered– that those were a favorite hiding place when you were boys. It's very quiet, very peaceful." She made sure the wife was looking at her.

Nathalie nodded quickly. "I'm sure the fair wage will attract someone sooner or later who's willing to work in an honest household," she said.

Outside Jean-Marc muttered, "I must remember to tell my brother of this new position."

"It's nothing you don't need, Jean-Marc," Nathalie said as she supervised the wagon-loading. She hurried them to the next stop for bed linens.

There the shopkeeper apologized profusely. A slight delay. The pieces would be finished any minute now.

Jean-Marc nodded. "You wait here," he told Nathalie, "and Matteo can guard the wagon. I want to show Abbie something."

Nathalie's chin came up. "I'm sure you have nothing that would interest Abbie," she insisted, standing in Abbie's way.

"It's perfectly innocent," Jean-Marc insisted. "It's nearby. It will take only a few minutes."

Nathalie gave him a measuring look while Abbie stood there puzzled. At Nathalie's nod, Jean-Marc grabbed Abbie's arm and hurried out of the shop.

Just a short ride over a hill lay a squat, half-stone and half-timber building. Here the quality of the neighborhood had deteriorated. The streets weren't cobbled, and ruts ran deep. Odorous filth oozed into the depressions.

Though they could still hear the enthusiastic shouting from City Market in the distance, here the shouts were only of children. Some sounded angry.

They rode into the entrance of the place, usually kept for deliveries, and discovered two gangs of young boys fighting. A score of them went after each other like wildcats, kicking and clawing– and some of them had knives.

Jean-Marc stood on his seat. "Stop!" he shouted and held his hands up commandingly. "Stop the fighting!"

One or two boys saw him, and their pause caused others to look up.

"Stop it this minute!"

"Dellamer!" "Monsieur Dellamer!"

The welcoming shouts from the boys halted the fight. Four of the boys whose blood streamed down their foreheads, ears and arms slunk off to the building that surrounded the courtyard.

"Here now, what have you been doing?" Jean-Marc asked the two tall, grinning boys who ran up to hang their arms over the sides of the carriage and stare at Abbie.

"Aw, we were just playing," the first boy told Jean-Marc. He couldn't be more than eleven. He was missing two teeth that Abbie could see, and he had a nasty blue-black bruise on his cheek. His clothing looked to be a good castoff, now worn and with more than a few ragged edges.

"How have I told you to act around ladies?" Jean-Marc snapped at the two. Others had gathered behind them. They all immediately stopped their stares, although they cast curious glances her way.

"Mademoiselle Bourgogne," Jean-Marc turned to her, "these are the inmates of stately St. Benedict Manor."

His announcement was met with laughter and guffaws.

"This is a refuge for orphans."

"Boys," Abbie put in.

He nodded. "Orphans of the male persuasion. The best bunch of brats in all of France."

That garnered cheers from all who heard.

Jean-Marc turned with a grin. "Now off with you all! I can smell that lunch must be near to being done, and I bet the chapel hasn't been polished this morn. You have better things to do than beat each other up just because you're bored. I'll be testing in arithmetic the next time I come!"

Most of the boys did disperse at that, waving back at Jean-Marc as he nodded at them.

Jean-Marc sat back down next to Abbie. "This is where I would have ended up," he told her quietly. "Believe it or not, this place has vastly improved since I was a child and newly orphaned."

"Has it improved because of some Dellamer donations?" Abbie ventured.

"It might have. The roofs leaked, there was only one blanket for every three boys, and the bread usually came with a maggot dressing."

Abbie shuddered.

"The boys here grew up in ignorance, and when they left they left no better– and often worse– than they'd arrived."

He turned to Abbie and took her hand in his. "Philippe saved me from this," he said. "He was still quite young, almost too young to run a large business by himself. Uncle was very sick. Bedridden. Philippe didn't have the time to take care of his younger brother– but he made the time. He took the time he could have spent on himself and spent it on me. He rescued me from this nightmare and didn't listen when his advisors and even Uncle told him to send me back."

Jean-Marc looked around the muddy courtyard with its discarded toys and tools. A toddler sat in a mud puddle and squalled until an older boy came along to pick him up.

"I owe Philippe my life. I know I should have died here if I'd stayed. Or I would have wound up lame, mean… beaten by life before it had even begun. Philippe saved me from all that.

"He gave up his own life so I could have one. I owe him everything. I even owe him you." He picked up Abbie's hand and kissed it, then held her fingers tenderly between his own before kissing her fingertips.

"Forgive me this," he whispered.

21

Babette lounged on a chaise, watching the workers clean. One of them was a rough-looking young man who helped move furniture long enough for the floor to be swept under it, then returned it to its previous spot.

He spared her a long, lingering up-and-down glance. She gave him a sly smile. Another man said something to him, and he returned to his work.

He ignored her.

Babette stuck out her lower lip and then got up to explore this luxurious mansion. The lower rooms had held knickknacks made of marble and gold– could it have been real?– that were gone now, locked away in rooms upstairs that she couldn't get into.

Drat it all, Abbie had even stolen her crucifix. That was her nicest piece of jewelry!

Idly Babette wandered through to the back of the house that faced the spacious courtyard. Peeking into a room lined with books and furnished with leather chairs, low tables, and at least a dozen candles, she saw Monsieur Dellamer.

Philippe.

Why hadn't anyone told her he wasn't a drooling, doddering old corpse of a man? Why hadn't they told her how rich he was?

Today he was dressed in boring black, but his outfit had golden accents that she knew must be real. His great necklace was scalloped to focus on large gemstones that caught the light and sent it in tiny, colored pinpoints to the walls of the room.

They would look so good on her.

"Well, hello," she cooed. He looked up, and she slid into the room in that slinky way she'd learned from the traveling minstrel's daughter.

He nodded. "Good day, um… Babette." His attention seemed more drawn to the book he was studying than to her. He actually glanced down at it before returning his gaze to hers. "May I help you?"

"I'm sure you can."

He waited a moment for her to go on and then frowned when she didn't. "Please tell me what you need, then. I'm afraid I'm quite busy."

She swayed her way across the room, circling it instead of going straight to him. She drew half-circles on the spines of the books with her fingertip as she passed them. "You're a diligent man, aren't you? Your business is a wealthy one."

"It's a hard-earned one." Again he glanced down at the book. "If you don't have anything I can help you with, I'm afraid I must get back to work. Perhaps the housekeeper can help you with whatever it is."

Babette placed her hand gently on his arm. The material was soft under her fingers. Velvet. "The housekeeper couldn't help me with this," she said softly.

He stared at her hand for two full seconds before bringing his gaze back up. It was as hard as his stern mouth. "Didn't Nathalie and Abbie take you with them?"

"They didn't tell me you were so good-looking," Babette gave him her slow, mysterious smile. "Probably too busy keeping all their little secrets." She rolled her eyes as if considering the ceiling. "Oh, the lies they do tell. The trouble that they get into when they have to cover them up. They will certainly get in trouble one day for them all."

She lowered her eyelids and gazed at his mouth. She licked her lips slowly. "Of course, I know their secrets, too. I could tell if I wanted to. If someone made it worth my time."

With a theatrical sigh she added, "Truly, they didn't tell me the important things, Philippe. They didn't tell me the truth about you. You're quite unlike any man I've ever met. You do live up to your reputation."

She lifted his hands from his book and pressed them against her breasts. "And I could live up to your every expectation, too," she whispered.

He stood frozen for a half-second, focused on his hands. Then he said, "What I expect from you is not to see your face until dinnertime." He shook off her hands and detached himself from her. "I expect never to see you again unless you are in the company of several of your relatives. I will not mention this to your uncle to save him the embarrassment of having a such a wanton as a niece."

Abruptly he closed his book with a snap, his jeweled rings flashing. Then with it tucked under his arm he marched out of the room. "Good day, Babette," he said.

How different this was from the plain parish churches back home! Monks sang a hymn that echoed through the great chamber, drowning out the drenching rain that fell outside. Hundreds of strangers dressed in their ultimate finery stood to either side of the central aisle. Older people rested in chairs with fur-trimmed blankets to keep them warm. More simple dress marked the men and their families who worked for the Dellamers, invited up from the warehouse and docks for the sacred event– and the feasting afterwards.

To the side of the main entrance a pink marble statue of Our Lady stood to bless the wedding party, surrounded by candles of which only a few were lit. The Dellamers and Bourgognes, with Nathalie to give Abbie encouragement, knelt to pray before they would proceed to the main altar and the bishop there.

Abbie squeezed her eyes shut, but she couldn't pray. She felt the presence of too many saints in here, all pointing at her in accusation. Lies. Lies!

This morning she had prayed long and hard to the Virgin: ten minutes before her tea of forgetfulness, twenty minutes afterward. In two more days she would no longer have feelings for Jean-Marc.

At least she understood his reasoning now. He had strong family obligations to his brother, perhaps as strong or stronger than her own obligations.

This new contract wasn't that much of a lie, was it? Things had twisted back on themselves, and though they were still tricking Philippe, they weren't tricking him much. Marrying a man she couldn't love– that wasn't a desecration of the holy sacrament. People did it all the time.

She was sacrificing her life for the Bourgognes' greater good. Would her suffering make her a better person? Would she gain a greater redemption through it? Did Heaven hold a vineyard where she would someday find her family? Could she bear a lifetime of lonely misery while awaiting her heavenly reward?

But the marriage contract was supposed to be for a good wife for Philippe as well as a contract to allow a partnership for shipping the Bourgognes' wine to the world. Now it was only a paper that enabled Abbie to return to her home. She didn't care about the rest of it. She didn't care about Philippe.

The statue of the Virgin looked kindly upon her, reminding her that salvation was still not out of reach. Salvation for her; salvation for them all. But still this was only a statue. Could the Virgin truly hear her prayers?

Abbie remembered that night of fierce praying on the Rhone. She hadn't prayed to any saint then. She'd broken the rules. That night it had been just her and God. God had answered her prayers.

And in return she had made a promise to God.

She would be a good wife. She'd be a willing wife.

Tears squeezed from between her clenched eyelids. She'd turned the marriage into a mere business transaction. She'd betrayed a holy promise to God Himself.

How long would she be punished for this? Would He throw her into Hell for all eternity?

They were cheating this innocent man of a proper wife with proper respect for and obedience to him.

But Jean-Marc, even Uncle Gus… These were both good men who were cheating Philippe, too. The bishop of this church had cheated when Philippe had given him a bribe to cut short the banns.

Even the best of people could do bad things. But should they? Did the ends truly justify the means? Wouldn't a little scandal now be worth not invoking God's holy wrath later?

How much punishment would all this involve?

God had caused the torrent of rain that fell on this, her wedding day. Would He reach out to destroy the clos in some way? Would He send disease to her grapes? A drought to wipe out her family's wealth? Sickness to strike the family again?

But even droughts and plagues were temporary. Kneeling on the cold floor it was difficult to imagine the eternal fires of Hell. Did they really matter? Wasn't the worst thing here that Abbie was lying to Philippe, who would be united to her as her husband in holy wedlock in just a few minutes? How much was her honor, her very soul, worth to her that she would do this to another human being? To her husband?

Lord, she prayed fiercely, *tell me what to do. I can't wait any longer. I have to hear You right now!*

Would He send an angel, a vision, to her? It was sinful to talk directly to God Himself, but this was an emergency.

She listened hard to the sounds around her, but all she could hear was the monks' choir, the soft muttering of the crowd, and the downpour outside. She strained to make out some heavenly summons from within her, but all she could hear was the voice of her own conscience.

She must save them all from themselves and the lies they'd been forced into. She must save herself.

But the contract… It finally stated that she'd be allowed to go home! Abbie clutched at her crucifix with the vine of Clos Bourgogne. She could never be home here in Marseille; she needed Clos Bourgogne. That was home. That was where the ghosts of her family waited for her to return.

Such welcoming ghosts, smiling at her. Laughing with joy at seeing her again. Holding out their arms to welcome her back to where she should never have left.

But that inner voice mercilessly drove at her. Above all, she had to save Jean-Marc from the desolation of Purgatory. He must not be allowed to suffer for her sins. He must remain whole and well.

He was more important than the wine, than the clos. He was even more important than family. Jean-Marc must go on to Heaven while she suffered eternity in Purgatory… or worse.

Help me, God!

She would never get home again.

"Philippe…" The word came as a whisper. Abbie cleared her throat. "Ph-Philippe," she said clearly. She shifted on her knees to face him. "I'm sorry, but

I don't love you. I don't think I ever will. You seem to be a decent man, but I love another and I will always love him, more than life itself. Please forgive me."

It took a long moment but Philippe's eyes at last opened and turned to her. There was no anger in them, but did the man ever experience a true emotion?

"I don't believe our contract calls for love," he said quietly. "I am glad you were honest with me." He turned back to the altar and closed his eyes in prayer–but opened them again.

"You are not pregnant with this man's child?" he asked.

Abbie shook her head, her eyes wide. "I am a virgin," she said.

He nodded and returned to his prayer.

A hand patted her shoulder reassuringly, and she knew it was Nathalie's. "Courage," Nathalie whispered to her.

There was more to be told. Abbie licked her lips, but the word she began her confession with was overshadowed by the same word uttered by another.

"Philippe."

Abbie turned to see Jean-Marc pulling on his brother's faux-slashed gown.

"Philippe, I'll be leaving as soon as this wedding is over. I wasn't going to tell you, but perhaps… I mean, I think that–"

Abbie's heart clenched. He couldn't leave now!

Philippe came out of his prayer immediately for this. "You're leaving? Why? You can't. I need you; the business needs you."

"I can't stay. I can't… I couldn't…" Jean-Marc bowed his head. "I am in love with Abbie," he said. "I am in love with Abbie."

He raised his chin and looked into her startled eyes. "I love you, Abbie. You are my life. You are my treasure, my diamond. Because I love my brother, I give him what I value most."

On his knees, he edged nearer to her and took her hand in both of his.

"Only you are good enough for him. I will see you wed, and then I am gone from here. My beautiful Abbie. I can't stand the thought of you and Philippe– Of you and–" Jean-Marc swallowed. "I am gone. But I will be able to leave knowing that Philippe is in the best of care. He will fall in love with you– how could any man resist you for long? And you, sweet, loving Abbie, will learn to love him, not me. It's for the best."

He gathered her hands and pressed them to his cheek. "Oh my dearest Abbie, trust me in this."

Philippe twisted to sit on the padded kneeler. "Let me understand this. Jean-Marc, you are leaving me and the business just because you love Abbie. Abbie, you do not love me and I do not love you. I can't–"

"You were supposed to marry me!" Babette said, springing up from her prayer position. "The contract was written about me. I love you, Philippe."

The expression Philippe bestowed upon her reminded Abbie of the time her father had taken a great gulp of soured wine. She almost fainted as her head spun. Jean-Marc loved her. The secret was out. Jean-Marc loved–!

Jean-Marc cleared his throat. "It is true to a point, Philippe. We originally started with Babette. But she had other plans, and since Abbie's Christian name is also Babette, well… I decided that Abbie was the better choice anyway."

"I certainly agree," Philippe said, looking everywhere but at the anxious Babette. "That girl is totally unacceptable. She would drain my coffers within the first business quarter and play me for a fool. Besides, I do not marry children."

"I am not a child! I am almost as old as Abbie!"

"She is not a virgin," Jean-Marc hastily added. "Quite possibly she is pregnant as well."

Babette let out a shriek that echoed throughout the cathedral.

"Shut up, girl." Uncle Gus shook her. "Haven't you done enough harm?"

"Doubly unacceptable, then," Philippe pronounced. He stood slowly, and the rest of the party followed his example.

But Abbie couldn't take her eyes from Jean-Marc. Sweet, brave, noble, and loving Jean-Marc! She'd never see him again. How could she bear it?

Something hurt her hands because she gripped it so tightly. Her crucifix. The one he had given her so dearly: her cross with its sliver of the Clos Bourgogne inside. The cross that held her soul.

"Here." She pressed it into Jean-Marc's hand. "I give my life, my freedom to you. This is my heart. Take my heart with you, dearest. Wear this for luck wherever you go and know that in my dreams I am there with you also. Think of me, Jean-Marc. Think of me!"

He cradled it and did not look at her. Finally he clenched his fist around it. "Philippe, you must marry Abbie," Jean-Marc choked. "She– She is virtuous, loving, wise, and she will bring the Clos Bourgogne back to its wealth. She will take care of you when I leave."

A priest walked quickly to them from the nave of the cathedral. The bishop waited at the altar, leaning and twisting to try to see what was holding up the ceremony.

"My son?" the priest asked Philippe. "Is there something wrong? Is there a problem?"

Philippe pursed his lips and then shook his head. "No. Nothing is wrong. If only you'd told me before, Jean-Marc, perhaps we could have done something. But now… Everything has been set, everything is arranged. We have the contract. Let us–"

He seemed to sag. Jean-Marc caught him from the right and Abbie from the left.

"Let us–" Philippe said again, but he fell to his knees, his fall cushioned by the support on either side.

From his knees he went to all fours, his head drooping almost to the ground. Philippe's voice came to them as a far-off wail. "I love another."

Abbie and Jean-Marc looked at each other.

Philippe raised up slightly but still stared at the floor. "I am mad for her," he said. "I cannot work for thinking of her night and day. It's been over twelve years, and I still burn for her. Her eyes, her hair, the way she moves, the way her lips speak. She is kind, she is beautiful and elegant, her hands are so graceful. She holds my heart."

He looked up, his eyes sorting through the small crowd. "Nathalie…" His voice sighed her name. "Nathalie Venise, I love you. I always have."

Nathalie's lower lip quivered. She brought one hand holding her rosary to her breast as she regarded the poor man.

"I offered to your father for you twelve years ago. He said I hadn't proven myself, that I was too young. He said my business would fail and you would be destitute. How I have worked to prove him wrong! Even when you'd gone and he had died, I'd hoped… I'd prayed… But now you have returned. I couldn't believe it was you, not after I'd been contracted myself."

He shook his head and closed his eyes. "If I had only known you were free again, I would have offered to your brothers. I would have paid any bride price, given you whatever you wanted. I'd have piled rare jewels and cloths at your feet. I'd have begged you and wept at the hem of your skirt until you took pity on me and answered all my prayers.

"But we had made the contract with the Bourgognes. Even as it was handed to me, you came back into my life. And now I was the unavailable one." Philippe swallowed and then drew himself up as if it pained him. "Perhaps I am mistaken," Philippe offered, "but I thought that if there had been no contract, and if I had approached your brothers, perhaps… Perhaps you would have found it in your heart to–"

"Oh, Philippe," Nathalie said with a glorious smile.

Jean-Marc snapped his fingers at the priest. "There will be a delay," he told him. "Tell them to stall. Start an extra mass before the wedding. Get us some paper and some ink."

They used the lower step of the small altar to write upon. Since all Nathalie's brothers were in attendance an altar boy collected them as the congregation tried not to stare back at the small crowd.

"I give up Abbie's dowry," Philippe said. "All of it. I will make up for what we have used already."

"I have no dowry to give you," Nathalie said.

"You are your own dowry," Philippe told her. How his face changed when he smiled! He was radiant, his eyes sparkling as he gazed upon his beloved. "We shall teach those boys of yours shipping and then we'll sell your family's wares across the known world."

"No," Jean-Marc said, "they will also make bottles and jars for the Bourgognes. Auguste, take back Abbie's dowry. Except for her mother's necklace. And whatever else she wants. All I want is a partnership in the clos with a stipulation that Abbie will manage the vineyard throughout the year. And she will train someone to manage your chardonnay vineyard."

"What does a partnership entail?" Abbie whispered to Jean-Marc. She had no head for business, just for the grape. But Jean-Marc continued.

"The vineyards will remain within the Bourgogne family, but profits will be split to include Abbie and me in them. The Dellamer shipping company will still carry your wine far and wide, ensuring a higher price and better profit for all of us." Jean-Marc tweaked his index finger at the priest who wrote so hurriedly. "Write that down," he ordered.

"But Christopher is—" Gus blurted.

"Christopher, I think, will go into partnership with me as well," Jean-Marc said. "Philippe, I want use of the river barges. And I'll want to build some more. There's much profit to be made upriver, especially with quality boats that can handle passengers in comfort as well as cargo. Christopher can help me. I think he will enjoy that. A good profit for all."

"Do you think so, Jean-Marc?" Philippe asked. Without waiting for an answer, he nodded at the priest. "Include that as well. Dellamer partnership with this Christopher…"

"Bourgogne," Abbie supplied the last name.

How all the saints were smiling at them! She could feel the very blessings of Heaven swirling about them like a shower of golden petals. Did she imagine the rustle of angels' wings overhead? She closed her eyes to offer a fervent prayer of thanksgiving that she would repeat all the days of her life.

Over the hunched back of the scribbling priest, she smiled at Jean-Marc.

He took her hand in his and pulled her close. "Is this contract more to your liking? What else would you wish? A crown so you can be queen of the vineyard? I will give it to you, and rubies and diamonds…"

Such bliss to rest her head on his shoulder! Her beloved forever now, even unto Heaven and all of eternity. "Perhaps we should include something about the honeymoon," she whispered. "Just to make sure it's as perfect as our marriage will be."

The smile he gave her was just between the two of them. "We'll take it in Burgundy," he said. "I want to see it in spring and summer and at harvest, just as you described it to me. We'll build a timber mansion… Or will we build that for Christopher and Maddy, and take the stone house for ourselves? That would please everyone better, I think."

"Oh, Jean-Marc, could we? Oh, but we can't go back to Burgundy. Not yet."

Jean-Marc stood speechless.

"I was thinking," Abbie mused. "That one man's tales of Rome were so interesting. And Eva's stories about Geneva were sweet. Do you think we might visit them? Or Venice. Nathalie's people are from there, you know, and she makes it sound like somewhere we might want to go…"

* * *

ABOUT THE AUTHOR

When you think of strong women and strange worlds, think Carol A. Strickland.

Although born in a small town in Illinois noted for its Nineteenth Century demonic possession cases, Carol claims that all those voices inside her head are a result of having stories to tell and books to write. Even so, her strange devotion to and study of Wonder Woman would seem to indicate an abby-normal brain.

A one-time comics letterhack and outspoken member of various comics message boards, Carol has found herself the basis for two comic book villains (at times her opinions have not been taken well by the books' creators) (both villains were soundly thrashed) (and both, for some perverse reason, were male) and had one superhero wear her costume design. (Light Lass!)

Carol has also become an award-winning painter. Along with her writing, she exercises this skill in her secondary hours (both of them) as she waits for the lottery to free her 9-to-5 time to more fulfilling pursuits.

Dear Reader,

Did you enjoy this book?

Your feedback helps me provide the best quality books and aids other readers like you to discover great books.

It would mean so much to me if you took two minutes to share your thoughts about this book as a review. You can leave one at the retailer of your choice and/or send me an email with your honest feedback: contact@carolastrickland.com.

And please check out my website at www.CarolAStrickland.com, which has links for social media as well as info about my other books.

Thanks so much for reading!

Carol Strick